Other Books by Linda Sunshine

Plain Jane Works Out
Plain Jane's Thrill of Very Fattening Foods Cookbook

Nonfiction, with John Wright:
The Best Hospitals in America

THE MEMOIRS OF

Bambi

A FIRESIDE BOOK · PUBLISHED BY

Goldbloom

OR,
GROWING
UP
IN
NEW
JERSEY

by LINDA
SUNSHINE

SIMON & SCHUSTER, INC., NEW YORK

A FIRESIDE BOOK
PUBLISHED BY SIMON & SCHUSTER, INC.
SIMON & SCHUSTER BUILDING
ROCKEFELLER CENTER
1230 AVENUE OF THE AMERICAS
NEW YORK, NEW YORK 10020
FIRESIDE AND COLOPHON ARE REGISTERED
TRADEMARKS OF SIMON & SCHUSTER, INC.
DESIGNED BY BONNI LEON
MANUFACTURED IN THE UNITED STATES OF AMERICA
10 9 8 7 6 5 4 3 2 1
LIBRARY OF CONGRESS CATALOGING IN
PUBLICATION DATA
SUNSHINE, LINDA.
THE MEMOIRS OF BAMBI GOLDBLOOM, OR, GROWING
UP IN NEW JERSEY.
"A FIRESIDE BOOK."
I. TITLE.   II. TITLE: GROWING UP IN NEW JERSEY.
PS3569.U65M4   1987   813'.54   86-21993
ISBN: 0-671-62288-9

THE AUTHOR IS GRATEFUL FOR PERMISSION TO REPRINT
SIX LINES FROM "DON'T LET THAT HORSE" BY LAWRENCE
FERLINGHETTI, A Coney Island of the Mind. COPYRIGHT ©
1958 BY LAWRENCE FERLINGHETTI. REPRINTED BY PER-
MISSION OF NEW DIRECTIONS PUBLISHING CORPORA-
TION.

Special thanks to

DEBORAH BERGMAN, MEREDITH BERNSTEIN,
MICHAEL DENNENY, CONALEE LEVINE-SHNEIDMAN,
SUSAN MOLDOW AND, ESPECIALLY, MARK BREGMAN
FOR THEIR
HELP, SUPPORT AND ENCOURAGEMENT
IN DIRECTING BAMBI GOLDBLOOM DOWN
THE JERSEY TURNPIKE OF LIFE.

Dedicated to all the girls
who ever hummed, sang or thought
"Someday My Prince Will Come."

Contents

THE CHEESE STANDS ALONE 1

*L*ate one night, *I* sat up in bed, smoking a cigarette and staring at my husband.

He was sound asleep, lying spread-eagled on his back; his mouth hung open and spittle drooled down his chin. Little pieces of gray lint stuck to the thick stubble on his cheek. As usual, he was snoring loudly. I flicked my ashes and sighed, asking myself the same question every woman has asked herself, at least once, during the course of her marriage. "Why," I whispered out loud, "did I ever marry this schlemiel?"

For the life of me I couldn't remember; all I could remember was the joyous sarcasm in my mother's voice when I told her I had agreed to be the bride of Seymour Weizentraubowitzman.

"Don't tell me, Bambi Iris Goldbloom, that after twenty-five years of causing me nothing but aggravation and heartache and tsuris—after making such a big megillah over this boyfriend and that boyfriend; after I had to put up with the motorcycle maniac, the hippie with the hair, the pothead . . ."

"Janice, I think the hippie *was* the pothead," my father correctly pointed out.

"Hippie, schmippie!" she exclaimed. "I can't believe my ears; my only daughter is finally doing the one thing I've been begging her to do all her life!"

"Yes, Mom," I groaned, not having the stomach for

my mother's dramatics. Seymour was the son of Mom's best friend, Sadie, and since I was eleven years old, he had been eating Friday-night dinner at our house.

Tears were glistening in my father's eyes. "You'll be married to a wonderful boy; a boy who'll give my little girl what she's always wanted most . . ."

"Live-in help," Mom said, finishing Dad's thought, as usual.

"I'm proud of you, princess," Daddy said, ignoring Mom, as usual. "You'll be taken care of for the rest of your life—I won't have to worry." He put his arm around me. "Now mother and I can die in peace."

"But not before the wedding," my mother promised, running to the phone to call my aunt Selma, the caterer and the florist. Mom had not been this happy since the day Daddy brought Frank Sinatra, our blue-eyed poodle, home from Le Dog Store, so I figured this wasn't the time to mention I was having serious doubts about marrying Seymour.

For one thing, I didn't like the fact we were going to live with Seymour's parents after the wedding. Oh, I realized we saved a lot of money by not having to pay any rent; but I thought my future mother-in-law's insistence that we all sleep in the same bedroom was a little overbearing. And when she and Seymour's dad insisted on joining us for the honeymoon ("We'll make it a family outing!"), I knew I was in for some serious In-Law Interference.

My wedding, however, was beautiful. I wore white; so did Seymour's mother.

We had a traditional ceremony under a massive hoopa, but it was not without incident. Mama Weisentrobowiztman stood next to the rabbi and talked throughout the entire ceremony. "Seymour, darling, you're slouching!" Sadie wailed, blowing her nose into a crumpled Kleenex. "Stand up straight (sob, sob . . . honk! honk!) when the rabbi speaks to you!"

This was the early 1970s so, of course, Seymour and

I felt obligated to recite something personal after our vows. After much deliberation, I had selected the wildly romantic poem "14" from my favorite book of poetry, *A Coney Island of the Mind,* by Lawrence Ferlinghetti.

When the rabbi was ready, he nodded at me to begin.

"Don't let that horse eat that violin cried Chagall's mother," I emoted, "But he kept right on painting."

I glanced up at my future husband.

"You done?" Seymour whispered and I nodded.

Seymour turned to his best man, his father, who handed him a heavy book. Opening the book, Seymour cleared his throat.

"Bile emulsifies fats in the duodenum," he read from *The Anatomy and Physiology Textbook,* "and is essential for the action of lipase and the absorption of fat-soluble vitamins."

Seymour paused thoughtfully, extracted a yellow magic marker from the breast pocket of his tux and highlighted a few words before continuing. "About five hundred milliliters a day are produced. Some of which is reabsorbed, while the rest gives the particular color to the feces."

Sandy, my matron of honor, gasped.

"Ah, I think we're out of time, Seymour," interrupted Rabbi Zindl. He picked up a stemmed Baccarat wine glass, wrapped it in a napkin and gently placed the goblet on the floor. "Break the glass, son," the rabbi said to Seymour.

My husband dropped his heavy textbook on the goblet, smashing the glass and several of the rabbi's toes.

"Mazel tov," Rabbi Zindl winced. "You may kiss the bride."

"No, he may not," I fumed, and gathering up the yards and yards of my bridal train, I turned and marched down the aisle by myself. Seymour chased after me.

"Is anything wrong?" Seymour asked when he finally caught up with me, outside the auditorium of the temple.

"I can't believe you read from your anatomy book."

"Why? I used the opportunity to get in a little studying. You want me to ace Anatomy, don't you?"

"You were supposed to pick something personal."

"Bile salts, Bams, I read about bile salts. What could be more personal than the digestive system?"

"Ah, Seymour," I groaned, throwing my bouquet on the floor, "did you have to mention *feces*, for Chrissakes?"

At my mother's suggestion, I swallowed two Valium and tried to forget the incident.

I guess the reception was pretty much your typical Jewish affair, although after several glasses of champagne it seemed quite special to me, particularly when Seymour and I waltzed across the dance floor to "our" song, *The Name Game*. "Banana fana fo fana," Seymour crooned in my ear.

There was a little shouting match over the seating arrangements—Aunt Selma, divorced for over fourteen years and now remarried to Uncle Shelley, refused to sit "within spitting distance," of her ex-husband, Uncle Melvin, and his second wife, "the shiksa whore." And, sometime later in the evening, a quick fistfight broke out over distribution of the centerpieces, but other than that, there was nothing out of the ordinary. Everyone ate themselves into a frenzy and danced until they either threw up, passed out or fell asleep at their table.

"It's just like the wedding scene in *Goodbye Columbus*," remarked my cousin Estelle, and in the end, everyone agreed it had been a lovely, lovely affair.

As a special treat for our wedding night, Mom and Dad rented the honeymoon suite at the Plaza Hotel for one night. "It cost an arm and a leg," Daddy said, "but nothing's too good for my little girl and my doctor son-in-law."

I learned a lot from my husband on my wedding night; mainly that Valium and champagne don't mix, which Seymour was patiently explaining to me a few seconds before I passed out in the stretch limo.

The next morning, I awoke on the couch in the sitting room of our suite. The phone was ringing and, when I picked it up, the hotel manager said, "You have twenty minutes to vacate the room."

I tried to sit up. My head was throbbing and I was all entangled in my wedding gown, which was now wrinkled beyond belief.

Stumbling to my feet, I went searching for my husband and found him fast asleep in the bedroom, stretched out on the massive satin bed cover. He wore jockey shorts that had "Tuesday" embroidered across the fly front and, let me tell you, they really turned me off. Today was Sunday.

Seymour was surrounded on the bed by neatly stacked piles of money, checks and bonds. Clutched in his hand was a pocket calculator.

I shook him awake. He rubbed his eyes, muttered, "We cleared $11,550," and sighed contentedly.

I burst into tears.

"Hey, it's not so bad, Bams." He patted my hand. "That's not counting the five grand from your Dad."

"What about my wedding night?" I wailed, unconsoled.

"Oh, *that!*" Seymour grinned, yanked my hand and pulled me on top of him. He kissed my nose and stuck his tongue in my ear. "Hubba Hubba," he cried as he grabbed my left breast and rolled on top of me. A $50 bond stuck to his forehead.

"Seymour, I don't think this will work," I said, struggling to remove his pocket calculator which was jabbing me in the small of my back, "We only have twenty minutes."

He fumbled with the buttons of my wedding gown. "Plenty of time!" exclaimed my new husband and, unfortunately, it was.

. . .

Seymour and I honeymooned at Brown's hotel in the Catskills where, as kids, both of us had spent many of our childhood summer vacations with our parents. My mother and father insisted that if Seymour's parents, Sadie and Sol, could horn in on our honeymoon, so could the Goldblooms, and the six of us drove up to Lake Kiamesha, stopping, of course, for pastrami sandwiches at Kaplan's Delicatessen on Route 17.

"Fear and loathing on the borscht belt," was how I later described the experience to Sandy.

The whole week was a mistake, right from the start, when our parents insisted Seymour and I eat at the young adults table. (We agreed to the arrangement solely because it was the only time we were allowed to be by ourselves.) After dinner, we had to go to the Jerry Lewis Nightclub, applaud Buddy Hackett and dance with our parents.

Afternoons, Seymour and I stood behind our parents and watched them play poker and, following a late lunch, took cha-cha lessons on the pool patio. We sat for a souvenir caricature, and then for the hotel photographer, because Mom wanted dozens of those little viewfinders with our photos inside. After a while, though, Seymour and I drew the line; we absolutely refused to attend Brownie Day Camp.

Although I enjoyed visiting Brown's as a newlywed, I was saddened to miss out on the best part of a Catskills vacation; namely, dating the waiters.

Home again, I spent the first three weeks of married life learning how to spell my new last name.

Space was tight with the four of us living in the Weizentrabowitzmane's tiny garden apartment. Seymour and I had to beg Sadie for permission to stay up late at night and watch Johnny Carson. (Neither Sadie nor Sol could sleep with the television on.)

As for our sex life, it had shrunk down to the few hours when Sadie left the house to get her hair done.

In vain, I repeatedly suggested to my mother-in-law that she find a new hair salon. "There's a great new shop that just opened in the Catskills," I would enthusiastically suggest. "Why don't you and Sol drive up for the weekend?"

But it rarely worked. Most of the time, Sadie liked to hang around the apartment and go through my personal belongings.

"We're all family now!" she would explain as she rifled through my mail, stopping to open an envelope or two. "There are no secrets between us in this house. What's mine is yours and what's yours is . . .", She looked up from the letter she was reading ". . . expensive! Thirty-five dollars in the underwear department!" she exclaimed, handing me the Bloomingdale's bill. "Why would anyone spend so much money for a piece of cotton and an elastic band? Sweetie, you don't need to shop Bloomingdale's for underwear. My cousin Simca, no, *your* cousin Simca, is a receptionist for a fancy-schmancy lingerie concern. You remember Simca from your wedding."

I shook my head, trying to sort out the endless succession of Weizentraobewitases I had met that night.

"Of course you remember Cousin Simca," Sadie insisted. "Simca, the spinster . . . the one who never married," she added, as if it were necessary to define the word *spinster* to a Jewish girl!

"Oh, that Simca," I said.

"A lovely girl," Sadie pointed her finger at me, "but never married, poor thing." Sadie sighed heavily as she picked up the phone. "Simca'll get you all the undergarments you need. Here, I'll give her a call," she started to dial. "Why should a daughter-in-law of mine pay retail? Am I right, tsatskeleh?"

Sadie pinched my cheek as she reminded me Simca's panties cost less than four dollars a dozen. "And they sell for $1.49 *each* in Alexander's," Sadie was proud to announce. She insisted Simca could fit me, over the phone, "just as well as any of those snoody brazeer salesladies in your fancy department stores."

I tried to protest but it was useless, since refusing to buy wholesale is akin to spitting on the Torah in many Jewish households.

I couldn't prevent Sadie from placing an order for six dozen panties and two dozen "brazeers." As a final gesture, Simca insisted upon sending along a half dozen girdles, "as my treat for the newlyweds."

Now, Mama Weisientraobiwitz's * intrusions on my sex life were one thing, but when she began interfering with my spending power by cutting back Seymour's allowance and canceling my Bloomie's card, I really got annoyed.

I found myself longing for my own mother; for the things that only a girl's *real* mother could give her: loving advice, warm support and a Gold American Express card.

Money and Sex, I suppose it always comes back to the basics. My husband was no help. In fact, Seymour tried to make me think that I was much too demanding on both counts. I could understand our fights about money but I just couldn't reconcile his attitude about sex.

Was I really asking too much to want to make love to my husband more than once a week, on Saturday afternoons, between 1:00 P.M. and 2:15 P.M.?

"Look at my mama and papa," Seymour would whisper in my ear late at night. "They never fool around and they've been married for thirty-two years. Doesn't that tell you the secret of a happy marriage?"

"No," I growled, "What's the secret of a happy marriage?"

"A good night's sleep," Seymour murmured, pecking me on the forehead and then turning over to blow a kiss good night to my mother-in-law.

"He's right, Bambi darling," Sadie crooned as she

---

* I still hadn't mastered the proper spelling of that stupid name!

reached up to turn out the light. "Now, sleep tight, children, and maybe tomorrow I'll go for a haircut."

"Promises, promises," I grumbled to myself.

When I caught Seymour reading a copy of *How to Make Love to a Married Woman* a few weeks later, I hoped things were about to improve. But the next day, I opened the book and read the subtitle: *Without Getting Caught by Your Wife*.

I began to suspect my marriage was in trouble.

Two days later, I worked up the nerve to ask Seymour why he was reading that incriminating book. It was late on a Saturday afternoon and we had just finished having sex (I had finally convinced Sadie to get a perm).

Seymour pleaded innocence. "It's reference reading," he insisted. "I'm just studying the subject so that I can help my future patients."

"Patients? What patients?" I asked. "Seymour, you're studying to be a veterinarian."

He was not defeated by this observation. "Bambi you've *never* understood the animal kingdom and—you know what?—I don't think you ever will!" With that, Seymour walked out of the bedroom.

I knew, right then and there, that our days of marital bliss were numbered.

In fact, we only lasted three more days. That afternoon Sadie came home with a bottle of Toni Home Perm and announced she'd never need her beauty parlor again.

I packed my things.

My parents were not thrilled when I landed on their doorstep with my seventeen-piece set of matching luggage.*

Mom opened the front door a crack, peered out at me and screamed. "What happened? Where's your diamond ring?"

"I threw it back in Seymour's face. I never want to see that jerk again as long as I live!"

---

* A wedding present from Aunt Selma.

My father peeked through the partially opened door from behind Mom. He looked stunned. "You gave back the ring?"

"What's the meaning of this, YOUNG LADY?" Mom demanded.

"Oh, it was just awful. I had to get out. It was worse than you can imagine. What a terrible family! Mommy, they were so cheap."

Mom unlatched the chain on the doorjamb and finally allowed me into the foyer. "How cheap were they?" she asked, suspiciously.

"They were so cheap that their refrigerator was constantly empty! And I'm not just talking about running out of milk." I lowered my voice to deliver the most damning evidence of Weizentrobitzmmar abuse. "Sometimes, at dinner, there wouldn't even be enough food for seconds."

My mother turned pale, and for a moment, I thought she might faint.

"Not enough food for seconds," she murmured softly, in disbelief, as she grabbed my arm for support. In a few moments, she recovered from her initial shock and took charge of the situation. "Herman, bring in the luggage," she said to my father. She took a deep breath. "Let's just thank our lucky stars you got out when you did, before you actually went hungry . . ." she shuddered at the thought, "or had to tell a guest there was nothing left to eat." Mother turned pale again, struck by the implications of her words.

"It's okay, Mom," I quickly said, trying not to upset her any further. "It didn't happen. I wasn't there long enough to have a dinner party."

"And thank God for that!" she exclaimed. "Can you imagine what the girls at my canasta game would say if a daughter of mine hadn't been able to properly feed her dinner guests? There'd be no living with Ceil!"

My father wasn't listening to my mother. "You returned the ring?" he asked again.

"Now, Herman," my mother said, in her most soothing voice, "it just didn't work out between the kinder. Don't blame Bambi, she tried her best."

"Tried her best!" Daddy exploded. "Janice, the girl was married for eleven weeks and the wedding cost seventeen thousand bucks. That's almost two grand a week!"

"$1,545.45 a week," Mother corrected him. "But what's money at a time like this? What's important is our little girl needs us and she's come back to the nest. What should we do, turn her out in the cold?"

"No, I suppose not," grumbled my father. He walked outside and carried my trunk in from the porch. "But I'll tell you one thing, Weisentrabuowman is going to pay through the nose for this!" he declared as he schlepped my smaller bags. "I'm canceling his college tuition loan. I'm repossessing that little sports car he demanded as a wedding present." Dad dumped my vanity train case on the floor. "And, as of tonight, he's definitely out of the will!" Daddy stormed off; probably to call his lawyer.

"I'm sorry, Mommy," I said, "but I had to leave that house. I couldn't stand it any longer."

"Oh, I understand, dear. But, you know, your father is right."

"Excuse me? Did I hear you correctly?"

"You really should've kept the ring."

I was too tired to consider my mother's advice, although later, upon reflection, I came to realize she was absolutely correct, that two-carat diamond was mine and, to this day, I regret not having it in my safe deposit box. That night, however, I couldn't think about diamonds.* It was the end of a long, hard day and I felt weary to the bone. "I've got to go upstairs and get some sleep," I said to my mother. "We'll talk in the morning." I kissed her on the cheek.

I knew that, in the morning, I would have to deal with the reality of being the first annulment in the

---

* I guess I was more upset than I realized at the time.

family. I was barely past my Sweet Sixteen and here I was, an unmarried woman.*

As I slowly climbed the stairs to my bedroom—the room I thought I had abandoned forever less than two months ago—tears came to my eyes when I thought about how the gossipmongers, like my ex-best friend, Tiffany, would have a field day when they heard about my separation.

I stopped at my bedroom door and inspected the familiar surroundings of my youth; the Elvis wallpaper, the Ulysses college pennant, fluffy Jerome Giraffe, my still glamorous Barbie doll—dressed to the nines in her strapless Gilda gown. I walked over and sat down on my bed. At almost the same moment, I happened to look over and notice my favorite book resting on my night table. I picked up the well-worn volume.

It had been a long, long time since I'd first read this inspirational work; many of the words had become indelibly impressed on my brain. It was a great comfort just to hold the dog-eared book in my hands. I turned to my favorite passage and, reverently, read aloud: "I'll think of it all tomorrow, at Tara. I can stand it then. After all, tomorrow is another day." †

I could almost hear the music swelling in the background. I sneaked a peek at myself in the mirror over my vanity table and, damn, if I didn't bear a striking resemblance to Miss Scarlett, at least the way I'd always envisioned her, which was more like Barbra Streisand than Vivien Leigh.

Slowly, I closed the book. Dramatically, I sighed aloud and, in the mirror, practiced my most fetching smile. I pinched my cheeks, like Scarlett always did, for color.

I thought about my past and the twists and turns of

---

* Editor's Note: This was years before Jill Clayburgh made it fashionable.

† Is there any other book in the world that can comfort the soul more than *Gone With the Wind* by Margaret Mitchell?

fate that had brought me back to this bedroom. Looking back, it felt as though, only yesterday, I was a little girl playing Mr. Potatohead and now, look at me, I'd become *Mrs.* Potatohead. One question burned in by brain: Why had I married Seymour?

Was it because, as a Jewish girl raised by adoring parents, I had been trained for only thing in life: to marry a doctor? Was it because of my lifelong rivalry with Tiffany, Seymour's ex-girlfriend? Was it the Mustang Daddy bought me as a wedding gift? Peer pressure? Insecurity? Or was it destiny?

I AM BORN (I LEARN TO EAT) 2

I was born in the very, very, very late 1940s.
In fact, it was practically the early 1950's by the time
I finally arrived.

"Twenty-six hours, I was in labor with you!" says
my mother, "you shouldn't know from the pain!"

Apparently, Mom's pregnancy was the longest test
of female endurance in the city of Hohokus, the state
of New Jersey or the planet Earth.

"I gained so much weight when I was pregnant
with you!" Mom likes to remind me. "Forty-seven
pounds! Oy! Was I uncomfortable!"

"Gained weight! You were a beached whale!"
Daddy screams with laughter. "Why, your mother was
so huge, we thought she might give birth to the Mormon Tabernacle Choir!"

"That's really not funny, Herman!" *

"Never mind about the weight," Nana Yetta dismisses my quarreling parents with a wave of her hand.
"This was some gorgeous baby! Momala, in all the
hospital, they'd never seen such a face! Even the
nurses couldn't believe how gorgeous!"

"Ach! A heartbreaker, even den," Grandpa Max insists, pinching my cheek until I beg for mercy. "Give
a listen, you vant to talk cute? Den talk about dose
dimples!"

Daddy smiles nostalgically. "Umm . . . the cutest

* Mother hates Dad's Mormon Tabernacle Choir joke.

little dimples, especially on those chubby thighs," he
chuckles. "Just like her mama!"

"She was beautiful!" Nana Yetta retorts.

"Beautiful? You bet she was beautiful!" Mother
sniffs. "After I labored for twenty-six hours, you think
I'd give birth to an *ugly* baby?"

I suppose it's true I was not terrifically anxious to
be born. Actually, I was very happy in my first home.
In many important ways, mother's womb represented
the perfect Goldbloom environment—lots of good
food and nothing to do all day but sleep and eaves-
drop. Sure, the space was a little cramped but I certainly had enough room to kick around.*

However, nature finally prevailed and I was evicted
from mother's belly; an event for which the entire
family rejoiced except, of course, for my mother's
cousin Mamie who was always such a Miss Sour
Puss, she never sent a two-cent postcard, much less
a present, when any of the second cousins were
born.†

Once born, the first thing I noticed was that people
talked to me as if I were a complete imbecile; not to
mention the ridiculous faces they made and all the
poking and pinching I had to endure!

Daddy took to bouncing me up, up, up in the air,
which scared the living daylights out of me, but I kind
of liked it anyway.

My two grandmothers were the worst two offenders
by far. Nana Yetta bounced me around like a sack of
potatoes and Nana Hannah hugged me so hard that
after one of her trips north from Miami Beach, I
smelled like Chanel No. 5 for a week. I really hated
that. I wanted to tell them to cut it out but, of course,

---

* In Manhattan, I once paid $1300 a month for an apartment with
much the same description.
† Everyone excused Mamie for being such a cheapskate because
she was, after all, thirty-two and had never married, through absolutely no fault of my mother, who constantly introduced Mamie
to such wonderful catches as Sam, the butcher, and Bernie, the
pants cutter in Daddy's office.

my powers of communication were limited to crying or spitting up.

I quickly realized that every time I made a loud enough fuss, someone would either pick me up, change my diaper or give me something to eat. So it doesn't take a genius to figure out why Mom dubbed me "Little Miss Fuss Budget."

At the tender age of six weeks, I attended my first formal religious service, my naming, at Temple B'nai Ben Beth Shalom Alecheim in downtown Hohokus.* Rabbi Zindl officiated and I was ceremoniously named Bambi Iris Goldbloom.

Over the years, I've taken a lot of flack about my name. I must have said "Yes, it's my real name" about a zillion times. Confidentially, I've always resented having to defend my name since it wasn't my choice; my name was my grandfather's doing.

You see, like many people in America at the turn of the century, Grandpa was forced to leave his home and change his name. At that time, Grandpa lived in Boston. His family, the Haveford Huntingtons, were old line WASPS whose fortune derived from rail-roads, oil and investment banking. Always the rebel, Grandpa tried desperately to break away from the confines of his upper class existence. For years, he struggled to gain entrance into the one business that could really change people's lives—the garment center. Grandpa had a premonition that the modern American woman would love to wear pants, if only someone would cut them with enough room in the seat. Unfortunately, as Maximillian Haveford Huntington, Grandpa couldn't even get an introduction to meet the notions salesmen on Hester Street, much less hondle over the price of cotton serge.

So, one day, after a bitter argument with his father, Grandpa bought a ticket on the Manhattan-bound train and arrived in New York penniless and disin-

---

* I'm told it was a nice affair; we served mondel bread, raisin cake, tea and Mogen David wine.

herited. His first stop was Ellis Island where he received a new name and a thorough delousing. His work was cut out for him; he immediately began to practice speaking English with a Yiddish accent and operating a seltzer bottle without spritzing all over himself.

Within seven months of moving into a rundown tenement on the Lower East Side, Grandpa had become Max Goldbloom, married the former Yetta Horowitz and cut his first line of pleated pants. He claims he never regretted the move he made from Beacon Hill to Henry Street.

"Vell, I'll tell ya, dere vas only one ting I really regretted about da' change I made in my life," intones Grandpa Max, in his near-perfect immigrant accent, "and dat vas giving up martinis to drink dat sveet Mogen David vine. Phooey on dat vine!"

In all fairness to Grandpa, I guess I'm just as happy about his decision since Bambi Iris Haveford Huntington would've been an even worse name to carry around high school. Officially, I was named for Mom's great-aunt Gertie. Mom skirted the issue of selecting a G name by giving me a Jewish name beginning with that letter, although it's virtually unpronounceable and I can't even begin to spell it, so forget it (that's what Mom did). She named me Bambi because I was such a "dear" and because *Bambi* was the bedtime story she was reading to my cousin David when she went into labor. Daddy always says it's a good thing Mom wasn't reading *The Adventures of Dumbo* and I quite agree.

As for my middle name, well, no one has ever satisfactorily explained how I was dubbed Iris, so I won't even bother to repeat any of the feeble excuses I've heard over the years. Let's just say Mom had only recently come off massive anesthesia and heaven only knows what transpired in her drug-befuddled brain.

By most accounts, I was an exceptionally beautiful baby. "A punim to make all the neighborhood kvell," according to Nana Hannah. I'm not bragging here, I'm simply recording, from memory, the stories I've heard as part of the Jewish oral tradition of constantly reminding a son or daughter of his or her babyhood, a ritual repeated at every family gathering.

Mom tied a red ribbon, a "kine-ahora bindel," to my baby carriage so that she could "touch red" whenever a passing stranger remarked on my fair looks. In this way, Mom was effectively able to ward off the evil spirits lying in wait, ever ready to pounce on my head and doom me to a life of ugliness.

At nine months of age, I uttered my first word, "shoe," much to the disappointment of my parents, who would've preferred "Mama" or "Dada." It was, however, an appropriate portent of the stacks and stacks of shoe boxes that would congest my closets in the decades to come.

In almost no time at all, I started displaying my Nana Yetta's genetic heritage by gaining weight, mainly in my already dimpled thighs.*

Then one day an extraordinary event took place; an event of such magnitude, it would forever change the course of my life.

The time was the very, very, very early 1950s and the place was an inconspicuous Chinese restaurant named "Chinese Restaurant and Take-Out" located in Newark, New Jersey. I was ten months old and too young to remember the event but my cousin, David H. H. Goldbloom, was an eyewitness and he vividly recalls that day:

IT WAS A SUNDAY AFTERNOON LIKE EVERY SUNDAY·AFTERNOON. THE FAMILY WAS GATHERED TOGETHER AT THE CHINESE RESTAURANT AND TAKE-OUT. EVERYONE WAS THERE, ALL THE COUSINS AND AUNTS AND UNCLES. ABOUT THIRTEEN VARIETIES OF CHOW MEIN AND OTHER DISHES WERE SPREAD OUT ACROSS THE TABLE.

---

* This is a special talent I've been able to preserve all these years.

NOBODY WAS PAYING ANY ATTENTION WHEN
LITTLE BAMBI CREPT OUT OF HER HIGH CHAIR
AND CRAWLED ACROSS THE TABLE TO GET TO
THE FOOD. SHE PICKED UP A SPARE RIB AND
STARTED GUMMING IT. IN NO TIME AT ALL, BE-
FORE ANYONE HAD EVEN NOTICED, SHE HAD
EATEN NOT ONLY THE SPARE RIB BUT ALL OF
THE MOO GOO GAI PAN AS WELL. WELL, NO ONE
KNEW WHAT TO SAY . . . NONE OF US HAD EVER
SEEN SUCH A LITTLE BABY EAT SUCH A HUGE
AMOUNT OF FOOD. THE WHOLE FAMILY WAS
SPEECHLESS . . . EXCEPT, OF COURSE, FOR
GRANDPA HYMIE, WHO WAS MADDER THAN
HELL BECAUSE MOO GOO GAI PAN WAS HIS FA-
VORITE DISH.

Aunt Selma, our self-appointed family historian,
also attended that climactic dinner and the event held
great significance for her, too. "Oy vey its meir! do I
remember that dinner . . . you think I should forget
such a meal?" Aunt Selma asks with a laugh. This, of
course, was when Aunt Selma was still in a good
mood; that is, before Uncle Melvin divorced her.*

"Bambi-la, the little pitseleh, she polished off all
that Chinese food," Aunt Selma continues, "you

---

* Their divorce caused a major rumpus in our house because
Selma was Mom's sister and Melvin was Dad's second or third
cousin. Dad and Uncle Melvin were also removed a couple of
times, a concept I never fully grasped.
　Aunt Selma and Uncle Melvin had met at my parents' wedding,
which, in later years, was a real sore point between Aunt Selma
and Daddy. To this day, Selma claims that if Daddy hadn't introduced her to Melvin, the shmegegge, she would've married
Lenny Goldfinger, who was only Grandpa Hymies's stockboy at
the time but eventually, after Grandpa passed away, Lenny took
over the entire fur company, lock, stock and barrel; inheriting
Grandpa Hymie's title, the "Chinchilla Czar of West Thirty-
Seventh Street." According to Aunt Selma, Lenny's wife was now
living the life of someone named Riley, in Forest Hills, which
galled my aunt no end although she tried not to dwell on her past,
preferring to talk about everyone else's, especially mine.

should've been there, you wouldn't've believed your own two eyes. That little, tiny baby grinning from ear to ear, happy as could be . . . from that moment on, we all knew Bambi was going to be a good eater!"

"Tock-a, Bambi was a good eater!" my mother repeats, rapping her knuckles on the table, "knocking wood" to hopelessly confuse any of those evil spirits Aunt Selma might've unwittingly invoked by saying something good about me.

As the proud parent of the precocious baby, Daddy, of course, had his own special reasons for remembering that dinner. "The meal cost close to sixty bucks! Grandpa Hymie, the bum, insisted on ordering another portion of moo goo gai pan even though I kept telling him the stuff didn't grow on trees. But that was my wife's family; they could eat the Gersteins * out of house and home."

Afterward, of course, Daddy felt just awful about calling Grandpa Hymie a bum; especially since Grandpa died two days later and the doctor said there was still lots of Chinese food in his system.

Nana Hannah never forgave my father for making such a big deal over the dinner check. She returned to Miami Beach and vowed never again to stay at our house when she came north to visit the grandchildren.

Daddy graciously accepted Nana's ultimatum as a fair and equitable punishment.

As for me, this Sunday dinner with the family was a true turning point in my life. Of course, I didn't know it at the time, but the valuable lessons I learned that day included reaching out for the things I wanted and what a thrill it was being the focus of everybody's attention. But perhaps most important, I learned how much I loved moo goo gai pan.

* The Gersteins were our landlords.

WINKY-DINK, KATY KEENE AND ME

3

My best friend in kindergarten was *Sasha Crest.* The Crests lived in the garden apartment underneath us and our mothers were best friends, or "bosom buddies," as Daddy used to say.

I really admired Mrs. Crest because she was a career woman at a time, in the early 1950s, when my mom, like most mothers, made a living doing laundry and cooking dinner. Sasha's mom held not one, but *two* glamorous jobs; she was an Avon lady and a Tupperware party giver.

How I loved playing with Mrs. Crest's sample cases! My favorite afternoons were when Mrs. Crest would take Sasha and me along to watch her perform a miracle make-over on a frumpy neighborhood lady or demonstrate how to "burp" a plastic canister to a roomful of excited housewives.

Inexplicably, to me at least, Sasha preferred coming over to my apartment to play. Although I was bored to tears watching Mom chop liver or polish the silverware, such mundane household chores fascinated Sasha. Thus, Sasha and I were virtually inseparable (bosom buddies without the bosoms) from the ages of two-and-a-half to seven-and-a-half, when Sasha's parents moved to Minneapolis and insisted Sasha move, too.

(In spite of the distance between us, Sasha and I stayed best friends for many years, up until the time we were twenty-five years old and realized we had not spoken to each other in more than a decade.)

Throughout kindergarten, while our classmates batted, kicked, threw and bounced balls of various sizes, shapes and colors and otherwise occupied themselves with sweaty outdoor activities, Sasha and I liked to stay indoors and play less taxing games. Our favorite activity, aside from naptime, was playing with clay.

We would spend hours on our clay projects, diligently working on the most minute details of our creations. While the other kids slapped together common, everyday things—snakes, starfish, ashtrays and .38-caliber guns—Sasha and I used the clay to recreate our favorite Avon cosmetics and Tupperware products.

Our teacher, Miss Kranski, would often stop by our work area to inspect our models, encouraging us to use our imagination with the clay. "These are wonderful creations, children!" she would say, admiring our latest works of art.

She pointed to the largest structure. "Tell me, what is this supposed to be?" she asked.

"A salad crisper," Sasha replied.

Miss Kranski seemed surprised by Sasha's answer.

"This miracle product will keep lettuce fresh for an entire week," Sasha said.

"If kept snugly closed in the fridge," I added for clarification.

"Why, yes, of course," our teacher hesitantly said, "and these fat pancakes are . . . ?"

"They're not *pancakes*," I howled with laughter at Miss Kranski's remark. "They're pancake makeup, in our latest high-fashion compacts." I picked up a compact and smiled my most winning Avon smile. "Miss Kranski, allow me to give you a demonstration of how our new foundation will magically erase those nasty crow's feet." I held a wet dab of clay to my teacher's face.

"I think not, dear," Miss Kranski muttered, rubbing the corner of one eye as she backed away from me.

"Well, then, at least take home a free gift, with our compliments," Sasha said, handing our teacher a clay egg separator. "No purchase necessary."

"Thank you, girls," Miss Kranski said.

Sasha and I, grinning with pride, nodded in unison.

Even though we could never persuade Miss Kranski to participate in a make-believe make-over or spend a dime on any of our Tupperclay (as we called them) products, we still thought she was a swell teacher. She was so nice and cheerful all the time that we even forgave her for the stale graham crackers and warm milk she served every afternoon.

At the end of the school year, I graduated Miss Kranski's kindergarten class with top honors and, to the envy of Sasha, I was allowed to lead the children in our graduation theme song, "The Itsy Bitsy Spider." (I was the only child who had memorized all of the intricate finger movements.)

How proud Sasha and I felt that graduation day as we got dressed in our classroom, donning our little cardboard hats and pretending to rouge our cheeks with a dried-clay compact of blush-on. We pressed our perfect little noses * to the classroom window, searching for a glimpse of our parents' faces among the crowd of adults who filled the back lawn of our Thomas Paine/Thomas Jefferson Elementary School. To this day, I can remember the way the sun was shining and the leaves were rustling in the warm summer breeze as I watched my father set up his cameras and organize his film crew.

Unfortunately, Daddy's two cameramen and his sound guy blocked the view for most of the other parents, but Daddy ignored the jeers of the crowd as he herded the children onto our makeshift stage.

"Move quickly, kids," Daddy directed. "Ya know how much these film guys cost per hour? Plenty, that's

* Neither Sasha nor I ever needed a nose job!

how much! We're not talking chicken feed! Come on, Tiffany, step lively!"

Worried about my father's payroll budget for this production, I hurried the class through "The Itsy Bitsy Spider" in just under one minute and thirty-seven seconds. Tiffany Jerkowitz started to cry because she couldn't sing that fast, but Miss Kranski said it was a graduation record.

Afterward, the parents milled around the backyard, photographing everything that moved. The children drank sun-warmed Kool Aid and tried to avoid getting kissed by fawning grandparents.

As usual, Nana Hannah trapped me in a stranglehold for a good ten minutes, after which I reeked of Chanel No. 5. Although Nana Hannah had flown in from Miami for the festivities, she still refused to speak to my father.

"Your Nana Hannah holds a grudge better than any human being on the face of the earth," Daddy commented, which made me real proud until Mommy told him to shut up and show a little respect.

I wasn't out of kindergarten for more than a week when my mother decided it was time I learned to read and, with a vengeance, she took up the chore of teaching me.

Our reading lesson was between 3:00 and 4:00 or whenever Ceil broke up the daily canasta game by cheating.

"Why do you keep playing with Ceil if she always cheats?" my father always asked.

"We need a fourth," Mother shrugged.

At any rate, Mother would call me out of the swimming pool right about the time Ceil started adding up the score. (Naturally Mom and I studied at the swim club. Where else would we spend the summer, since my father was "too much of a tightwad to take us to the Catskills for more than two lousy measly weeks." Aunt Selma got to spend the whole summer at

Brown's because her alimony settlement had put her on easy street for the rest of her life or until Uncle Melvin dropped dead, which wouldn't be such a great loss either.)

Mommy and I always sat under the umbrellaed tables that circled the pool. I can still remember the way Mom looked in one of her bathing suits made with real whale bones which had such firm foundations they could stand up all by themselves. Mom sat up super-straight in her beach chair because, I think, her suits fit so tightly she couldn't bend at the waist, although sometimes she sort of swayed a little from side to side.

Mom's poolside outfit was accented by a matching sarong and a schmatta she tied around her head to prevent her frosted hair from discoloring. She would slather Nivea cream over her arms and legs while insisting I wrap seventeen towels around myself so that I "shouldn't catch a chill."

"Look, your lips are turning purple!"* she was wont to screech, turbaning my head with yet another towel, and making disapproving clucking noises with her tongue.

Once securely bundled up and fully protected against the ninety-degree heat, humidity and burning sun, I began grappling with Uncle Wiggly and Dr. Seuss.

I didn't show much interest in either volume, especially Dr. Seuss, who, in my opinion, knew even less about good English than I did. "And you don't have to stop. You can think about SCHLOPP," Mom pointed to each word as she read from *Oh, The Thinks You Can Think*. "Schlopp, schlopp, beautiful schlopp. Beautiful schlopp with a cherry on top."

---

* Mother always paid particular attention to the color of my lips. As I grew older, my lack of lipstick would drive her into a frenzy. "What's the matter, you can't put a little *color* on your lips?" she'd cry, pressing a tube of lipstick into my hand. "Here, try this, my favorite color: Screaming Fire-Engine Coral."

"What does schlopp mean?" I asked my mother.

"I'm not sure, dear. It's a made-up word."

"A made-up word? Is that legal?"

"I suppose so."

"But how do I know which words are real and which are made up?" I slammed the book closed. "What kind of doctor is this Seuss clown anyway?" I asked, but my mother didn't seem to know.

In general, children's books just weren't my cup of tea. Oh, I liked it well enough when my parents or my babysitter would read to me at bedtime, but if I was going to make the supreme effort of learning to read, it was clear Mother would have to come up with more interesting fare than schlopp stories or the goody-two-shoes adventures of Madeline and Eloise, neither of whom would've lasted five minutes at Thomas Paine/ Thomas Jefferson Elementary School, as I told my mother.

Mom tried another tactic. She splayed a bunch of magazines before me: *My Weekly Reader, Jack and Jill, Highlights, TV Guide*. Nothing worked. Try as she might, Mother just couldn't motivate me to learn to read.

Then, one hot afternoon, we were struggling with M-N-O when a cabana boy walked by and dropped a menu on our table.

"What's that?" I wanted to know.

"It's a menu, darling," Mom said. "Let's get back to the M words . . . man is spelled M-A-N."

"Mommy, isn't menu an M word?"

"Why, yes, darling, it is!"

From that day on, I was taught to read by studying menus. I quickly ran through the club menu, learning how to spell four different kinds of salad—chicken, egg, shrimp and green. From there I graduated to sandwiches. ("Pumpernickel" was my first four-syllable conquest!) My vocabulary increased rapidly when the club started serving several varieties of omelets.

To expand our home library, Mom swiped menus from the exotic restaurants she and Daddy frequented on their evenings out.

Late one night, Mom tiptoed into my room, carrying her shoes in her hand. I awoke to the rustling sound of crinolines against nylon.

"Which menu did you bring me tonight, Mommy?" I sat up in bed all attentive, anticipating another gourmet spelling lesson.

My mother laughed softly as she sat at the edge of my little four-poster bed. "Chez Antoinette," she whispered, opening the huge, red-tasseled menu.

"This is Chateaubriand." She spelled it out for me. "C-H-A-T-E-A-U-B-R-I-A-N-D."

"Chateaubriand,"I repeated softly. "C-H-A—"

Suddenly, we were interrupted by my father, rudely snapping on the overhead light. "Janice, why're you teaching her that?" he growled and, crossing the room, tore the menu from my mother's hand.

"Chopped Steak," he read aloud. "C-H-O-P-P-E-D S-T-E-A-K. Repeat after me, Bambi." He looked at my mom. "You too, Janice!"

"Chopped steak," Mom and I repeated in unison with my father. "C-H-O-P-P-E-D S-T-E-A-K."

"When you get married, princess, your *rich* husband can buy you Chateaubriand," Daddy declared, and tossed the menu on my night stand.

"Herman, why do you teach her things like that?" My mother cried. "You know I'd never let her eat chopped steak in a restaurant. Who knows what kind of beef they use?"

My parents were fighting as they left my room and I could hear the echoes of their argument in the hallway. I knew they would argue late into the night but that, in the end, they would kiss and make up.

"Your Daddy will never leave me," Mommy always assured me. Her reasoning had something to do with some kind of fun that only Mommy could give Daddy. I think she called it "trust fun." Anyway, the important thing about this fun was that Daddy couldn't have it without Mommy because of a paper Grandpa Hymie wrote before he went to heaven.

It was all too complicated for my six-year-old brain so I put all worries about my parents out of my head as I turned over in bed. I went to sleep dreaming of swirling crinolines, exotic restaurants and Chateaubriand. Of course, I didn't have the slightest idea what Chateaubriand actually was, but I knew if it was as expensive as Daddy said, I would probably love it.

With very little effort, Mommy eased me away from menus and into books. Every night we would read a page from the family bible: *The Joy of Cooking.* I especially enjoyed the fanciful line drawings that dotted the pages of *Joy.*

One day Daddy took the cookbook into his office and xeroxed my two favorite pages so that I could hang the drawings over my bed. Late at night, I lay awake in bed and, by the amber glow of my little Minnie Mouse night light, gazed dreamily at the treasured illustrations of "Divisions of Commercial Cuts and Retail Cuts of Beef" and "Bone Structure and Commercial Cuts from the Carcass of Lamb."

In no time, my spelling skills far surpassed those of the other children in my class. I was the only first-grader who knew the essential difference between "knead" and "need" or the distinction between a Pink Lady and a perfect Manhattan.

Also, I was the only kid in the entire school who was semi-fluent in French, being able to spell, define and use in a sentence such words as *niçoise, hors d'oeuvre, croquette, mousse,* and *vinaigrette.* (I once got an A plus for writing a little poem that rhymed *flambé, puree, soufflé and pàté.)*

My mother was so enthusiastic about my literary talents that she began saving all of my papers, a practice she has continued to this very day. To date, Mom has squirreled away every word I ever put to paper and every piece of paper that has ever slipped past my hands.

Although her collection was of great assistance in the preparation of this book, I had a tremendous logistical problem sorting through all of the material. Mother showed little discretion about what she chose to hoard. A good portion of her enormous collection is more or less useless. For example, I had to wade through cartons and cartons of scratch paper containing endless games of hangman, three miles of gum wrapper chains and four sacks of empty potato chip bags to find my first formal letter, a piece of fan mail I wrote, at the tender age of seven, to my television idol, Winky-Dink.* Luckily, I knew enough, even then, to make a carbon copy. Reprinted in its entirety, the letter read as follows:

> DEAR WINK,
> I THINK YOU ARE THE BEST ON TV. I LIKE YOU. YOU ARE GRATE [SIC]. WHO'S YOUR FAVORITE MOVIE STAR?
>
> > LOVE, YOUR FAN,
> > BAMBI GOLDBLOOM

I was heartbroken when Winky didn't answer my plaintive letter. Quite frankly, Winky's failure to recognize and acknowledge this obvious case of puppy love generated in me a life-long prejudice against stick figures. After Winky's cruel rejection, I stopped watching "Winky-Dink and You" and I turned my attention to two-dimensional characters like Supergirl and Casper the Friendly Ghost. From there, I made the logical progression to Archie, Millie the Model and, my favorite, Katy Keene.

By the time I was in my late sevens and early eights, I simply adored the statuesque Katy Keene, who had

---

* I got Wink's address from my official Winky-Dink Kit, which, as you may recall, included a green plastic sheet that fit over the television screen and a box of special crayons.

everything in the world a girl could want: lots of handsome boyfriends, a super-successful modeling career, a fabulous wardrobe and tons of jealous girl-friends. But the best part was that her clothes were actually designed by her readers, who would submit their drawings to the publisher of *Katy Keene Comics.* If Katy liked a particular outfit, and decided to wear it, you would get a credit line with your name and hometown printed in the comic, a real honor, to my mind. Over the years I sketched hundreds, maybe thousands of different outfits for Katy, and, every week, submitted my work. I suppose, as I look back now, this was the beginning of my eventual career on Seventh Avenue, but Katy's influence was even more crucial to my family. Because, as my father always says, "Thanks to Katy Keene, my business went bank-rupt in 1959."

BEST FRIENDS AND BARBIE DOLLS

4

I *had barely recovered from the Winky-Dink crisis before Sasha's mom was promoted to Tupperware's Midwestern Regional Party Organizer and the whole Crest family moved away.*

Sasha took the move really hard. Not only would we be separated; she would be forced to live in *Minneapolis!**

"They've probably never even heard of hula hoops," Sasha wailed, sobbing on my shoulder.

I tried in vain to console her.

It was on a Tuesday that Sasha packed all her Barbies, Slinkies, coloring books and six brand-new hula hoops into a huge moving van (headed for Minnesota), climbed into her parents' green Chevy† and left me stranded without a best friend to play with.

I was shattered. My life would never be the same. How could I survive without Sasha?

I moped around the house in a state of total despair, even going so far as to lose my appetite for dinner,

---

* Keep in mind this was the fifties, years before Mary Tyler Moore transformed Minneapolis into a swinging-singles kind of town.
† This was before Ralph Nader, so Sasha didn't know enough to buckle up.

which greatly alarmed my parents. I locked myself in my room and designed Katy Keene clothes all evening. (My only consolation was that Sasha's move inspired me to design a line of travel clothes—plaid clam diggers with a matching plaid circle hat box—which ran in the Spring Previews issue of *Katy Keene*.)

I tried playing with Bruce Berger, my next-door neighbor. I thought Bruce was cute because his round face was covered with freckles. He looked a lot like Howdy Doody, without the strings, of course. But, really, boys were no fun at that age. Bruce's idea of a good time was to punch me in the stomach until I got mad enough to hit him back.

Bruce's twin sister, Ethel, was a likely candidate for the best friend position except for her annoying tendency to repeat everything anyone said.

"Hi, Ethel," I'd say.

"Hi, Ethel," she'd answer.

"How are you?"

"How are you?"

"Ethel, quit doing that!"

"Ethel, quit doing that!"

"I'm not kidding, Ethel!"

"I'm not kidding, Ethel!"

At which point, Bruce would intervene by punching Ethel in the stomach; not without my approval, I should add.

It wasn't until the following Thursday that I was able to find a viable replacement for Sasha. (Hey! Two whole days seems like forever when you're seven years old.)

My new best friend's name was Q* and she was one of the most popular girls in the class even though everyone was scared to death of her. Q had an evil temper and she was more than a little spoiled. In fact, she hated to share anything with anyone. "You're breathing my air," Q would say if you stood too close to her.

* Not her real name!

Choosing Q as a best friend was a tough decision, because she scared me, too. Part of it had to do with Q's family life. The daughter of the richest orthodontist in town, Q lived in a big white house at the top of a hill. However, the house was so well decorated that Q's mother refused to let anyone so much as touch their expensive furniture. (Guests were given surgical gloves, masks and gowns upon arriving at the house.) And, even worse, like her mother and three older sisters, Q was always on a diet so snack time at her house meant a gloomy choice of Melba toast, gluten bread or Metrecal.

But Q had one redeeming quality that far outweighed her sour disposition. Sure, she was mean, nasty and selfish, but I could overlook her character flaws because Q possessed the most fabulous Barbie wardrobe in town.

Q's Barbie had a collection of clothes that was simply to die; her doll was as well dressed as Katy Keene.* Every piece of clothing was either designer-labeled or hand tailored by her mother's personal dressmaker. Q's portable pink Barbie closet included three tiny fur coats: a real Blackglama mink, a fox jacket for less formal wear and a fake fur for knocking around.

Q's Barbie had never even heard of Loehmann's. (My poor Barbie could barely find one silk blouse in her closet that didn't have the label slashed out.)

I was willing to put up with all of Q's unpleasant ways to get my hands on some of those outfits. However, no matter how much I pleaded, Q refused to let me borrow the red satin Gilda gown that I just adored.

"Your Barbie is too fat!" Q whined. "She'll bust all the seams like she did with the sequined ensemble."

"The sequined dress got ripped because you grabbed it out of my hands when your Ken made a pass at my Barbie!" I spat back, knowing how sensi-

* I copied some of Q's Barbie wardrobe for my Katy Keene submissions and received a nasty note. "Katy does not wear cheap knock-offs," wrote the publisher.

tive Q was to Ken's obvious attraction to my Barbie over hers.

"Your Barbie should learn to wear some underwear if she doesn't want to get picked up by every man in pants," Q viciously attacked my doll. "And I think a panty girdle might be in order these days."

"She does not need a girdle!" I screamed, flying off the handle, as Mom would say. "She's lost a ton of weight since she wore the sequined dress. Just look at the way this cowgirl dress is hanging on her! She's all skin and bones!"

Q inspected my Barbie in her Western outfit. "Your Barbie should go back to exercise class." she sniffed, handing her back to me with disdain. "Just look at all those lumpy dimples on her upper thighs."*

I grabbed my Barbie from Q. "We don't have to hang around here and be insulted by our EX-best friends," I angrily declared. I gathered together my Barbie's authentic Annie Oakley suede jacket and matching cowgirl boots. "We're leaving," I announced.

In a huff, I picked up my schoolbooks and put on my coat. My Barbie got into her pink Corvette, slammed the door and drove off without me.

Mother couldn't help but notice our agitation when we got home. "Barbie's hair is a mess!" Mom cried. "Was she driving with the top down?"

I nodded angrily as I threw my books onto the kitchen table.

"Why, she must really be in a dither to drive so carelessly. Just look at her hair, that beehive is all but ruined. What on earth happened?" Mother handed me a chocolate chip cookie. I didn't really feel like talking and I knew Mom was using the cookies as a bribe but these were *warm* Tollhouse cookies. "It's

---

* It was only the 1950s, the term "cellulite" had yet to be coined (not that my Barbie suffered from unsightly cottage cheese dimples back then). Now, of course, my Barbie's in her late forties and she won't even *discuss* upper thighs anymore.

that stupid Q!" I confessed, "She gets me and Barbie so mad. She's jealous because her Ken is in love with my Barbie."

Mom glanced at Barbie.

"It's not my Barbie's fault," I said in defense of my beloved doll, "if Q's Ken is attracted to her, is it?"

"Well, no, of course not," Mom laughed gently. "Love is like lightning, you never know where or when it will strike."

I had never thought electricity had anything to do with love but what did I really know about such things?

"Sweetie, tell me something," Mom said, flinging a dishtowel over her left shoulder.* "I always thought you didn't like Q."

"Yeah, so?"

"So, I don't understand why she's your best friend all of a sudden."

Are all mothers this dense? I wondered to myself for the hundred thousandth time.

"How could you ask me a question like that, Mom?" I asked, exasperated. "You, of all people, should understand. Look at your friend Ceil!"

"But you don't play canasta," Mom argued. "You don't need a fourth to play Barbie dolls."

"Oh, no?" I countered. "And what if *Barbie* wants to play canasta?"

Mother nodded philosophically, "Umm, I guess I see your point," she finally agreed. "But, even so, I wish there was something I could do." She stared thoughtfully out the window.

I wondered what kind of crazy scheme was brewing underneath those tightly rolled pincurls.

"I know," she snapped her fingers. "Maybe I should call Q's mommy and invite Q over for dinner tonight?"

As usual, my mother hit upon the one solution that

---

* For some unknown reason, Mom could not cook unless she had at least one dishtowel draped over her left shoulder.

had absolutely no relation to the problem. "Forget it,"
I said, "Barbie would barf all over the dinner table if
Q showed up tonight." To emphasize my point, I
manuevered Barbie's chin to her chest, simulating
Barbie's official barfing position. I made mock-vomit-
ing noises. Barbie, always the showoff, stuck her fingers down her throat and pretended to throw up. She
got a little carried away with herself and actually
started gagging so I clapped her soundly on the back.

"All right, dear," Mom said. "I can't say I fully understand your attitude but I guess school has changed
a lot since my day."

Mom then proceeded with her usual litany about
her own school days, in the olden times, when she
had to walk two miles through the snow (even in the
summer)* to get to school and her afterschool activities included scrubbing the kitchen floor and doing
the laundry because Nana Hannah's cleaning lady
didn't do as good a job as my mother.

I let Mom ramble on (I had no choice) as she
prepared dinner and I polished off the remaining
cookies.

Mom was up to the part about how everything was
so much simpler and people were so much nicer back
then when Dad walked through the door, and a few
minutes later, we all sat down to eat while my mother
continued her saga of childhood during the Depression.

Daddy looked up from his plate of spaghetti long
enough to agree with my mother's assessment that
food not only cost less back then, it even tasted better.

As always, I wasn't really listening. I was wondering how I could cajole $3.75 out of my father in order
to buy Barbie her own authentic Gilda dress. And, I
had to ask myself, if I got my Barbie her own Gilda
dress, would I still want Q as a best friend?

Ironically, I needn't have worried, As it turned out,
my friendship with Q was to last only another two

---

* That crazy Brooklyn weather!

weeks—until one Wednesday morning when I forgot to save her a seat on the school bus and she swore she'd never, ever, ever, *ever* speak to me again as long as she lived, and, thirty years later, I can honestly say Q was as good as her word.

After Q unceremoniously dumped me, the next few years of my childhood passed by relatively uneventfully.* My best friend problem was solved when Sandy Rasabinsky moved into the garden apartment across the courtyard. I suppose it was fate, Sandy was looking for a best friend, so was I. Neither of us asked too many questions. It wasn't the greatest best friendship in the world but, after what I'd been through with Sasha and Q, I was more than willing to settle for simple companionship.

Sandy and I formed our own exclusive club called BASCO (Bambi and Sandy Club Only). We agreed not to admit any new members, which was good because no one asked to join except for Ethel, whom we unanimously blackballed.

Events in my social life pretty much run together in my mind; a whirlwind of playdates, Howdy Doody shows, homework, jumping jacks, ballet classes, Katy Keene designs and the air raid drills we continually rehearsed in school just in case the Russians decided to drop the A bomb on Hohokus, New Jersey. Our instructions, in case of *real* emergency, were simple:

> Don't stand near the windows.
> Don't run in the halls.
> Don't talk to your neighbors
> Don't panic.

I remember a class trip to the Bronx Zoo, my first Broadway show,† Cousin David's bar mitzvah, an A

---

* I'll try to hurry the story along, because, if I don't, we'll never get to the sexy parts.
† *Peter Pan.* And I don't care what Mommy said, I could, too, see the ropes.

plus for a third-grade oral book review   and a frozen chocolate dessert Aunt Selma made for someone's birthday. But, basically, I led a pretty quiet life. Quiet, that is, until the fifth grade.

Fifth grade was the year we moved.

STUPID CUPID

I was eleven years old when my father made a major career shift. Daddy went from manufacturing pants to cutting skirts. Fortunately for us, he switched just in time to be in the forefront of a leading industry trend: culottes.

Daddy did so well with culottes that we were able to move out of our two-bedroom apartment and into a seven-room split-level across town. (The house came with its own Fallout Shelter dug into the backyard, which, we all agreed, we'd never need but—who knew?—it certainly couldn't hurt.)

Moving is always traumatic for a kid but, mostly, I took it in my stride. Of course, I had to give up Sandy as a best friend (I cried a little when Sandy and I said goodbye but, confidentially, I was not all that upset). I could easily overlook this hardship because Mommy promised me that, once we moved into our new house, I would get the one thing I had been dreaming about ever since I was a toddler.

"And this is going to be your very own bathroom," Mommy said when we visited the development, where rows and rows of new split-levels were being constructed. Of course, at the time, Mom was pointing at an area of roped-off floor, but I had enough imagination to visualize what the tub would look like. (Sparkling clean, if my mother had anything to say about it!)

"And will my very own medicine cabinet go here?" I asked, pointing to an imaginary wall.

"Yes, darling," Mommy wrapped her arm around my shoulder and hugged me. "And, as soon as we move, Nana Yetta promised to buy your first set of monogrammed towels." A tear rolled down Mommy's cheek.

My own set of towels! I thought excitedly. "They won't be seconds, will they, Mommy?"

"Over my dead body!" she declared with her usual conviction. "As long as I'm around, my little girl will never dry her tush with factory seconds!"

I could barely wait to move.

We spent weeks packing our things and then dusting, cleaning, scrubbing and polishing the apartment.

"The new renters shouldn't think we were slobs," Mommy said as she waxed the floor in the hall closet.

Moving day came one dark, cold April evening.

Daddy instructed Mommy, the moving men and me to be very, very quiet as we slipped past the apartment of Mr. Gerstein, our landlord.*

"We don't want Mr. Gerstein to be sad because we're moving," Daddy carefully explained to me. "He'll really miss us if we tell him we're going away." I whispered Daddy's instructions to my Barbie as we silently waved goodbye to the courtyard where Sasha and I used to sell our Tupperclay.

Like most of the neighbors' houses in our new development, our split-level was way above our means and we couldn't afford a stick of furniture. At first, my mother didn't complain. "Empty rooms are better than no rooms," she would philosophically remark. The unfurnished rooms didn't bother me either because I enjoyed having the open space for rollerskating when Mom was out shopping.

Actually, Mom and I had fun fantasizing about the kind of furniture we would buy when Daddy had the money. I suggested we replicate Aunt Selma's deco-

---

* Imagine my surprise on discovering, much later in life, that some people moved during the day! In the daylight!

rating scheme, which featured a color television as the central piece of furniture, but Mom was thinking more on the lines of Princess Grace Kelly's Monaco palace decor.

After a while, though, Mom started pestering my father about buying furniture for those empty, echoing rooms.

"If fancy furniture is so important, why don't you use some of your *trust fun* money to buy it?" my father asked.

"That's emergency money!" Mother emphatically retorted.

"So, nu? This isn't an emergency? We're eating on the floor because we can't afford a dining-room table and you're *saving* for an emergency. You know, you're meshugge." Daddy turned to me. "Your mother, me-shugge!" he exclaimed.

Pointing to his head and making little circles with his finger, Daddy uncrossed his legs and awkwardly stood up. "Meshugge! The woman's definitely meshugge!" Daddy mumbled as he wandered off upstairs.

"Your father's a little upset tonight, dear," Mother sighed, scraping lamb chop bones off Daddy's plate. "Some silly story in *Women's Wear* said culottes are out this season."

"Oh, no!" I cried, more knowledgeable than my mother about the power of *WWD*. If culottes were really dead, we were in deep trouble.

Worried that I'd have to take a cut in my allowance if Daddy had to finance a warehouse full of dead culottes, I followed my father upstairs to my parents' bedroom. Daddy was sitting on the edge of one of the two army cots my parents were temporarily using as beds.

I tiptoed into my mother's closet and started playing with Mom's shoes. "Daddy, are you okay?" I timidly asked, trying on a pair of Mom's red stiletto heels, my favorite item in the closet.*

* In the house!

"Of course, princess." He bravely smiled. "Come here and give your old dad a kiss."

I wobbled over to my father and, throwing myself in his arms, I planted a resounding kiss on his cheek. For several minutes, I sat quietly on Daddy's lap, contemplating his problem. "Daddy, is it true *WWD* is predicting the death of culottes?" I shyly inquired.

"I'm afraid so, kitten." Daddy murmured. "But don't worry, they'll be back in fashion next season."

"But you're only as good as what you cut *this* season," I said, repeating my father's favorite phrase.

Daddy sighed as he absentmindedly tousled my hair.

"Daddy," I said, trying to distract him, "you know what Tiffany Jerkowitz was wearing today in school? These really neat kind of shorts; I think she called them *skorts*. Wait here a minute."

Barefoot, I ran into my room and grabbed my latest Katy Keene drawing. I raced back to my father and showed it to him. "See, Daddy? They're like real short culottes but they flare at the bottom."

Daddy stared, for the longest time, at my picture of Katy in her green skorts* and orange halter top. "Skorts?" Daddy asked.

"Skorts!"

Well, talk about out of the mouths of babes!

You probably know the ending to this story, it's the plot line of practically every Margaret O'Brien movie you've ever seen and loved. Of course Daddy went into manufacturing skorts and, as they say in Hollywood, the rest was history.

Daddy cut zillions of skorts that season and, as has been so well documented, skorts turned out to be the "Worst Fashion Faux Pas in the History of Seventh Avenue," according to Eugene Shepard in his weekly *WWD* column, *Let's Talk Tacky!* "This season, skorts were an even bigger bomb than the great culotte debacle of last season," wrote Shepard.

---

* I had wanted to make them lilac but my purple crayon wasn't pointy enough.

Daddy went bankrupt; the bank repossessed our car and filed suit to reclaim the house. Credit collectors rang our doorbell at all hours of the night; fat men in shiny suits threatened to break my father's legs.

One night I caught Daddy eyeing my felt-lined jewelry box. The next morning my fourteen-carat gold charm bracelet mysteriously disappeared.*

Daddy started playing the ponies and fooling around with cheap women. He broke down in tears every time we watched *The Millionaire* on television.

Mommy found empty bourbon bottles in Daddy's sock drawer but, through it all, she stuck by his side.

In the end, we were saved by Mother's faith in my father, and, more important, by her trust fun.

"This, epis, is an emergency!" Mom finally concluded.

The next season, Daddy quit his low-life ways. He started coming home again after work and the Betty Boop-voiced women stopped calling the house. Daddy cut culottes, and just as he had predicted, culottes came back into fashion with a vengeance. We got that new dining-room table and Mommy seemed much less tense after Daddy bought her a real bed (with a mattress *and* box spring).

As for me, well, I was happy. One night, I left an offering for the tooth fairy and, in the morning, found my charm bracelet stashed under my pillow.

Moving had changed my father but it also changed me.

I was learning to adapt to a whole new school, a whole new teacher and no best friend to fill me in on all the local gossip. It wasn't an easy year for me, which is why, I suppose, I fell madly in love with Jerome Wall.

---

* The charms included a dancing ballerina, a French poodle, a heart, a chi, a square calendar "page" with my birthday x'ed out, a little car with a trunk that really opened and a shoe (to commemorate the first word I'd ever spoken).

THE GIRL FROM RIVER HEIGHTS

*I*n the fifth grade I had three great passions: Nancy Drew, stuffed animals and Jerome Wall.

I was also madly in love with my poodle skirt, but I don't classify that as a passion; even though Mom complained the skirt was going to walk away by *itself* if I didn't send it to the dry cleaners once in a while. (A poodle skirt is a piece of clothing that is impossible to describe without sounding moronic so I'll save myself the embarrassment.) Fifth grade was also the year Seymour started eating Friday-night dinner at our house, but I'm getting ahead of myself.

First, I have to explain about love at first sight or you won't understand anything that happened that year.

I walked into Room 7, my first day of fifth grade, and there he stood. He had a sandy-colored crew cut and wore a well-bled madras short-sleeved shirt. His eyes were the deep, rich color of blue Play Dough.

I was mesmerized by the handsome stranger and as he walked toward the front of the class, I immediately began envisioning him in a tuxedo, walking down the aisle in temple, a yarmulke on his head.*

* I said a quick prayer—"Please, make him be Jewish!"

At the blackboard, he picked up a piece of chalk and wrote "Mr. Wall". Then he turned to face the class. "Good morning, class," he smiled. "My name is Jerome Wall."

I instantly became aware of the complications: I was eleven and a quarter years old, Jerome Wall was probably closer to thirty. I wondered if our age difference would be a problem as I opened my brand new Woolworth's notebook. "Mr. Jerome Wall," I wrote at the top of the page. "Mrs. Bambi Goldbloom Wall, " I scribbled underneath his name and nodded with approval because, even though it wasn't "*Dr.* and Mrs. Wall," still, it had a definite ring to it.

I practiced alternative names like "Mrs. B.G. Wall" as Mr. Wall took attendance. I had practically filled the page when he called my name.

"Here . . . over here!"

When Jerome smiled at me, he looked just like Cubby on *The Mickey Mouse Club*. "Bambi? Like the deer?" he asked.

"Like the other dear, the one that sounds the same but is spelled different." (Unlike some of my girl-friends, I was never afraid to display my intelligence to men.)

Mr. Wall whistled softly under his breath, obviously impressed, I thought.

"Brown nose," Bruce Berger hissed from the back of the classroom.

Mr. Wall either ignored Bruce or didn't hear him as he continued calling out names.

I turned around and stuck out my tongue at Bruce. "Eat dirt and die, Bruce Berger," I said.*

As the weeks went by, I began to realize Mr. Wall's teaching techniques were hardly conventional, and I'm not just saying that because he was the cutest teacher in Hohokus. For instance, Mr. Wall liked to tap dance in front of the class to the tune of "M-i-s-s-

---

* My technique with men had yet to be refined.

i-s-i-p-p-i!" He said we might never remember anything he taught us but we would certainly recall his singing and dancing.*

I couldn't figure out how Mr. Wall felt about me. He seemed to appreciate the apples, cheese and wine I left on his desk every day but, in most ways, he treated me the same way he treated Tiffany Jerkowitz and all the other girls in the class. By October, our unresolved relationship was driving me nuts. One rainy afternoon, I decided to wait outside school and confront him. I pretended to play hopscotch in the schoolyard, which wasn't easy, because the rain kept washing away my chalk marks.

I was rechalking the wet cement for the twenty-third time when I saw Mr. Wall walk toward his car. I walked around the swings and stood in front of his car until Mr. Wall offered me a ride home.

In the car, Mr. Wall commented on how wet I was (I was dripping rain all over his plastic seat covers) but I didn't want to spend all afternoon discussing the weather.

"Mr. Wall," I said, as I coquettishly banged my rain boots under the dashboard of the car. "I'd like to ask your opinion about something."

"Bambi, does this have anything to do with yesterday's math test?"

"No," I said, wondering if his mind was always on business.

"Listen, I thought your argument that sevens and eights are irrelevant to the numerical system was clever, but I really think you need to learn how to multiply *all* the numbers from one to ten."

The last thing I wanted to discuss was the multiplication table. "Mr. Wall, I wanted to ask your opinion of younger women," I blurted out.

He seemed momentarily stunned as he swerved the car away from a passing garbage truck (just in the nick

* He was right!

of time, I should add). "Younger women?" he laughed nervously.

I couldn't tell if Mr. Wall was being coy or stupid. (It suddenly occurred to me that he might be an idiot —with his tap dancing in class and all—but I put that thought squarely out of my mind.)

Unfortunately, I lived pretty close to school so, just at that moment, we reached my house. Mr. Wall zoomed into my driveway at about seventy-five miles an hour and hit the brakes so hard that my books went flying into the windshield. "So, I'll see you in school tomorrow," he said.

"Yeah, sure," I muttered.

Sliding across the seat, I took my math book from Mr. Wall and, accidentally touching his hand, I received a huge electric shock. I was reminded of my mother's description of love ("It's like a bolt of electricity") and I realized this must truly be love, the real thing.

"Static electricity," Mr. Wall commented.

"I *know*!" I happily agreed.

I could hear tea cups rattling in the kitchen as I walked into my house and assumed Mom was sitting at the kitchen table with her best friend Sadie. I would've bet my entire weekly allowance of seventy-five cents that they were talking about Sadie's creep-ola son, Seymour.*

"Janice, my Seymour keeps playing that spin-the-bottle game!" Sadie whined.

"Said-a-la, all children play spin-the-bottle!"

"With a bowl of goldfish?"

"Goldfish?"

"Goldfish!"

"Oy vey!"

"You ain't kidding, oy vey!"

* They were always talking about Seymour.

Mom was silent for a few moments. "Sadie, darling, I think maybe the boy spends too much time by himself. Why don't you send him over here for dinner on Friday night? Maybe we'll get Bambi to make him more social."

I wanted to race into the kitchen and ask Mommy why I had to get involved with her harebrained scheme and Sadie's spaz son but I knew I'd only get the standard, "Because I Said So and I'm The Mommy, That's Why!" reply so, instead, I ran upstairs and slammed my bedroom door.

My mother walked to the foot of the staircase, "Bambi? Is that you?" she called.

By way of an answer, I turned on my radio and blasted her with a Frankie Avalon refrain. As she traipsed back to the kitchen, I could hear her muttering something to Sadie about how girls were no picnic, either.

I threw myself on the bed, squashing the thirty-seven stuffed animals piled over the bedspread.* Jerome Giraffe let out a horrifying squawk, so I threw him across the room to shut him up. "I'm in no mood, Jerome!" I added, just so all the animals would be clear about my state of mind. There was dead silence on the bed.

Seymour was such a weirdo. Take my birthday, for instance, which he was invited to only because my mother said, "Either he gets invited or there's no party, period!" So Seymour brings me this humongus present, all wrapped up with a green satin ribbon, and I was thinking maybe he wasn't such a faggot after all when I opened it and found—you'll never, ever guess what, so I'll spare you the suspense—a case of Puppy Chow!

"This is to feed all those stuffed animals of yours," Seymour said, like I really needed his retarded sense of humor.

---

* Daddy called my room the Plush Menagerie. (I didn't get it.)

When we were alone together in my room, Seymour always wanted to play doctor, which I wouldn't have minded, because I've got a scientific mind, but Seymour wanted to play doctor with my stuffed animals, especially Molly Moo Cow.

"Someday I'm going to be a rich Park Avenue vet," he would boast.

I kicked Roger Reindeer and Ulysses Unicorn off the bed and grabbed Nancy Drew's latest adventure, *The Clue of the Dancing Puppet*, from my yellow wicker night table. Nancy Drew was the only one who could help me forget Seymour and the gnawing feeling that, static electricity or not, my relationship with Mr. Wall was still far from resolved.

How I envied Nancy Drew and her career as a young sleuth! First, she had the world's greatest Dad, Carson Drew, a widely-known lawyer who would always supply Nancy with an interesting clue when she was running into a dead end. Of course, Nancy's mom was dead, which should've made her sad, except she didn't seem to mind,* especially with a gem housekeeper like Hannah Gruen who was always baking blueberry muffins and never once told Nancy to clean her room, do her homework, get her elbows off the table or take her hair out of her eyes.

I loved Nancy's blue roadster and the way she'd tool around River Heights with plump Bess and George, Bess' slim cousin, who really seemed to enjoy her boy's name. For her dates with dreamboat Ned, Nancy was always slipping into green chiffon dresses and gold high heels. For my "dates" with Mr. Wall (like the one we'd just had driving home from school), I was doomed to wear plaid tartan skirts and blouses with dumb Peter Pan collars!

Wardrobe notwithstanding, the best part, the part I really envied, was that interesting things always seemed to *happen* to Nancy. Everywhere she turned,

* I understood perfectly.

Nancy would stumble over hidden staircases, mysterious letters, broken lockets, haunted attics, secret diaries or unclaimed signet rings; and when she wasn't solving major mysteries, she was helping crippled children or accidentally uncovering minor mail fraud cases.

It was frustrating for me to compare my mundane life to Nancy's. I searched high and low for clues but the only things I ever stumbled over were those stupid pink flamingoes Mom installed all over our front lawn.

I couldn't find any crippled orphans in Hohokus who needed my assistance and Mom wouldn't let me volunteer as a Candystriper because of all the germs, so I threw my energies into selling Girl Scout cookies, which wasn't very profitable because there were fifteen other Brownies on my block, so where was I going to sell them?*

Let's face it, Hohokus was no River Heights.

So that afternoon, as on many other afternoons, I escaped from my life by plunging into Nancy's. I had almost forgotten my problems by the time I finished reading *Dancing Puppet*† and Daddy came home from work.

At dinner that night, Mom told me and Dad about inviting Seymour for Friday-night supper and I go, "Like I can hardly wait!" and Mom goes, "Don't Use That Tone of Voice With Me, Young Lady!" and Dad goes, "Can't I ever get any peace around here?" and he goes into the living room and Mom goes into the kitchen and I go into the den and it was a pretty typical dinner, if you know what I mean.

In the den, I watched my favorite show, *77 Sunset Strip*, and Edd "Kookie" Byrnes was combing his distinguished DA while parking Stu Bailey's convertible

---

* Actually, I did okay in cookie sales because Daddy sold 230 boxes to his office staff and Mom dumped another 300 boxes on her country-club cronies.
† I won't tell you the ending in case you haven't read it yet.

when our phone rang. It was Tiffany inviting me to a
sleepover party on Friday night. I asked my mother if
I could go to Tiffany's party and she said, "Of course
not, I just told you Seymour was coming for dinner on
Friday night!"

Soon we were yelling so loud that my father came
in from the living room and, eventually, he diplomat-
ically settled the argument by saying I could go to
Tiffany's party *after* I had dinner at home with Seymour.

Spazola Seymour came over on Friday, and it
wasn't too awful because Mom let us eat our dinner
on trays in front of the television so we wouldn't have
to miss a minute of *The Roy Rogers Show,** which
Seymour just loved. I didn't mind because I really
admired Dale Evans' wardrobe; Seymour, of course,
was smitten with Trigger, but what else would you
expect?

As it was Friday night, Mom had to light the Sabbath candles but Roy Rogers had already started and
we couldn't budge Seymour from the show, so Mom
propped the candles on top of the television and re-
cited her Sabbath prayers to the strains of "Happy
Trails to You!"

Seymour and I hardly said a word to each other all
during the show.

After Roy and Dale rode off into the sunset, followed by Nellybelle, their jeep, I packed a Two Guys
shopping bag with my flannel nightgown, nail polish,
cuticle remover, nail files, pink hair rollers, rattail
comb, end papers, hair net, Dippety-Do and latest romance comics. Daddy drove me to Tiffany's house
where the sleepover was well in progress.

When I told Tiffany why I was late, she was green
with envy. "He's soooo cute, you're so lucky!"

"Cute? Seymour? Are you nuts or something? He
still wears a coonskin cap, he eats scrambled eggs

---

* This was years before Roy franchised himself into hamburgers
and fried chicken.

with ketchup for dinner and, even if his life depended on it, he couldn't play a decent game of *Clue*."

"I know," Tiffany sighed. "I really go for guys who aren't competitive about games."

"Seymour's a real intellectual," said Kimberly Katz. "Like Ricky Nelson." *

"That's right," Tiffany said. "Now listen, Bambi, just because you're in love with Mr. Wall—that's no reason to be mean to Seymour."

All the girls giggled. "I am not in love with Mr. Wall," I lied.

"Are too! Why else do you clean his erasers every afternoon?"

"I enjoy chalk dust, okay?"

"You better watch out for Miss Singer," Kimberly crooned. "I hear she and Mr. Wall are a real hot item in the teachers' lounge."

This was not the first bit of gossip about Mr. Wall and Miss Singer I'd heard in the past few weeks.

All the girls in school were crazy about Miss Singer, the principal, because she was the spitting image of Loretta Young with her high cheekbones, sunken eyes and elaborately teased brunette hair. We just loved the way Miss Singer would sweep into the auditorium, twirling around as she stepped on stage, just as in the opening of *The Loretta Young Show*. With a fanciful flounce of her full, petticoated skirt, Miss Singer would glide toward the podium and all the girls would exchange envious smiles.

"Mr. Wall and Miss Singer are probably French kissing at this very moment," Tiffany said, knowingly.

In order to disguise my jealous feelings, I pretended Tiffany's remark was beneath my notice. "Stupid rumors," I yawned, nonchalantly waving my hairbrush. "Come on Ronnie, I'll set your hair," I of-

---

* Ricky's tragic demise in an airplane crash, many years later, was a real downer for Kimberly. "Poor Harriet," Kimberly kept saying when we recently met for lunch. "I'm almost glad Ozzie isn't around anymore; this would've *destroyed* him!"

fered, cleverly distracting everyone's attention, because Ronnie had this incredibly kinky red hair and
setting it was like unraveling Brillo.

After that, the party really got going, we played the
album *Gypsy* at full volume and acted out all the
parts. My favorite song was "If Mama Was Married,"
but Tiffany made us perform "Everything's Coming
Up Roses" about a million times.

It was back to usual after the sleepover. Seymour
started coming over every Friday night, which was a
real drag until I got the bright idea to invite Tiffany to
dinner as well. After we ate, the two of them played
with my stuffed animals while I locked myself in the
closet and read Nancy Drew by flashlight so I
wouldn't have to watch Seymour perform an appen-
dectomy on Harry Hippopotamus.

In school, I kept an eagle eye on Mr. Wall and Miss
Singer but, as far as I could tell, they were only good
friends. I mean, he never brought her long-stemmed
roses or chilled bottles of champagne in silver buckets
so I figured they couldn't really be romantically involved or anything. But I wanted to be sure.

I remembered Nancy's dilemma in *The Clue of The
Black Keys* where she searched a deserted cellar for
"incriminating evidence" and I decided to follow her
example. One day, during lunch recess, I snuck back
into the empty classroom.

As luck would have it, Mr. Wall walked into the
room just as I was going through his wallet.

"Bambi!" he exclaimed.

"Oh, hi Mr. Wall," I said, quickly shoving the wallet back into his top drawer.

"Why're you going through my wallet?" he asked,
dashing my hopes that he hadn't noticed what I was
doing.

"Just wondering if you had change for a five."

He didn't buy it.

I got sent to Miss Singer's office where she didn't
want to hear about the *Black Keys* or Nancy Drew.

She lectured on and on about a teacher's right to privacy.

A few days later, Mr. Wall announced his engagement to Miss Singer. Feeling totally deceived, especially after banging Mr. Wall's erasers for a whole term, I decided I wasn't in love with him anymore. I threw away the ten notebooks I had filled with "Mrs. Bambi Wall." I even stopped reading Nancy Drew because of the painful memories she inspired, although I never lost my respect for her.

(Recently, I heard a rumor that Nancy Drew had given up the detective business to marry Ned and stay home with the kids but I could hardly believe it. Nancy was the original working sleuth, a role model for every little girl who grew up in the fifties and sixties. Surely a woman with Nancy's spunk would've kept active, even with a house full of kids. My bet was she had set up some kind of consulting business on the side; bringing in additional income by solving local crimes in her spare time. I still, however, wonder whatever became of George.)

Obviously, my relationship with Mr. Wall had not turned out the way I had hoped but, as I was to learn many times over, that's usually what happens with love at first sight.

TRUE CONFESSIONS: SIN, SEX AND SUFFERING IN SLEEPAWAY CAMP

I once asked *M*om why adults were always writing drippy songs about love. She said, "You'll understand when you grow up," which, of course, made me think she didn't know the answer either.

After my relationship with Mr. Wall ended so abruptly, I decided to forget about men forever and ever. Love was a pretty stupid thing, I concluded, wondering why grown-ups made such a big deal out of it.

It was real confusing to me, I mean, you should've just heard my Aunt Selma go on and on about her latest *bow* (a pretty goofy label for a boyfriend, if you want my opinion).

His name was "Uncle" Shelley and I couldn't imagine how he could be anybody's bow, or boyfriend, for that matter, because he was like totally bald, which meant he was too old, I thought, to be dating.

"Uncle" Shelley really wanted to marry Aunt Selma but the delay in their matrimonial vows was the result of my aunt's unwillingness to let Uncle Melvin off the alimony hook, or so I heard her tell my mother over and over.

"Melvin will piss blood through a stone before he

stops paying for what he did to me!" was how Aunt Selma delicately put it.

Eventually, my mother ("the original Mrs. Butt-in-ski," according to Daddy) convinced Aunt Selma she was no spring chicken and marriage-minded waxed fruit manufacturers like Shelley didn't grow on trees. Daddy got a real kick out of the pun—waxed fruit on trees and all—but Mommy told him to mind his own beeswax and Aunt Selma said, "Men, they're all the same," and shook her head, kind of sadly, I thought.

Aunt Selma finally relented, so Shelly became my real uncle, without the quotation marks, and Uncle Melvin celebrated by buying himself a white Caddy with the most gigantic set of tail fins you've ever seen.

I didn't understand why Selma's wedding made Nana Hannah weep with joy or Mom's cousin Mamie turn green with envy or why Mom thought the whole wedding was so darned "romantic." If you ask me, the whole affair was just a lame excuse for the adults to get sloppy drunk and crack stupid jokes about Aunt Selma's peach colored wedding dress or about Uncle Shelley staying awake for the honeymoon. But, in all fairness, I was still pretty bitter about Mr. Wall, so maybe my view was prejudiced.

It wasn't until a couple of years later that I understood things a little bit better; after I went away to sleepaway camp for the first time, that is, and learned a lot about men and women and French kissing.

Mom and Dad signed me up for Camp Kenico because Tiffany Jerkowitz's Uncle Julie owned the camp and had given Daddy a 15 percent discount off the regular camp fee. After that, Tiffany and I spent endless afternoons talking about the approaching summer and promising each other we'd remain best friends forever and ever, no matter who else was in our bunks, no matter what happened during the summer. We made all kinds of vows and oaths of undying friendship. And, just for insurance, to cover any unforeseen circumstance, Tiffany invented a secret password to be used in the unlikely event of a quarrel or disagreement.

"If we ever, ever get mad at each other—"

"Which we won't," I quickly interjected.

"Which we won't," Tiffany agreed. "But, just *in case* we do; one of us will say 'Pepsi-Cola.' "

"Pepsi-Cola?"

"Right. And then we instantly make up. Agreed?"

"Agreed." We sealed the pact by touching pinkies, crossing our hearts, exchanging wads of Juicy Fruit and smacking Tiffany's kid brother, Jason, on the head three times.

Unfortunately, Tiffany and I were two incredibly naive kids at the time, so, of course, we didn't know that *nothing* ends a best friendship faster than spending a summer together in sleepaway camp.

Mom and me started shopping for my camp wardrobe around the second week in March and, despite my pact with Tiffany, I was real nervous about leaving home for the whole summer. My only previous camp experience had been two weeks at a Girl Scout camp in Pennsylvania; the worst two weeks of my life, if you really want to know. I swear, the mosquitoes at Camp Rammahammaquoy were the size of tennis balls, and forget that back-to-nature stuff, there's a lot to be said for indoor plumbing; mainly, it doesn't stink to high heaven and you don't get splinters. So, even though the Camp Kenico brochure included a full-color picture of their porcelain toilets, I was a real basket case about the approaching summer. One minute I was so scared I thought I'd die, and the next, I was so excited I thought I'd die. But, I must confess, I loved the shopping part.*

Mom, I think, was feeling a little uneasy about sending me off for the entire eight-week session and

---

* I know Thoreau once wrote, "Be wary of any enterprise involving new clothes." (I read it on a box of Celestial Seasonings tea.) Of course, I realize Thoreau was an important writer but, let's face it, he never saw Don Johnson in a Georgio Armani jacket.

I took full advantage of her guilt by insisting she buy me everything new: bathing suits, Bermuda shorts, pedal pushers and even my first bra, about which we had a major fight in Bamberger's, after she said, "You need a bra like I need a hole in the head." So, I threw a full-fledged temper tantrum, right there in the teen lingerie department, and probably just to shut me up, Mom let me purchase the undergarment.

By the end of our shopping spree, I had seven pairs of sneakers (in assorted colors) and enough clothes to stock a small Salvation Army truck.

Mom spent May and June sewing name tags on all my stuff; at least until the day Daddy found my name sewn on his Fruit of the Looms and said she was getting carried away.

It took us three days to pack my bags and we only managed to close the second trunk with me, my mother and Nana Yetta sitting on top of it.

"Does she really need *two* down quilts?" my father fumed as he desperately tried to close the duffel bag.

"You want she should freeze off her gazats?" Nana Yetta asked.

At dinner, the night before I left for camp, Mom told Dad about the training bra.

"Herman, guess what our little Bambi bought in Bamberger's?"

As always, Dad refused to play Mom's guessing game, so she told him about my new underwear. "It's the itsy-bitsiest littlest thing," she crooned. "A size quadruple A!"

"Maaaaaaaaaaah!!!!" I screeched.

"She's embarrassed," Dad stage-whispered to my mother.

My mother looked surprised. "What's to be embarrassed?" she asked, displaying her usual sensitivity. "Bambi thinks she's got boobs!" she announced to Dad, Grandpa Max, Nana Yetta, Aunt Selma, Uncle Shelley, Mom's cousin Mamie, Stuie (Mamie's blind date whom Mom had picked up at a UJA luncheon),

Sadie, Sol and Seymour Weisentrabowitzen and the nine other people who were having dinner with us that evening.

Rabbi Zindl turned beet red and almost choked on his chicken soup while stupid Seymour laughed so hard that Coca-Cola sprayed out his nose and stained Mom's best hand-crocheted tablecloth (my only consolation).

I was too mortified to say anything. Instead, I clenched my teeth and wondered, for the millionth time: How did I ever get into this family?

Mom pointed her fork at me. "Your face will freeze like that, Bambi Goldbloom!" she warned.

The stony silence at the table was broken by Uncle Shelley. "Hey Herman! Why do Jewish husbands always die before their wives?" he asked.

"I don't know, Shel. Why?"

"Because they want to!"

I was pretty happy to get away from my mother after that dinner so saying goodbye at the Port Authority bus station the next morning was a relief. My parents, Tiffany, Jason and Mr. and Mrs. Jerkowitz were squeezed in a tight circle amid dozens of trunks, suitcases, crying adults and screaming campers trying to board the bus. It took twenty minutes for the seven of us to finish with our goodbyes. I promised Mom I'd be a good girl and have a good summer. Dad slipped me a twenty dollar bill through the bus window right before we pulled away from the station.

"Free at last," I said to Tiffany as we settled into our seats and I opened my traveling case. From the bottom of my canvas bag, underneath all my cosmetics, bottles of calamine lotion, rolls of toilet paper and a change of underwear,* I found my beach towel, which I unrolled to get to the carefully wrapped brown paper package stashed inside. I tore through

* Mom made me pack clean underwear just in case the bus crashed and I was rushed to the hospital.

the seven layers of paper that had taken me two hours to tape closed and, finally, got to one of my copies of *True Confessions* magazine. Soon I was well into the heart-rending lead story: "Dirt Poor and Desperate: We Traded Our Baby For a Tractor!" I glanced out the window and sighed with contentment. At last I could read my magazines in the daylight!

I was starting to read the next story, "Restless Nurse: By Day She Helps Sick Women—By Night She Helps Herself to Their Men," when Tiffany and I met our first Camp Kenico counselor.

Her name was Roz and she seemed real friendly when she introduced herself, informing us that this was her twenty-second summer at Camp Kenico, and that she held the record for the longest camp attendance. Sitting down next to us, Rozzie, as she liked to be called, started talking about camp life, which I thought was nice of her until I realized she had been speaking for a whole hour and hadn't even asked us our names or anything. When she started singing a medley of camp songs from the past two decades, I could barely stifle a yawn. By the time Roz was half-way through "One Hundred Bottles of Beer of the Wall," all the other campers on the bus were screaming "Knock it off, Roz!" and Tiffany and I were praying Roz was not our bunk's counselor. Fortunately, our prayers were answered.

Our counselor's name was Staci, "with an i," she said (which I am absolutely certain she dotted with a little happy-face circle, or a heart, if you know what I mean). Staci was real perky, like a cheerleader. "Like *That Girl!*" Tiffany marveled. "Yeah," I agreed, because Staci had the exact same nose as Anne Marie. Staci's nose was the tiniest nose I'd ever seen. I couldn't stop staring at this perfect little turned-up button of a nose, which, somehow, didn't fit in with the other, more prominent, features on her face.

"I'm a Five Towns girl!" Staci said, which didn't mean anything to us until we had been in our bunk for about seven and a half seconds.

Camp Kenico was literally crawling with Five
Towners, and I thought they might all be related be-
cause every one of them had a nose identical to
Staci's. It wasn't until later that I learned the Five
Towns were enclaves for rich Jews on Long Island*
and the noses were five thousand dollars a pop (you
should pardon the expression), courtesy of Dr. Morris
Diamondstein, chief of plastic surgery at Woodmere
General Hospital.

At first, Tiffany and me were awed by the girls from
the Five Towns. They were so cool, so sophisticated,
so Papagallo. They peroxided their hair, shaved their
legs and plucked their eyebrows. (Jersey girls were so
hairy by comparison.) They also smoked an occasional Newport and seemed to know everything there
was to know about sex. I had yet to kiss a boy with my
eyes closed. (And poor Tiffany thought "petting"
meant being kind to your cocker spaniel, so I loaned
her "Restless Nurse" to expand her horizons.)

Sometimes, the Five Towns girls were nice to us,
explaining things like what Kotex was used for or how
to avoid locking braces while kissing (which wasn't
exactly a problem for me, but was educational for Tiffany). But, most of the time, the Five Towners acted
real cliquey and excluded the Jersey girls from their
group. They used to play a lot of "No Soap Radio"
jokes on us: They'd tell a joke and the punch line was
"No Soap Radio" and they'd all crack up; so we would
laugh, too, even though we didn't get it, but that was
the point, there was nothing to get (Get it?) and the
joke was on us.

Usually, after they stopped laughing at us, Tiffany
started to cry and then the girls felt bad because Tiffany's uncle Julie owned the camp and it wasn't such
good policy to drive his niece to tears. "You can't help
it if you weren't born in the Five Towns, Tiffany,"
Marci Schwartz said, and Tiffany, to my amazement,
agreed.

"Marci's not so hot, Tiffany," I said when Tiffany
_____
* Phonetic pronunciation: "Lawn Guyland."

and I were alone. "You don't have to agree with *every-thing* she says."

Tiffany wagged her finger. "Pepsi-Cola," she re-plied, squeezing my hand.

I laughed and, with a shrug, dropped the subject.

I steered clear of the Five Towns girls after falling for the "No Soap Radio" ploy more times than I care to admit. Tiffany, however, kept trying to get those girls to be her friends; like when she let them borrow anything in her cubby and, boy, did they take advan-tage of her. Tiffany got to wear her madras Bermuda shorts because they were all bled out and no one else would be caught dead in them; which was good be-cause the shorts were just about the only piece of clothing she got to wear all summer. I thought Tiffany was acting pretty nerdy and, after biting my tongue for the longest time, I finally told her off one morning when she wouldn't let me borrow her gorgeous yel-low sweater because Wendy Pinkowitz, from Cedar-hurst, offered to be Tiffany's best friend if only Tiffany gave her the garment. And, can you believe it? Tiffany tossed away that sweater like it was a stale black Chuckle.

Unlike Tiffany, I didn't need to give away my clothes to make friends, because I had fourteen copies of *True Confessions, Modern Romances, True Ro-mances* and a beat-up edition of *Peyton Place* under my mattress. My bed was pretty lumpy but I was one of the most popular girls in the teen division; even some of the counselors, the ones who could read, were real friendly to me.

After our skirmish over the yellow sweater, I avoided Tiffany and pretended not to notice she and Wendy had become inseparable. Between ignoring Tiffany and being ignored by Wendy Pinkowitz, I was learning it wasn't easy to live with eight girls in one small bunkhouse. (The fights over dibs to the bath-room mirror were not to be believed!) One day Marci Schwartz offered to be my best friend, but she wanted

Peyton Place in exchange. I really had to admire her chutzpah but, since my Daddy had always taught me "never part with your principal," there was no way I was going to hand over my most popular asset. I turned down Marci's offer.

I tried to forget my girlfriend problems by throwing myself into Arts and Crafts, where I made all of those really neat and useful things like mosaic hot plates, pot holders, whistle lanyards and lollipop stick sculptures. I also auditioned for the camp play, where, just like in those old Mickey Rooney movies, someone actually said, "Let's put on a show!" which everyone agreed was a pretty dumb thing to say since the whole point of Dramatics was to do just that.

After several callbacks I bagged the roll of the Wicked Witch in *The Wizard of Oz*, which was really flattering but, even more exciting, during rehearsals of the play, I met Igor Stein who was a CIT (counselor in training) in the boys' division, lifeguard at the lake and Tin Man in the play.

Igor was cute, in a clean-cut, Paul Peterson kind of way. He was always neat and tidy, his hair slicked back with a little dab of Brylcream, just as you'd expect from the son of Donna Reed. True, Igor wore thick glasses and his Bermudas were several seasons out of fashion but, more important, he had a really great sense of humor. Igor was always giving me noogies or spraying himself for cooties, which, I know, doesn't sound all that great now, but it was pretty funny back then.

After our first meeting in Dramatics, I ran into Igor again at the lake. Our bunk went swimming during fifth period and, at the dock, I spied Igor stacking kickboards. I walked over to say hi and he pushed me into the water where my feet touched all that slime and gook at the bottom* and I got totally grossed out and told Igor I hated him and he apologized and helped me out of the water. Then we made up and he

* Give me a chlorinated pool any day!

threw me into the lake again. (As I said, he had a really cool sense of humor.)

I was floundering around in the water, screaming real loud so that all the girls would know I'd been dunked by the gorgeous lifeguard, when Tiffany swam over and we had our first civil conversation in days. "Igor's the cutest lifeguard in camp," Tiffany gurgled between breaststrokes.

"Thanks," I beamed.

"I think he really likes you—he dunked you twice!"

I was delighted by the note of envy in Tiffany's voice.

"Pepsi-Cola?" she asked.

"Pepsi-Cola," I agreed. I was so happy about Igor's attention that I excused Tiffany's despicable behavior over the yellow sweater and the way she'd dumped me for Wendy Pinkowitz. It wasn't until much later in the summer that I would realize what a dumb mistake that was.

By the time *Oz* was in dress rehearsals, Igor and I were going steady, which meant we sat next to each other during Friday night services in the mess hall and I wore his whistle lanyard when he wasn't on lifeguard duty at the lake. (In Arts and Crafts I hand-wove a special lanyard for Igor's whistle.) Of course, I had to listen, day and night, to the girls in my bunk singing: "Bambi and Igor sitting in a tree, K-I-S-S-I-N-G!" but that was one of the drawbacks of any camp relationship.

Little did the girls know that the issue of kissing was a major sore point between Igor and me. Listen, I was no Nellie Novice, not after reading "The Love Game I Played on My Bingo Night Out!" and having played my fair share of spin the bottle in Bruce Berger's basement, but I guess Mom's frequent "germs in saliva" lecture had wreaked havoc on my attitude about necking. Igor, however, was getting restless and even I was developing weak wrists from our endless

nightly handshakes. Finally, I broke down and promised Igor that, on the night of the play, I would let
him kiss me, on the mouth, and I even hinted at the
possibility of introducing tongues into the action. Igor
threw himself into rehearsals, offering to help all the
Munchkins learn their lines.

The Wizard of Oz was a major success, even though
Wendy Pinkowitz messed up her big entrance by trip-
ping over my broomstick. In all modesty, I must
admit, I was outstanding as the Wicked Witch, modeling my character after Mom's cousin Mamie, Miss
Sour Puss. *Camptown News* hailed my portrayal as
"wicked witchcraft," and oldtime campers still talk
about my reading of the "I'm melting!" line.

Backstage after the performance, Igor and I got into
some serious kissing, I even closed my eyes real tight.
It was totally romantic except that his aluminum foil
costume had all these dangerously sharp edges and
he could hardly find my lips under my black hula-skirt
wig. When I was back in my bunk that night, I tried
to decide which was better, the applause from the
audience or Igor's kisses, but it was really too close to
call.

(For many years after my triumphant performance
that night, I believed I was destined for a career on
the Broadway stage. Then, in the tenth grade, I lost
the role of Eliza Doolittle to Tiffany and gave up my
theatrical aspirations. Frankly, I couldn't take the rejection, especially after witnessing Tiffany's mediocre
interpretation of the Cockney Pygmalian.)

Igor was on my mind all the time after our first kiss
even though we didn't see nearly as much of each
other as I would've liked. At Camp Kenico, it was hard
to see the boys because their bunks were located
across the lake and it was a pretty wide lake. But we
were girls away from our parents for the first time, so
it was going to take more than a body of water to keep
us away.

After several days of furtive planning, we went to

sleep fully dressed one night, our shoes paired at the foot of our cots. Awakened at 1:00 A.M. by Marci's clock radio, we slipped out of bed, put on our shoes and crept into the night. We hiked two hours, around the lake, to fulfill our secret mission—spread toilet paper across the lawn and over the trees at the boys' bunks. We figured that, in the morning, the dew-drenched paper would clump like sticky papier mâché onto every green leaf on campus and it would be a real mess to clean up. We were inspired. We called it a Panty Raid, although I don't know why as no panties were involved; but I guess it sounded sexier than a Toilet Tissue Raid.

Everything went off perfectly except, when we were hiking through the woods, Wendy thought she saw a bear and she got so scared she peed in her pants, which was totally embarrassing, so Wendy made us all become blood sisters and swear we'd never, ever tell anyone about her "accident." I probably shouldn't be discussing this now except these were all Jewish girls, mainly from Long Island, and everyone was too squeamish to become real blood sisters by actually cutting themselves or shedding real blood. But Wendy insisted, so we compromised by spitting on our fingers and touching hands; making us, I guess, spit sisters, which in my opinion, is not as binding as being real blood sisters.

For me, the most exciting part of the Panty Raid was meeting Igor behind his bunk where we French kissed for the first time. Despite what my mother had told me, I thought it was real nice even if it wasn't real sanitary. Eventually, Igor and I became experts at French kissing, learning to breath through our noses so that we could hold one kiss for almost twenty minutes, but that night we both concentrated on not drooling any more than was absolutely necessary.

On the way back to the bunk, the girls said they were mad at me for telling Igor about the raid.

"You acted just like a slut," Wendy "Toilet-Mouth" Pinkowitz said.

"Yeah," Tiffany agreed.

"You're all just jealous because I got to neck with Igor while you guys unrolled toilet paper for an hour and a half," I said, and all the girls but Wendy and her sidekick, Tiffany, gloomily agreed.

As for the Panty Raid, it turned out to be a major success. We had been right about the toilet paper, it was a mess to clean up. We discovered this after Uncle Julie made us do most of the cleaning. He came storming into our bunk at dawn, woke us up and drove us over to the boys' camp. We couldn't figure out how he knew it was our bunk until we saw him waving Tiffany's yellow sweater, which Wendy had lost in all her confusion that evening.

We got docked for the Thursday-night movie in the mess hall, which was no great punishment because it was the fourth time Uncle Julie ran *The Long Grey Line*, a really retarded Tyrone Power movie. In our bunk, we spent the evening, as we spent many late nights, fantasizing about our future husbands.

The girls asked me a zillion questions about Igor but they didn't know I had a secret love fantasy I had never, ever told to anyone. That night, sugar-drunk on too many root beers and Tootsie Rolls, I finally confessed I had only one dream man: the Prince of Wales.

"When Charles and I marry, I will become the first Jewish queen of England," I informed my bunkmates, and they all sighed with envy because everyone knew the queen of England got to wear a tiara, with real diamonds, rubies and emeralds.

Of course, everyone in my bunk fell in love with Staci. In fact, we loved and admired all the counselors (except for Rozzie) because they were real role models for us. We wanted to follow in their footsteps and do exactly what the counselors did; namely sleep all day and fool around with the guys all night. But in spite of our heroine worship, most of the time the counselors ignored us, at least until Parents' Day when they suddenly became our best friends and even helped out with work chores.

Work chores were performed every day after breakfast. We had a circle pie chart hung in the bunk that divided the morning's tasks. Dustpan was the easiest assignment and cleaning the bathroom was the worst. Most of the girls in the bunk had never even touched bathroom porcelain with their bare hands, so you can just imagine the fuss we made over having to scrub a toilet. Marci Schwartz called her mom in Lawrence and asked if Annie Ruth, their cleaning lady, could come to camp and do day work on the mornings Marci drew bathroom duty. Mrs. Schwartz said, "Of course, darling, I didn't spend $465 so my daughter could scrub toilets all summer," but Uncle Julie nixed the plan because he thought it might set a bad precedent.

But the morning of Parents' Day, the *counselors* scrubbed the toilets, and let me tell you, they did one heck of a job. Later, we realized the counselors were only trying to impress the parents and possibly up the ante on their tips but we didn't care. Listen, any excuse to get out of the bathroom detail was okay with us.

Chores were always followed by Inspection, which meant counselors would come around and bounce quarters on our cots. On Parents' Day, however, the counselors dropped dollar bills that we could keep if we promised not to mention anything about how the counselors' beds would squeak all night when their boyfriends from Camp Massanaqua came to visit.* We pocketed the money and kept our mouths shut.

After Inspection, we waited expectantly by the dirt road for our parents to arrive. We were dying with excitement because our folks would be bringing bushels of care packages and we could finally unload those pot holders and mosaic ashtrays on our mothers. I shouted with excitement when Mom and Dad

* I suspected these nocturnal visits constituted a genuine Panty Raid but I could find no literature in any of my confession magazines to verify my hunch.

pulled up to the mess hall in Uncle Melvin's white Caddy because all the girls were impressed with the size of those fins on the Coupe de Ville. Then I noticed Mr. and Mrs. Jerkowitz were sitting in the back seat of the Caddy.

"I guess our parents drove up together," Tiffany said.

"Umm," I muttered. (Tiffany and I were barely speaking since the night of the Panty Raid.)

Breaking away from my circle of bunkmates, I ran into my mom's arms, almost crushing the case of Oreos she was carrying. Daddy gave me a fifty dollar bill for looking so much like a real camper.

I hadn't seen my parents for more than a month and was amazed to discover I was actually glad to see them again. I tucked the cash in my training bra.

"Aren't you going to say hello to Mr. and Mrs. Jerkowitz?" Mom asked.

I dutifully pecked Tiffany's parents on their respective cheeks and steered my parents toward the bunk.

"Is there something wrong between you and Tiffany?" Mom asked.

"No, of course not," I hastily replied. As we walked away from the Jerkowitzes, I changed the subject by telling my parents about Igor.

"Igor Stein?" Daddy howled with laughter. "What kind of name is that? Is he Frankenstein's brother?"

"Now, Herman," Mom said, but I could see she was having a hard time supressing a smile.

I changed my mind about being glad to see my parents. "Daddy, if you embarrass me in front of Igor I will totally die!" I said, in all earnest.

"Now, now, kitten, would I embarrass my little girl?"

I wanted to tell him that I was no longer a little girl, especially since Igor and I had French kissed, at last count, seventeen times, but I didn't think that particular piece of information would help matters very much.

I was really nervous when we ran into Igor about half an hour later.

"Mommy, Daddy, this is my friend," I said, staring hard at my father, "Igor Stein."

"Igor Stein? What kind of name is that?" my father asked, his eyes dancing with mischief.

"Jewish, sir," Igor innocently replied.

"Ah! Wonderful name, son, wonderful name! Janice, did you hear, the boy's Jewish."

Mom, who was standing about two inches from Dad, said, "Yes, Herman, I heard. Isn't that lovely?"

After Igor left us, Mom, Dad and I toured the camp and Dad got a great kick out of tipping every counselor who knew my name. Robin, the water ski instructor, was embarrassed to take Dad's twenty, warning that after his numerous unsuccessful attempts to get me balanced on skis, tipping him was like throwing money down a well, but Daddy insisted.

Some of the campers put on a little show for the parents, a kind of tournament of games—baseball, soccer, tennis and Ping Pong. We all watched as Igor jumped into the water to "rescue" a "drowning" camper. Daddy energetically applauded Igor's life-saving technique but not half as loudly as Tiffany.

Dripping wet, Igor emerged from the lake and Tiffany ran over to him with a towel. "Wasn't he wonderful?" she said to a group of parents and campers on the dock. Everyone clapped their hands and Tiffany planted a kiss on Igor's cheek.

"Looks like Tiffany has her eye on your boyfriend," Daddy chuckled.

My father's remark really startled me. I thought about all the times Tiffany had commented about Igor's good looks and his "swimmer's shoulders." Was Jerkhead Jerkowitz (my new nickname for her) after my guy?

"Now Herman, don't start making a federal case," Mom said. "Come on Bambi, let's go get your care packages from the Caddy."

From the trunk of the car, Dad unloaded several cartons of cookies, cakes and candy and helped me carry everything back to my cubby. (I was proud to have the biggest care packages in my bunk.) Right before dinner, all the campers said goodbye to their parents and watched them drive off in their assorted Caddys, Fords and Buicks. The counselors stopped smiling at us and everyone over sixteen flew off into town to spend their day's loot.

All the campers skipped dinner that evening because there was so much good food in the bunks. After lights out, everyone got sick from all the junk food and spent most of the night in the bathroom, so the next morning, there was a huge fight over bathroom duty and everything was pretty much back to normal.

For the next few weeks, I watched Tiffany and Igor as intently as I'd spied on Miss Singer and Mr. Wall in grade school. I began to notice the way Jerkhead fawned all over my boyfriend. "Igor, you're just a panic and a half," Tiffany would scream, giggling hysterically whenever Igor made a match burn twice on her wrist. I had never appreciated Igor's match trick until the night I noticed Tiffany's arms were studded with dozens of tiny burn marks. How often was he showing her this trick? I wondered to myself. I didn't want to give Tiffany the satisfaction of knowing I was concerned about her and Igor so I kept my suspicions to myself, at least until Color War when things came to a head.

During Color War, the whole camp split into two teams, the Gold Pintos and the White Ponies.* For two weeks, the Gold and White teams competed for points in various sports. There were no prizes or anything for the winners but I am certain the Viet Cong never fought as viciously for victory as the campers at Camp Kenico. For instance, once, during the swim meet, a White Pony kid got a cramp while doggie pad-

---

* Horses were Uncle Julie's favorite animals, which is why he spent so much time on the phone talking to his friend, Bookie, about the ponies.

dling across the lake and the Gold team lifeguard (not Igor!) hesitated long enough to make sure the kid lost the race before diving into the water to rescue him. Nobody involved in Color War blamed the lifeguard but the doggie paddler was really upset and his parents threatened to sue Uncle Julie.

Everyone was totally into the spirit of Color War; Pintos and Ponies refused to even talk to each other. My problems with Tiffany started when she and I were appointed opposing team captains of our bunk. Naturally, we had our share of conflict, especially since Tiffany took everything so _personally_. She really overreacted when I short-sheeted her bed, sending my parents a Bloomingdale's bill for her satin sheets and then, just for spite, dumping some indescribably smelly thing from the woods into my cubby. Staci had a conniption fit because she had to remove the gunk (I certainly wouldn't touch it!) but, since Staci was on my team, Tiffany ignored her reprimands, claiming, "No White Team person can be impartial, and if you don't stop yelling at me, my Uncle Julie will fire your ass out of this camp."

Unexpectedly, Staci smiled. "Tiffy! You sound just like a Five Towns girl!" she exclaimed with a note of admiration in her voice.

Wendy proudly patted Tiffany on the back.

Later that afternoon Tiffany shaved her legs for the first time and the whole bunk, except me, celebrated.

Igor was on the Gold team so we didn't get to spend much time together and, besides, every time I saw him, Tiffany was hanging on his swimmer's shoulders. "Igor is such a help to the team," Tiffany bragged to the other campers during lunch.

I pretended not to hear her.

"Honestly, I don't know what we'd do without him, Bambi," Tiffany said as she grabbed a bowl of soggy potato chips out of my hand.

I tried my best to give Tiffany a really dirty look and then acted as if I was too involved with my duties as Color War Captain to pay any further attention to her. "Okay, White team, it's time for the Competition Relay Races!" I clapped my hands. "Let's get out there and MURDER those Pintos!"

My enthusiasm must have been effective because, pretty soon, the entire mess hall was shouting "Murder! Murder! Murder!" as all the campers marched off to the baseball field.

Halfway through the potato sack race, Tiffany sauntered over to me. "I need to borrow Igor's whistle," she said, making a grab for the lanyard hanging around my neck.

"Touch this whistle, Jerkowitz, and you're chopped liver."

She laughed. "Igor *said* I should get it from you."

I couldn't believe my ears. "And I *said* you can't have it." I went searching for Igor and found him crawling out of a potato sack on the finishing line.

"Did you tell Tiffany she could have the whistle?" I demanded.

"Yeah," Igor replied. "She said she needs it to start the Pass-the-Cantaloupe event."

"But, Igor, I wove this lanyard with my own two hands."

"Oh, well then, keep the lanyard and just give Tiffany the whistle."

"But this is your official life-saving whistle. What if Tiffany gets it full of spit?"

Igor laughed. "Tiffany will go easy on the saliva. Won't you, Tiff?"

Tiffany stood next to Igor. "That's right, Iggie," she said, touching his sweaty chest.

I tore the whistle off the lanyard and threw it at Tiffany.

"Pepsi-Cola, Pepsi-Cola!" Tiffany chanted.

"Pepsi-Cola, my ass!" I said, which, if I'm not mistaken, were the last words I said to Tiffany all summer.

Color War ended in a blaze of glory the next day

when Gold and White sang against each other in the Camp Sing. Each team sang three original songs: March, Comedy and Alma Mater, which we'd endlessly rehearsed for two weeks. Before the potato sack races, I'd loved rehearsing our songs because, of all the singers, I was the only camper on the White team who was asked to be a mouther; that is, to only mouth the words to the songs instead of singing them out loud. Although I sang with great enthusiasm and volume, my voice tended to throw the entire back line off key. I had felt privileged to sacrifice myself to the greater glory of the White team but, now, everything about Color War seemed like a sham to me.

The Gold team won Camp Sing, but the White team won Color War. There was a lot of murmuring that the war had been fixed but I think the rumors were started by Rozzie, the Gold team general and a sore loser if ever I saw one.

I was cool to Igor when he congratulated me on my team's victory. He leaned over to kiss me but I withdrew.

"Can't I get a kiss from the victor?" he asked.

"Kiss your whistle, Igor," I said.

"But, Bambi, I thought you were my steady."

"You thought wrong."

"You mean we're breaking up?"

"You've got it."

Igor sighed deeply. "Now I know I have a heart because it's breaking," he said, quoting his exit line from *The Wizard of Oz*.

I was touched by Igor's words and almost relented. "I'm melting!" I thought to myself but then I glanced across the social hall and saw Tiffany waving Igor's whistle, on *her* lanyard, like a cowgirl twirling a lasso. "Bug off, Igor," I said and returned to my triumphant White teammates. One thing I had learned from Mr. Wall and Miss Singer was that being a heartbreaker was a lot more fun than being heartbroken.

There were only a few more days left of camp but

Igor tried his best to worm his way back into my good graces. I was not receptive. At the lake, I nearly broke Igor's arm when he tried to push me into the water.

At the final camp dinner, Tiffany won the Miss Congeniality Award for our bunk but I'm certain that was only because she gave away all her clothes instead of packing them.

On the ride back to New York, Tiffany and Igor sat together in the back of the bus, giggling and spraying each other for cooties. I sat as far away from them as possible, in the front seat behind the driver, with Rozzie.

For most of the ride, Rozzie walked up and down the aisles, trying to get the campers to sing and leaving me alone to plot my revenge on Jerkowitz. I was trying to think of something really mean to do to her once we were back in Hohokus. I couldn't come up with much besides placing a phone order for seven pizzas delivered to her house or scribbling her phone number in the bathroom of our parents' country club, neither of which seemed quite right. Suddenly, Steven Levy strolled over and sat down beside me. I was shocked because Steven Levy was absolutely the cutest waiter in camp and he'd never so much as said hello or saved me an extra dessert all summer. (Rumor had it Steven had spent most of his summer trying to unhook Marci Schwartz's training bra.)

Steven had blonde hair, green eyes and was really suntanned. He had that California Beach Boy look, even though he came from Bayonne.

I looked into Steven's black sunglasses and forgot all about Igor.

Steven was a little shy when we started to talk but, after a while, he confessed that ever since seeing *The Wizard of Oz*, he liked me all summer but had assumed I was already taken since I always hung out with Igor.

I laughed and told him, quite frankly, Igor and I had been dating, but I'd ended it because Igor was too immature. "A real Noogiehead," Steven agreed and then told me he'd always thought I was too good for Igor, which made me realize it was great to talk to a really intelligent boy for a change, instead of some dumb lifeguard. Flirting with Steven made me feel so good that I robustly joined in when the kids on the bus sang the White Team's March song all the way down the Henry Hudson Parkway, which, of course, Steven didn't notice because, that summer, I had learned to be a really expert mouther.

When we pulled into the Port Authority, Steven asked for my phone number, my address and a date on New Year's Eve. He wanted a kiss, right there in the Port Authority, but I told him it was too early in our relationship and my parents were watching. He said okay and started quietly singing, "Bambi and *Steven* sitting in a tree, K-I-S-S-I-N-G!"

I waved goodbye to Steven as I walked over to my parents, standing next to the soda machines with little Jason and Mr. and Mrs. Jerkowitz.

I said my hellos and distributed kisses to everyone except Jason, who had dribbled Coke all over himself.

"Who's with Tiffany?" Mrs. Jerkowitz asked and we all turned around to watch Tiffany and Igor kissing by the bus. They parted and Tiffany raced over to her parents.

"Wasn't that your boyfriend, Igor?" Mom, with her usual tact asked me.

Tiffany, of course, loved it.

"Igor?" I said with a laugh. "No, I dumped him ages ago. Steven Levy is my new boyfriend."

Tiffany's jaw fell open but she quickly recovered. "Igor asked me out for next Saturday," she said to her mother.

"Steven asked me out for New Year's Eve," I said to my mother.

"Igor gave me his lifeguard whistle," Tiffany dangled the whistle. "*For keeps*," she added, in case I missed the point.

I ground my teeth together and could've kicked my-self for not asking Steven to give me his Kenico wait-er's apron.

I suppose our parents picked up the tension be-tween me and Tiffany, because everyone stood around looking at their shoes for a few seconds. Then Mr. Jerkowitz sipped his can of orange soda and jin-gled some change in his pocket. "Wanna soda, girls?" he asked, pointing to the machines. "Coke? Pepsi-Cola?"

"NO!" Tiffany and I screamed with such force that all the adults jumped and Mr. Jerkowitz dropped his can of soda on poor Jason's foot.

Mrs. Jerkowitz took Jason off to the bathroom to tend to his bruised instep while Dad and Mr. Jerko-witz unloaded our camp trunks from the bus. When it was time to say goodbye, Tiffany and I coolly nodded at each other.

As Mom, Dad and I walked away from the Jerko-witzes, I heard Tiffany blowing Igor's whistle and I winced.

Igor's whistle haunted me for the next few years as Tiffany wore the damn thing to school all the time, at least until the day, by accident, Jason inhaled instead of exhaled and nearly choked to death on the little ball. By then, however, Tiffany and I were totally es-tranged and I was in love with Rocky Rissotto, who was too cool to wear a clean tee-shirt, much less a stupid whistle.

I HAVE A MEMORABLE BIRTHDAY

"*Sweet Sixteen and never been kissed,*" exclaimed Daddy one night about a month before my birthday and I blushed beet red, thinking about several hot and heavy Friday nights at the drive-in with Steven Levy.

Daddy made this naive remark the evening Mom and I were writing out invitations for my Sweet Sixteen party, which was a pretty exciting event in my life, my very first catered affair. For weeks, I had to make several crucial decisions about the party. With boys or without? With relatives or without? Steak house or Chinese restaurant? What to give as party favors? Who to invite for a sleepover after the party? I was learning it was no easy task to totter on the brink of becoming a "Real Young Lady," as Daddy said.

I settled on the China Star on Route 17 because Susie Blaustein's Sweet Sixteen was scheduled the week before mine at the Manero's Steak House and because I had never lost my fondness for moo goo gai pan. No relatives, I decided, and no boys, because Steven and I weren't talking at the moment. Several weeks before, we'd had a major fight when his hand "accidentally" wandered over to my left breast while we were watching *Psycho* at the drive-in. Steven claimed seeing Janet Leigh in the shower scared him so much he lost control for a moment, which was hardly a good enough excuse since he'd had a similar "accident" watching *One Hundred and One Dalmatians.*

Anyway, I pared my invitation list down to twenty-four of only my very best friends. Mom and I bought two dozen sugar cube corsages as favors, which were really pretty but proved to be impractical when I tried to press my corsage between the pages of my social studies textbook. The cubes dissolved into grains of sugar, and I couldn't get the flies out of my locker for months.

Even after all the major decisions had been made, the invitations had been mailed and I had bought an outfit for the occasion (a stunning orange shirtdress and a matching headband), the most difficult part of planning the party was still at hand. Mommy said I was getting a "Lesson in Real Life" when I sat down to work out my seating chart.

I had more or less grown up with the twenty-four girls who were coming to the party but, over the years, we'd traded best friendships so often that I needed to draw up a big chart to figure out who was still speaking to who. It had been tough enough when we were kids, but now that boys had formally entered the picture, everyone was trading best friends right and left. (I assumed it was no coincidence the most popular girls were the ones with the cutest older brothers.)

For instance, Ronnie was not speaking to Susie because Susie's seventeen-year-old brother, Hank, had once cruelly called Ronnie "Four-eyes." Unfortunately, Ronnie was practically blind without her coke-bottle glasses, which were a heavy cross to bear in the 1960s, before contact lenses. Ronnie was real self-conscious about her glasses and the fact she'd never had a date in her life didn't add to her confidence. So

I had to make sure Ronnie and Susie didn't sit anywhere near each other. Well, that would've been easy enough if it weren't for Bobbi Krautman, Ronnie's next-door neighbor, a lifetime friend, who was also Susie's best friend at the moment. Bobbi wanted to sit between Ronnie and Susie.

Susie wanted to sit between Bobbi and Lesley, which was another problem because Lesley had once accepted a ride home from school with Bobbi's boyfriend when Bobbi was out sick for the day and so, of course, Bobbi refused to talk to Lesley and Lesley was mad because Bobbi never gave her a chance to explain how she'd only taken the ride as a favor to Bobbi. Lesley's explanation was pretty lame-brained but we all sided with Lesley, not so much because of her logic as because Lesley was the prettiest girl in our crowd, the only natural blonde among us and a bona fide cheerleader, so she knew lots of cute guys on the football team.

I settled the Bobbi/Lesley problem by using Kimberly Katz as a buffer between the girls, but that didn't solve my biggest problem: where to seat Tiffany. Mom insisted I invite my "camp friend" to my Sweet Sixteen and Tiffany's mother insisted she attend, so we were both sort of stuck with each other. Actually, I didn't mind inviting her because, by then, I had gotten my revenge by reviewing Tiffany's lead role in *My Fair Lady* for the school paper, and noting her performance marked "the first time in theatrical history Eliza Doolittle spoke with a heavy North Jersey accent."

For a while I thought about having everyone sit at separate tables but Mom said that kind of thing just wasn't done and, somehow, I devised a plan that looked workable and I think it all would've been perfect except Kimberly got the flu and canceled at the last minute. Lesley refused to move down a seat, as did Bobbi, so there was this empty seat on the left side of the table, which drove my mother nuts. Mom must've nudjhed Bobbi a hundred times to move over a seat.

Fortunately, I had placed Tiffany at the last seat at the end of the table, far enough away so it wasn't all that obvious she never said happy birthday to me, not even once.

Everyone dressed up for the party in their stockings and heels, circle pins, ankle bracelets and pearls. Susie Blaustein wore the same shirtdress as I did, which could have been a problem except that her dress was blue and she didn't have a matching headband.

We spent the first hour at the China Star talking about Kimberly, who, of course, was an easy target since she wasn't there. All the girls agreed it was lousy of Kimberly to cancel at the last minute, since Mom had prepaid for twenty-four luncheon specials and no refunds were allowed.

"If Kimberly was really your friend she would be here," insisted Bobbi.

"In a wheelchair, if necessary," added Lesley.

Everyone agreed Kimberly lacked character and class and had absolutely no loyalty to her friends.

I tried to defend Kimberly since she had sounded awful when she called that morning and, right before she hung up, I thought I heard her mom say something about a temperature of 104 but, let me tell you, the tide of sentiment was really against her.

"Let's all hate Kimberly," Tiffany proposed and everyone promised they would.

After we ate, it was time to unwrap my presents so all the girls moved their chairs into a semicircle around me. I tore open my gifts in a frenzy of excitement and greed and was delighted by the loot. I got lots of cute clothes, except for an ugly polyester blouse from Bobbi, who was the world's worst dresser, and a wrinkled paisley scarf from Tiffany, who hadn't even bothered to remove her Camp Kenico name tag from the corner. My favorite present, though, was a new charm for my bracelet: a "16" encircled in pearls from Mom and Dad.

While I opened the presents, Susie took notes, writing down everything I said. Then, when the last present was unwrapped, she read the remarks out loud, as the honeymoon dialogue between husband and wife. (She read the wife parts in a real high-pitched voice.) Back then, double entendres were our main form of entertainment (other than the drive-in, of course) so everyone really cracked up over comments like, "This is exactly what I've always wanted" and "I sure hope it fits."

Lesley gathered together all the ribbons and bows and attached them to a paper plate, making me a Sweet Sixteen bonnet, which I wore long enough for my mom to take a picture.

I invited Lesley and Ronnie to sleep over after the party, since Ronnie was my best friend and Lesley was the girl I most admired at the time. This decision proved to be fortuitous later on when the sleepover got raided in the middle of the night by Steven and his two friends.

Ronnie and Lesley helped me pack the presents in Mom's car and then drove home with us. We had a real good time rehashing the party as we listened to the record player. Before long we were deep into our standard argument over the Beatles, fighting about who got Paul.

As with many climactic events in history (the assassination of JFK, the first moonwalk), I can clearly remember the exact moment and what I was doing the first time I ever heard the Beatles. It was a Thursday morning, sometime during tenth grade, and I was on the school bus. Someone had a transistor radio, and from the back of the bus came the electrifying refrain, "Yeah, yeah, yeah."

Well, the whole busload of kids was dumbstruck; we'd never heard such meaningful lyrics.

"Who's singing that song?" asked Tiffany Jerkowitz.

"A group called the Beatles," answered Bruce Berger.

"The Beatles?" we all roared with laughter. "What kind of stupid name is that?"

In the weeks, months and years to follow, the Beatles would become our favorite topic of discussion. Mostly, as I said, we would argue over Paul.

"He's my favorite," Ronnie whined.

"He was your favorite last week; this week he's mine." I insisted.

"Oh, please, please, pretty please with sugar on top, can't I have Paul? I'll be your best friend."

"You already *are* my best friend."

"Oh, Please . . . PAALEEZEE???" Ronnie's whine was perfected to such an annoying pitch, she could drive Rabbi Zindl to eat on Yom Kippur, so to stop her whining and because we both felt sorry that she never could get a real guy, Lesley and I gave her Paul, as always.

"All right," I said. "I'll take George." George was almost as cute as Paul so, most times, he was an acceptable runner-up for the number-two slot. John was also cute but he was a little too intellectual for most of the girls in Hohokus. Of course, Ringo was the booby prize, since he wasn't cute, couldn't sing, didn't write songs and didn't make clever quips to the press. No one ever wanted Ringo.

Next, we made phony phone calls on my very own pink Princess phone, a present from Mom when we'd redecorated my room the previous winter. My new color scheme was pink on pink and I was especially proud of the wallpaper which was pale pink with line drawings of Elvis Presley and musical staffs printed all over it. I should add, it was exceedingly ugly paper and Mom had argued desperately against plastering the Elvis motif over my walls.

"You don't even like his records," Mom complained, which was true. However, since my mother really, really hated the paper, you can understand why it was the only pattern I would consider.

By midnight Ronnie was having a swell time calling Hank Blaustein and hanging up the phone after Hank said, "Hello." As Lesley and I listened to Hank screaming, "Quit this or I'll call the COPS!" I was startled by the sound of tapping against my window. I glanced out and saw Steven Levy and his two friends, Ray and George, standing among the newly landscaped azalea bushes. Steven was signaling me to let him in the back door.

After listening at my parents' bedroom door to make sure my father was snoring, I tiptoed downstairs and opened the back door very quietly. "What're you doing here?" I whispered to Steven, poking my head outside.

"I tried to call but the phone's been busy for the past three hours. Is Ronnie sleeping over?" (Ronnie was notorious for her phony phone calls.)

I nodded my head. "I just remembered I'm not speaking to you," I said and closed the door on Steven's face.

I waited a moment and then peeped through the Venetian blinds on the door window. Steven was rubbing his nose and there was a kind of pained dullness in his eyes so I opened the door again.

"Look, just let me and the guys in," Steven pleaded, "we'll all go down into the basement and talk."

I hesitated. This was pretty risky business.

"I have your birthday present," Steven said, waving what looked like a jewelry box in my face.

It was hard to resist Steven's sweet-talking. "Wait here," I said. "I have to ask the girls."

I ran upstairs and explained the situation to my friends, who were staring out the window.

"They look like turkeys," commented Lesley, who could afford to be choosy.

Ronnie said, "The tall one isn't bad."

"That's Ray, he's a wrestler. And George is also a real jock. He's captain of the darts team."

"Let's do it," Ronnie said.

"Nah, I'm not in the mood," Lesley yawned.

"Ah, come on, Lesley," Ronnie pleaded.

"Don't start with the whining, Ronnie," I said, startling myself because I sounded exactly like my mother.

Ronnie had her hands clasped in prayer and was rapidly whispering, "Please, please, please." She looked so pathetic that Lesley gave in.

Then Ronnie realized she'd set her hair with empty orange juice cans (her hair was so kinky she could never find big enough rollers), and that in her quilted silver bathrobe, she looked a lot like the frozen food department at Shop Rite. "Tell 'em to wait till we get dressed," Ronnie said, furiously pulling Minute Maid cans out of her head.

I relayed the message and the boys waited by the backyard swings until we were presentable, which took about an hour and forty-five minutes because the orange juice cans had left ridges all over Ronnie's kinky hair and we had to get Mom's iron and steam press Ronnie's hair until it looked halfway decent.

In the basement, I introduced Lesley and Ronnie to Ray and George. Ray and George hovered around Lesley while Ronnie kept busy sneaking Cokes out of the kitchen. Ronnie suggested we hold a seance, which Ray and George agreed to if Lesley would be the one they levitated. Lesley, who was used to being chosen in such situations, lay down on the floor while George, Ray and Ronnie kneeled around her.

I don't know if the seance was successful because, at that point, Steven and I slipped behind the soft water tank so that he could give me my present in private.

I was delighted by the name necklace Steven had bought. The gift meant a lot to me because I knew it had to be special ordered since "Bambi" was never among the names manufacturers chose when they produced name necklaces, rubber stamps, coffee mugs or bicycle licenses.

I let Steven attach the hook in back and forgave him for the mishap at the drive-in. He promised never to lose control again and suggested we avoid any more Hitchcock movies.

The necklace was going to look great with the other things Steven had given me in the two years we had been going steady: his ID bracelet, his class ring (which I wore on a chain around my neck), his letter sweater and his varsity jacket. I was sort of a walking billboard proclaiming the name Steven Levy. The payoff was that Steven had already agreed to take me to my senior prom, a mere two years away. (Mom and I had already started shopping for my prom dress.)

Steven and I spent a long time behind the soft water tank and I really showed him my appreciation by letting him kiss my neck all the way down to the collar bone until he started to make those funny groaning noises that usually signaled he was about to lose control.

I clamped my arms firmly to my sides to protect my chest from his wandering hands.

"I think I hear my father coming," I whispered.

"Your father?" he gasped. Steven was sufficiently in awe of my father to beat a hasty retreat with his two friends.

Upstairs, in my room, I showed Lesley and Ronnie my name necklace.

"Uh-oh!" Ronnie exclaimed, touching my neck instead of the necklace.

"What's the matter?" I asked. "It's fourteen carat."

"Oh, Bambi," Lesley said, in this real sympathetic voice. She held my shoulders and turned me around so that I faced the mirror behind my bedroom door. "Hickey," she said gently, pointing to a huge black-and-blue mark smack dab in the middle of my otherwise unblemished neck.

I was so shocked that I could barely speak; my parents would have a total conniption fit if they ever saw what I was seeing.

"Sweet Sixteen and never been hickeyed," Lesley teased.

"What were you and Steven doing under the pool table?" Ronnie asked.

"We were behind the soft water tank, not under the pool table!" I proclaimed. "And we weren't doing nothing!"

"Well, you must've been doing something," teased Lesley. "Hickeys don't grow on soft water tanks."

"I thought Steven was biting my necklace," I said in all honesty. "I didn't even feel anything."

"Maybe it's time for a new boyfriend," observed Ronnie, as she gingerly touched my neck. "You definitely should've felt *this*."

I was so upset I started to cry. To my mind a hickey was like a Scarlett Letter, because only the trampy girls in class, the ones with the teased beehives, walked around with purple marks on them.

Would this hickey ruin my reputation in school? I wondered and started to cry even louder, which generated a lot of sympathy from Ronnie and Lesley; they told me not to get emotional and went to work helping me to cover up the telltale mark. We spent the entire night plastering my neck with Erase and white lipstick but the more makeup we applied, the worse I looked.

For two days, I was able to hide the embarrassment of Steven's passion by wearing my aqua turtleneck sweater, but on the third morning my mother got suspicious.

"Bambi, why're you wearing that turtleneck under your pajamas?" Mom asked.

"No reason, I'm cold," I said nonchalantly.

"Cold? It's June! Are you sick?" She put her lips to my forehead like I had a fever or something.

Suddenly we were having a big fight because Mom said I had to stay home from school if I was so cold, and there was a big baseball game after school I couldn't possibly miss. So I had no choice but to remove the turtleneck, tell the truth and let the chips hit the fan, if you know what I mean.

"Oy vey!" Mom screeched, dropping her "Best Mom in the World" coffee mug on the floor. "What's that *thing* on your neck?"

"What thing?"

"That purple thing!" she screamed, knocking over the milk carton as she lunged for my neck.

"What? This? Oh, it's nothing. I had a little accident this morning."

"What kind of accident?" Mom yanked back my head to make a closer inspection.

"I, um, hit myself in the neck with a hanger."

"A hanger? With teeth marks?"

"A skirt hanger."

I finally escaped Mom's admonishments about being such a klutz and hurried out of the house, vowing never, never to neck with Steven again.

I was able to forget the day's troubles for a little while because the baseball game that afternoon was really exciting. Ho High was competing for the state championship against our arch-rival, Newark Tech. Ronnie and I joined in our traditional school cheer against the technical academy:

> THAT'S ALL RIGHT, THAT'S OKAY,
> YOU'RE GONNA WORK FOR US SOMEDAY!

Although we won the game, and then the championship, that afternoon will always stand out in my memory as the day I saw Rocky Rissotto for the first time.

Ronnie and I were standing under the bleachers when this gorgeous guy zoomed past us on the biggest and loudest motorcycle I'd ever seen or heard.

"Who is that?" I asked Ronnie.

"Rocky Rissotto," she said. "King of the Boppers."

I should explain that in the mid-sixties, our high

school was divided into two ethnic groups: the Rah Rahs and the Boppers. The Rah Rahs were the fore-runners of today's Yuppies and the Boppers were self-styled Punks with greased, as opposed to green, hair. In movie-star terms, the Rah Rahs were Sandra Dee and Troy Donahue while the Boppers were James Dean and Priscilla Presley before she divorced Elvis.

Rocky guided his motorcycle under the bleachers where Ronnie and I were standing and he gave me the once-over about nine times, staring blatantly at my neck.

"Wanna ride?" he asked, licking his lips in a real sexy way.

I did, but I didn't think it was safe to get on his motorcycle in my pleated kilt skirt held together with one flimsy safety pin.

"I can't," I said. "I'm with my friend."* I pointed to Ronnie, who had pulled off her thick glasses and was squinting sweetly at Rocky.

"You wanna ride?" Rocky said to Ronnie, who gig-gled real stupidly and stumbled over in the general direction of Rocky's bike. Her arms were extended in front of her and she felt her way around until she knocked against the rear fender.

As Ronnie lifted her leg to climb aboard, I grabbed her arm and tackled her to the ground. "She's only kidding," I laughed, locking Ronnie's arm in a stran-gle grip behind her back. "Right?"

"Umm . . . sure," Ronnie gasped.

Rocky grinned and then shrugged his shoulders, causing the pack of Marlboros stuck in his tee-shirt sleeve to slide to the ground. He revved his motorcy-cle to a deaf-defying timbre (which really impressed us), yanked on the handles of the bike and wheeled off. Coughing from the dust thrown up by the bike, Ronnie and I scrambled for Rocky's forgotten pack of cigarettes. Naturally, I got hold of the cigarettes first

* There was an unwritten best-friend code at the time that you never left your girlfriend alone.

because Ronnie, who wasn't wearing her glasses, missed the pack by a good six feet.*

I saw Rocky again a couple weeks later at Mc-Donald's† and since I was wearing my Levis, I accepted his offer of a ride.

Much to the chagrin of my parents, this was the beginning of a serious romance between me and Rocky Rissotto, which, as you may have noticed, is not a Jewish name.

At first, Rocky and I snuck out on our dates because my mother threatened to drown herself in the dishwasher every time I mentioned his name in her presence. Then my parents decided they were protesting too much and even though they disapproved, granted me permission to bring Rocky home. Of course, this caused a bit of a strain as Daddy would grind his teeth whenever he heard Rocky's motorcycle coming down the street, while Mom dropped to the kitchen floor to practice rolling over in her grave.

My father seemed real suspicious of Rocky and always gave him the third degree as soon as he walked in the door. "Made any career decisions yet, Rocky?" Dad would always ask.

Rocky, a recent high school graduate, spent a lot of time deciding which career to pursue. Of course, he spent more time greasing up his bike and waiting to get drafted, but nevertheless he always answered my dad's questions like a real gentleman.

"No, sir, not yet," Rocky would tell my father. "I don't really care what I do, I could be a garbage man as long as I was the best garbage man I could be."

I thought Rocky had a really good attitude but whenever he alluded to garbage, my mom would choke up and glance longingly at the dishwasher.

---

* I kept that pack of Marlboros hidden in my underwear drawer for the next two years.
† This was the first McDonald's ever opened in Hohokus (before Big Macs were even invented). I was proud of my constant participation, which helped to boost sales of over "one million burgers sold," before the year was out.

I rather liked the way Rocky annoyed my parents. Dating him made me feel like Maria in *West Side Story* and I took to singing "I Feel Pretty" while I got ready for my dates.

My parents forbade me to ride on Rocky's motorcycle so we spent a lot of our dates in my basement making out to Johnny Mathis records. Every fifteen minutes or so Daddy banged on the basement door and shouted, "What are you two doing down there?"

"Playing pool," I would reply while Rocky pitched a billiard ball across the pool table. Daddy always waited to hear the balls knocking together before closing the door again.

I broke up with Steven after the first time Rocky and I slow danced to "Chances Are." (Steven thought I was overreacting to the hickey. Little did he know the black-and-blue mark had practically brought Rocky and me together!) I knew I was taking a chance by giving up a sure thing for the senior prom but I was really in love with Rocky and you know how reckless love makes you. I returned Steven's letter sweater, his varsity jacket and his class ring, but I kept his ID bracelet as a souvenir.

Rocky and I dated all through my last two years in high school. I took to wearing black eyeliner painted from my lashes to right below my eyebrows (with perfect little triangles drawn on the outer edges of my lids), lots of white lipstick and black chiffon scarves, which I wrapped and tied around my neck like Sophia Loren. I learned to blow smoke rings. But, mostly, Rocky taught me about sex.

Rocky suffered from a condition he called "blue balls" which would attack him every time we got into heavy necking. As he explained it, blue balls came from not being able to go all the way and they hurt so much that a guy could actually have a heart attack and die from the pain.

Blue balls notwithstanding, Rocky didn't have a

snowball's chance in hell of going all the way with me; not with my Gidget sense of morality. Although I might not look or act the part when I was hanging with the Boppers, underneath those tight black sweaters and black straight skirts, I was a good Jewish girl who wanted to be a virgin on the day my husband broke the glass under a hoopa.

But, occasionally, I got so weary from Rocky's constant complaining that I allowed him to rub up against my thigh long enough for his blue balls to subside. I didn't particularly like the rubbing as it uncomfortably reminded me of Aunt Selma's German shepherd attaching himself to my leg, but it seemed a small price to pay for having Rocky as my boyfriend.

Before I met Rocky, I thought the world was divided into two religions: Jewish and Gentile. So I was amazed when Rocky told me how there were lots of Christian religions: Roman Catholic, Protestant, Lutheran, Episcopalian, Methodist, Baptist and so on. Rocky, who was a Roman Catholic, took me to Mass, which was my very first time in a church. ("My Virgin visit," I reverently thought, getting into the swing of things.)

At first, it didn't seem all that different from the services at temple, except, of course, that the women wore hats instead of the men. The priest conducting the services dressed in a robe and spoke in a foreign language, just like Rabbi Zindl. Everyone in the church squirmed around and pretended not to be falling asleep during the sermon, just like Dad and Uncle Shelley. The major difference seemed to be that people were continually kneeling, which I wasn't too keen on—the Jewish version (just standing up) was more comfortable, and certainly a lot easier on the kneecaps.

Suddenly, everyone stood up and started filing down the aisle. I could see they were going up to the stage and getting little crackers from the priest.

"Oh, goodie," I thought to myself, "it must be time

for snacks." Thinking how pleasant it was to serve refreshments during the services, I also stood.

Rocky grabbed my arm and tried to stop me from going down the aisle. He said it just wasn't right, me being Jewish and all.

Well, that turned me right off. I'd always heard Gentiles were stingy with food, but this was ridiculous. I certainly couldn't sanction a religion that didn't feed everyone. I ignored Rocky's arguments and went up to get my cracker anyway.

The kindly priest overlooked my chi necklace as he put the little cracker on my tongue. Now, I don't mean to complain, but I have to say the cracker tasted pretty awful. In fact, it had almost no taste at all. ("Needs a little salt," I thought to myself, "and a dab of chopped liver wouldn't hurt.")

I waited around for seconds but none were forthcoming. "That's it?" I mumbled to myself. "Ah, excuse me, sir?" I motioned to the priest. "May I have some more?"

"One to a customer," he said, reminding me of the old Catskill joke, "The food is lousy, and such small portions!"

Rocky swiftly ushered me out of the church and, after that, we hardly ever discussed religion again.

That was also the year Daddy gave me my first driving lesson in our Bonneville convertible. It took us ten minutes to get out of the driveway and Daddy remarked I didn't need to drive quite so slowly. But then Mom took me out for a lesson and, remembering Daddy's advice, I turned the corner in front of our house without stepping on the brake. The car turned on only one of its four wheels, sending Mom flying across the front seat.

After that, Mom and Dad left my driving indoctrination to Driver's Ed, which was, bar none, the most interesting class ever taught at Ho High.

Mom's car made me really popular my senior year,

especially after I got accepted to college and the greater part of my high school curriculum consisted of driving down to the shore.* Even Tiffany begged to come along and I was feeling generous so I let her.

As usual, we ran the tolls on the Garden State Parkway and, at Bradley Beach, stole lunch food from the local A & P.

On the beach, we stripped to our bathing suits and slicked down with baby oil. In those days, there were two schools of suntanning protocol: those who swore by baby oil and those who insisted that baby oil with iodine was far superior.

Stretched out on our towels, we talked about our forthcoming prom and our dates and ate olive loaf and Wonder Bread sandwiches.

"You're so lucky," Tiffany said to me. "Rocky is so cute."

I did not fail to remember that Tiffany had said the same thing about Igor.

On the drive home, Les, Nita, Cyn, Bev, Kar, Tiff and me compared sunburns and tried to out-kvetch one another as to who was in greater pain (swollen eyelids generated the most sympathy). But real status was measured by who had the greatest "difference" in skin tone from their bathing suit lines. Of course, the world is different now—those magazine articles about skin cancer and premature wrinkles have really put a damper on any enthusiasm for a day in the sun.

That day, however, I had to cede the sunburn competition to Tiffany, who had burned the backs of her legs so badly that she had to sit in the car with her ankles propped up on the dashboard.

Once home, we changed clothes and headed for upstate New York where we could legally get drunk on

---

* For anyone who's never lived in New Jersey, the shore is where Bruce Springsteen used to play before he was famous, when only Jersey kids knew him because they went to school with one of his cousins. Now, of course, Bruce, Mr. Superstar, has singlehandedly legitimized not only the shore and the entire state of New Jersey but being born in the U.S.A. as well.

whiskey sours and Tom Collinses. At the bar, Tiffany remarked on Rocky's muscular biceps, so I accidentally spilled a whiskey sour on her striped bellbottoms.

Prom night, I spent hours dressing for my date with Rocky. I had my hair set at the beauty parlor where Mr. Michele had styled a perfect doody-roll flip topped by a crown of curls. I wore Mom's diamond earrings and an emerald green and white satin dress encrusted with rhinestones; so cool, it was to die. Unfortunately, I couldn't wear high, high heels because Rocky was a tad on the short side,* but my one-inch heels were dyed green to perfectly match my dress.

I waited for fifteen minutes after I heard Rocky ring the doorbell, and, then, I slowly descended the stairs to allow Rocky and my parents the full benefit of my three hours of preparation.

Mom took one look at me and applauded wildly. "Chills!" she declared, showing the goosebumps on her arms to Rocky and Daddy. "Chills!"

Rocky handed me a lovely green carnation corsage, which he carefully pinned to the spaghetti strap on my dress.†

The prom theme was "A Night of Knights" and it was totally romantic. The gym was decorated like the interior of a castle with a papier mâché drawbridge, a flying dragon spouting orange crepe paper breath and colorful medieval shields. We had our prom pictures taken by a real photographer and danced to the music of Rhonda and the Romantics, who were sort of a white version of Gladys Knight and the Pips, except that unlike Gladys, Rhonda didn't sing on key. In fact, I had the sneaking suspicion Rhonda was tone deaf, and that, if this was Color War, she'd be asked to be a mouther.

---

* And my father wouldn't let me out of the house in stilettos.
†You could hardly notice the trickle of blood where he stabbed my shoulder.

The prom was followed by a few hours of madness and mayhem at the Cresskill Bowling Lanes, where the guys drank beer from bowling shoes and the girls gathered in the ladies room. Then we drove into New York City to a little club in the Village where we felt so cool sitting among the Beatniks wearing torn tee-shirts and dirty jeans.

As I straightened the bow tie on Rocky's rented tux, I wondered if the Beatniks could tell we were from out of town. I assumed not, because they were smiling at us and acting real friendly—borrowing cigarettes and letting us buy them drinks.

It was one of the best nights of my life and one of the last times I ever saw Rocky with a full head of hair. Two weeks later, Rocky was drafted and his head was shaved to the skull, which, I have to admit, detracted a lot from his Bopper image. Rocky shipped off for Fort Leonard Wood and I shipped off to college where I soon discovered there was life after high school and Rocky had lied about all that blue balls business.

I BEGIN LIFE ON MY OWN ACCOUNT AND DON'T LIKE IT
9

I can't even begin to describe the panic that gripped the senior class when it came time to take SAT exams. You would've thought everyone's future depended solely on getting high scores (which, of course, it did). I was much calmer than any of my friends because my expectations were a lot lower. As I had been reminding my parents since the fifth grade, I never tested well.

The scramble for college acceptance was similarly hysterical. Perfectly sane kids threatened to nose dive off the roof of Ho High if they didn't make Ivy League. Naturally, oddball Seymour was the only kid in school who wasn't worried about getting into college, especially after he practically aced his SATs with the highest score in the whole class.

"I've been studying for that test since the sixth grade," Seymour explained during one Friday-night dinner at my house. He extracted a pipe from his breast pocket, which he stuck into his mouth but did not light, because his mother, Sadie, forbade him to smoke.

"Such a brain, that Seymour," my mother sighed. "Too bad he didn't help Bambi study."

"I offered a hundred times," Seymour said, somewhat dejectedly.

"You're not supposed to study for SATs," I said in my own defense. "Besides, I had other things to do." I smiled at Rocky, who sat next to me.

"Yeah," Rocky agreed, squeezing my knee under the dining room table.

If it hadn't been for Rocky I never would've survived those dinners with Seymour, who seemed to consider my house his second home. Rocky used to say Seymour had a wild crush on me.

"Seymour isn't interested in girls," I insisted. "He's only interested in Mom's cooking." So, it came as a real shock when I discovered, years later, that Rocky's jealousy had been well founded.

Daddy, as always, acted as if Rocky wasn't even there. "So, Seymour, have you decided . . . Harvard or MIT?"

"Fairleigh Dickinson."

"You're going local?"

"Mom wanted me to live at home and the commute to Boston seemed impractical."

"Such a good son," Mom sighed, "Seymour, dear, have some more noodle pudding."

"But Janice, the boy turned down Harvard," Dad shook his head in disbelief. "For Fairleigh Dickinson."

"Fairleigh Ridiculous," joked Rocky.

"I guess college was never your thing, huh, Rock?" Seymour asked, a touch condescendingly, I might add.

"Me? Spend four more years in school?" Rocky howled and even my parents laughed at the idea.

Like all my friends, I sent away for lots of college brochures and eventually applied to Ulysses College in upstate New York because their application form was real short and didn't require a written essay. I was requested to provide my name, address, favorite movie star and $150. Half the graduating class of

Ho High applied to Ulysses. We all got accepted, including Tiffany Jerkowitz, which didn't exactly thrill me.

Daddy, of course, was heartbroken, not because of Tiffany, but because tuition at Ulysses amounted to over thirty-five hundred dollars a year. Mom reminded him I was more likely to snag a rich husband at an expensive college, which somewhat softened the financial blow.

A few days before freshman orientation, Daddy rented a U-Haul to transport my seven trunks of clothes, nine cartons of records, and portable refrigerator to my tiny 6 by 6 feet dorm room. Mom, Dad and I spent the weekend at a small motel near Ulysses and, on Sunday, after a brief tour of the campus and a thorough inspection of the cafeteria kitchen, I gently reminded my parents it was time for them to return to Hohokus.

"Don't smoke any unlabeled cigarettes," Dad instructed me for the thousandth time as we walked to the parking lot.

"Try not to fight with Tiffany and promise you'll be a *good* girl," Mom pleaded.

"I promise."

"You promise?"

"Daddy, she's driving me crazy with the promising!"

"Who's *she*?" Mom indignantly demanded. "The cat's mother?" *

"Janice, kiss the college girl goodbye and let's get going. I want to make the Thruway before dark."

Mom kissed my cheek so hard that I thought she might dislocate her nose. "You'll be a good girl?" she asked again because I don't think she believed my promises for one minute.

Daddy laughed as he pried my mother off me, guided her into the car and slammed the door. He

* It was not the first time Mom confused me with this rhetorical question, the meaning of which still eludes me.

kissed my forehead one last time. "You won't forget about the cigarettes?"

"Daddy!"

"Right," Daddy said, patting my shoulder. He got into the car, started the engine and drove away slowly.

Leaning out the car window, Mom waved her wad of Kleenex. "Don't forget to call every Sunday!" she hollered as the car disappeared down the road.

I met my first roommate, Mona, about an hour later. I tried to be nice and helped her unpack her stuff, which consisted mainly of framed photographs of her fiancé. "Pre-med at Harvard," Mona bragged, kissing a black-and-white head shot of a blonde, haggard looking guy with a stethoscope stuck in his ears.

Mona was so neat and orderly that she put away all her clothes and did her laundry in the same amount of time it took me to unpack my Barbra Streisand albums.

Mona and I went to dinner in the cafeteria, where I discovered my roomie ate only cottage cheese and tomatoes. "This has virtually no calories," she said.

"Neither does cardboard but I wouldn't eat paper for supper either," I joked, but Mona didn't laugh. She was dead serious about her diet, and went on to explain how she had to fit into her size eight wedding dress when her fiancé graduated from med school sometime in the next decade, if she was lucky.

Mona talked a lot about her fiancé, her impending wedding and what she expected from future bridesmaids. "Waterford crystal is always appropriate, don't you think?" she asked about a dozen times while we sat in the auditorium for freshman orientation.

Ulysses College was a comparatively new school and Dean Stanley, the president of the college, wasn't much older than the student body. He gave a stirring speech as part of orientation saying, in part, "Don't expect miracles from college, study hard, do your best, watch out for unlabeled cigarettes."

Ulysses boasted a huge physical education department and an impressive agricultural program so most of the guys were jocks studying to be either phys ed teachers or forest rangers. Now that might not seem all that impressive—speaking strictly scholastically—but, let me tell you, there were more hunks per square foot in that auditorium than at any science fair I'd ever attended.

The girls, for the most part, were like me: well-dressed and ready to get pinned.

In the crowded auditorium, Tiffany sat about six rows in front of me and we pretended not to notice each other, a practice we continued for the next four years.

I quickly learned that living in a dorm was almost as hard as surviving a summer with bunkmates. After two weeks, I requested a new roommate because Mona was driving me absolutely nuts. She'd plastered the walls of our room with photos and brochures of various honeymoon hideways in the Caribbean. Even worse, she'd set a dressmaker's dummy in the middle of the room so that she could work on her bridal gown. I could barely find my jeans under all those bolts of white satin and tulle netting.

My next roommate's name was Désirée. Well, actually, her name was Diane but she had changed it when she entered college. For a while she tried to convince me to change my name and suggested Bambée would be more sophisticated than Bambi. I tried out the name in a few classes but when one of my professors pronounced the new spelling "Bombay" I decided to stick to my original moniker.

Désirée got pregnant about one month into college and dropped out. After that came Cheryl Stanton, who majored in political science. Cheryl was real involved with politics so we had nothing in common and, after a couple of weeks, she decided to move in with the girlfriend of the president of the SDS.

Every time I asked for another roommate, I reminded the house mother that it wasn't my fault I couldn't keep a roommate for more than two weeks. "There's a lot of weird girls in this school, Mrs. Sharp," I said, but she just bit her lip.

"You were an only child, weren't you?" Mrs. Sharp asked as she rummaged through her card file.

"Yeah." I wondered what that had to do with the price of tea in China.

Naturally I joined the traditional freshman activities of drinking tap beer and eating roast beef subs by the gross. I pursued my academic studies* and learned how to pass an exam by filling an entire blue book without understanding the test question. I enriched my mind with the important works of Kurt Vonnegut and Ayn Rand, and my ear with the musical accomplishments of John Denver and Elton John. But, mainly I searched for love and romance and dating was my primary concern.

There were lots of nice freshman guys in my classes but I wouldn't be caught dead dating someone my age so I had to maneuver ways of meeting upperclassmen. My friends and I attended mixers, fraternity parties, afternoon teas and rush dances and, when really desperate, engaged in blind dating.

Listen, having a blind date was usually the pits but not having a date was a fate worse than death. It wasn't like high school where a girl could hide out at home if she didn't have a date Saturday night. In a dorm, you eventually had to leave your room, even if only to use the bathroom, where you were certain to encounter a gorgeous, thin blonde girl dressing for a formal night out on the town.

My first fix-up was with a boy named Bobby Lowenstern, who took me to a fraternity party where all the guys were smashed on this really foul-smelling punch and the girls were daintily nursing mixed drinks.

* I had pretty much decided to major in fashion appreciation but Daddy insisted I learn something so I majored in English and minored in fashion.

Bobby introduced me to a few of his brothers, showed me his room and immediately downed three mugs of the punch while I sipped a rum and Coke. Then we slow danced to the classic love song *Purple Haze* by Jimi Hendrix.

"Are you thinking what I'm thinking?" Bobby whispered huskily in my ear.

"I don't know," I replied. "Were you wondering what's for dinner, too?"

I guess it wasn't the correct answer because Bobby drove me back to the dorm about ten minutes later. Unfortunately, the rest of my blind dates that year pretty much followed the same pattern.

Going to college in the late sixties and early seventies was a unique experience, really "mind-blowing" to use a phrase from the time. All over the country, college kids were rioting, picketing, marching, demonstrating and sitting in to protest the war in Vietnam. Cheryl Stanton and her group of friends tried to get us to join in, but campus unrest at Ulysses was minimal, since most of the students were more concerned with deep knee bends or gypsy moths than foreign affairs. Sometimes a rabble-rouser shouted Vietnamese propaganda on the quad but we silenced such activists with a well-aimed pitcher of beer tossed off the balcony. It's not that we were unsympathetic to politics, it was just that the noise interfered with our primary occupation: keeping track of slutty Rachel on *Another World* and *Another World Somerset*.

One of the best things about college was that it introduced me to a whole new world of afternoon soap operas. Few classes at UC were even scheduled after 2:30 in the afternoon, as the teachers shared our enthusiasm for the infamous Rachel-Steve Frame-Alice triangle.

By 2:25 sharp, the entire female population of Ulysses and a few of the early feminist guys were crowded around the TV set in anticipation of seeing what devious scheme Rachel Cory had hatched to seduce poor Steven Frame away from his sappy wife, Alice.*

One afternoon, we were shocked when Rachel appeared on TV in the guise of a different actress. All the other actors on *Another World* went about calling this new woman Rachel.

"This is an outrage!" shrieked one of the students.

"They can't do this," shouted Dr. Virginia Layton, our biology professor.

"We should do something!" yelled Dean Stanley— one of Rachel's biggest fans on campus.

"Let's protest!"

"Let's march!"

"Let's picket NBC!" screamed Cheryl Stanton.

"Let's get something to eat!" shouted Tiffany Jerkowitz.

The kids organized a March on NBC and the dean canceled classes for several days. ABC and CBS ran feature coverage of the students picketing their rival network. On campus, we drafted a petition, signed by 4,582 students, and everyone wrote angry protest letters to their congressmen, but none of our efforts did any good. NBC stuck with their Rachel and, after a while, we learned to adjust, because the new actress playing Rachel was just as bitchy as the old Rachel. One of the major lessons we learned from this experience was that protesting might end the war in Vietnam but it couldn't budge NBC.

I hate to admit this but, frankly, I wasn't all that thrilled with my first year of college. Oh, I knew it was supposed to be among the best years of my life but, in sum, the tests were a drag, I went through all those obnoxious roommates, my social life was nothing compared to dating Rocky in high school and the food was atrocious.

I griped bitterly to my parents but I got no sympathy; my father in particular brooked no complaints when he was in for almost five grand.

---

* I read an interesting thesis recently that traced the origins of Alexis Carrington all the way back to Rachel Cory.

Mom was even less understanding since she was suffering her own trauma at the time. In pyschiatric terms, Mom was afflicted with the empty nest syndrome and was acting, according to my father, "like a chicken without its head." Mom spent most of her time driving around Ho High School, offering to lend her car to any kid with a driver's license. When a junior front-ended the Bonneville, Daddy realized something had to be done to alleviate Mom's loneliness, so he bought her a French poodle, paying a hundred bucks extra for a pup with blue eyes, which Mommy named after her favorite blue-eyed movie star, Frank Sinatra.

Trouble with the dog began almost immediately. Within a week, Frank's eyes turned brown and, since Mom couldn't think of a sexy actor with brown eyes, the dog's name stuck.

Then one morning, the demented dog tried to drown himself by swimming halfway across Lake Kiamesha. Too exhausted to swim back to shore, Frank was going down for the third time when Dad dove into the ice cold lake and rescued the drowning dog. Next, Frank nearly jumped to his death when he leaped out the window of Aunt Selma's second-story apartment. A couple of weeks later, his two front legs in a cast, Frank made a desperate attempt to overdose by eating a dozen Dunkin' Donuts. This poodle was really determined to die. Mom wanted to put Frank on Librium or get him into psychotherapy but Daddy refused to cough up the dough for treatments.

Finally, the suicidal maniac got his wish, after giving my cousin Estelle an instant nose job when he viciously bit off her left nostril. At the insistence of Nana Yetta, Frank was sent to doggie heaven. None of us mourned too much except, of course, for Mom, who now had a doggie ghost haunting her empty nest.

"You're on your own with this one, Janice," Daddy said.

I saw Frank's demise as a metaphor for life, especially after studying Albert Camus at UC. Like most of my college friends, I was deep into the meaninglessness of existence and heavily under the influence of the authors we read in Existential Lit. I tried to explain *The Stranger* to my mother, but Frank's death had made her extremely short-tempered.

"Camus-Shamoo, don't be such a worry wart," she scoffed. "Go. Find yourself a husband. Get married."

"Mom, there's more to life than marriage."

"Bite your tongue!" Mom shrieked. "You want Seymour to hear you?" Seymour was devouring Mom's stuffed derma in the kitchen. "Where do you get these ideas? What're they teaching you at that high-priced school?"

I don't know if it was because of her empty nest or because I was not yet engaged, but relations with my mother deteriorated steadily during my college years, especially during my Jonathan Livingston Siegel period.

At the beginning of sophomore year, I fell madly in love with Jonathan, a junior. Jonathan was the first Jewish guru hippie at Ulysses; his main claim to fame was the summer he spent in India, traipsing through the Himalayas and searching for inner peace. To fit his vagabond self-image, Jonathan wore his hair shoulder-length with a red bandana tied across his forehead and wire-rimmed glasses. He often dressed in a white sheet and thonged sandals, even before sheets and sandals were made fashionable by the Beatles.

I took to dressing just like Jonathan, only I chose designer sheets in a fashionable butterfly pattern. Mom was appalled when she and my father visited me at school.

"When I spent a thousand dollars at Bergdorf's for your wardrobe, I didn't realize you wanted to shop in the linen department," she quipped.

Jon's appeal totally eluded my mother. In fact, the only good thing she ever said about him was, "I'm sure he would be very cute, if only he'd take a bath once in a while. And a haircut wouldn't kill him either."

I paid no attention to my mother. I liked Jon because he was really deep and seemed to know all the answers. "When you get really depressed about your life, think about all the people who are so much worse off than you," he advised.

"What about the people who are better off?"

Jon said I wasn't seeing the forest for the trees, a metaphor he lifted, I think, from Linda Ronstadt.

Rocky wrote me an occasional letter from Vietnam. He wasn't enjoying the war as much as he'd expected before he was drafted. Rocky drove an ambulance in a place near Saigon, the name of which I've forgotten although it sounded a lot like Long Been Gone. "Life in Vietnam is no picnic," he wrote, "though the grass is A-One."

Rocky had a hard time relating to my problems with curfew, sign-outs and Public Speaking class, and he thought *The Teachings of Don Juan* which I had sent him in a burst of sophomoric enthusiasm,* was the worst book he'd ever read. "The rantings of an acid-head," he wrote. "Castenada could learn a lot more about life by visiting the First Battalion, Third Marine Division, fifteen miles west of the Da Nang Air Base."

Rocky and I saw each other one last time when I was home for Christmas vacation. He had returned from Vietnam a changed man, no longer interested in riding his motorcycle. He got a job at the Nabisco factory in Fair Lawn, where he supervised the Oreo cookie division, and talked a lot about job security.

A few months later Rocky married Cookie La-Touche, the girl he dated before meeting me under the bleachers at Ho High. Mom and Dad were so delighted by Rocky's marriage that they sent a two-hundred-dollar Bamberger's gift certificate to the new Mrs. Rissotto.

---

* Rocky was lucky he didn't get *The Prophet*, by Kahlil Gibran.

• • •

Throughout my years at Ulysses, my social life was the main topic of conversation when I called home late Sunday nights. Mom always asked the same question, "So, where'd you go last night?"

"Nowhere," I replied.

"What did you do?"

"Nothing."

"Who did you go with?"

"No one." *

Satisfied that everything was status quo, Mom would then pass the phone around the canasta table. "Say hello to the ladies," she would instruct and, after that, I would be told to talk to Seymour, who had become so accustomed to eating dinner at my parents' house that he continued the practice after I had left for college.

Seymour and I never had very much to say to each other over the phone. He was a biology major so we mainly talked about the latest escapades of Dr. Kildare and Ben Casey.† "Man, woman, birth, death, infinity," Seymour said during the numerous lulls in our conversations. It wasn't until a few years later that Seymour and I had a more profound conversation.

Junior year, I finally moved off campus because I just couldn't take living in a dorm anymore. I shared a two-bedroom apartment with Sandy Rasabinsky, my old best friend, who had transferred to Ulysses from a small college in Ohio. Sandy and I loved our little apartment and were always fixing it up by rearranging our cinder-block bookcases.

One afternoon I was busy alphabetizing my enormous record collection when there was a knock on the door.

"Seymour!" I exclaimed upon opening it.

Seymour stood on the front porch. His reddish hair

* I tended to eliminate a lot of the particulars when discussing my dates with Mom.
† Vince Edwards was like a god to Seymour.

was Beatle-length and he wore torn jeans and a dirty flannel shirt. Except for the pen and pencil set in his shirt pocket, he almost looked cool.

"What're you doing here?" I asked.

"I drove up to see Tiffany; she invited me to some dance this weekend." Seymour walked into the living room.

"Tiffany Jerkowitz?"

"Umm, but I really drove up to ask you something." He sat down on the pillow couch.

"You? And Tiffany? I don't get it."

"Don't get what?"

"I didn't know you two went out, is all."

"Oh, sure. We've been screwing around together for years." Seymour picked up my *Hair* album and glanced at the liner notes. "Got a Coke or anything to drink?"

I went into the kitchen and when I returned I said, "Screwing around? As in sleeping together?"

Seymour tossed *Hair* on the coffee table. "Tiffany's been putting out for me since the tenth grade."

Well, I was dumbstruck. I didn't know which shocked me more: Tiffany screwing around since tenth grade or Seymour.

"Thanks," Seymour said, taking the soda from my hand.

I sat on the floor in front of Seymour. He began slurping down the soft drink so I went back to sorting through my albums. I was wondering whether to file *Tea for the Tillerman* under T or S (for Cat Stevens) when Seymour burped loudly.

"So, Seymour," I said, "what'd you want to ask me?"

"Oh, yeah, I almost forgot, I was curious if you'd be interested in something."

Probably not, I thought. "Like what'd you have in mind?"

"Nothing much. I thought we might go out for a cup of coffee, maybe lunch or dinner. A weekend in the city, a week in Jamaica. I was thinking we could live together for a couple of months, have the wedding at your parents' country club, a couple of kids, a dog and a cat, early retirement and then we could die in each other's arms."

I made a major decision right then and there. I filed Cat Stevens after Nina Simone.

"A cup of coffee sounds okay," I said to Seymour.

"Great. We'll have coffee this afternoon and tomorrow you can pick out our silver pattern."

"Whoa, Seymour. Are you asking me to marry you? I mean, seriously?"

"To marry me, to have my children and to die in my arms."

"But . . . what about Tiffany?"

"Are you kidding? I'd never marry a girl who sleeps around as much as Tiffany."

Men, I thought to myself, you can't live with them and you can't punch them out when they say something stupid.

"But, Seymour, I don't get it. Why me?"

"Why not you?" he laughed. "Okay, the fact is I . . . sort of . . . you know . . . love you."

"You do?" I think this was the biggest shock of the day. "Since when?"

"Since always. Since we used to watch Roy Rogers and Dale Evans. So, whadda ya say? Happy trails for us?" He softly whistled the Happy Trails theme song while I tried to answer his question.

"I can't marry you, Seymour," I said, not being able to think of anything more original.

"Why not?"

"Well, for one thing, I'm lavaliered to Jonathan Livingston Siegel."

"So dump the guy. I hear he's a pothead anyway."

"From whom?"

"Tiffany."

"Yeah, well, what does that little slut know?" I stood up and then sat down again. "OK, forget Jon. I still can't marry you because . . . how can I say this? Listen, you remember all those times you'd be playing with my stuffed animals and I'd be reading my Nancy Drews and you'd slice open Jerome Giraffe's seams—"

"Not his seams," Seymour interrupted, "his subclavian artery."

"Whatever, after you opened his artery—and ruined his stuffing, I should add—remember how I'd start to cry and scream that I hated you?"

"I sure do. Those were the days, huh?" He grinned happily.

"You missed my point. Seymour we're like totally incompatible. Besides, I don't love you."

"You don't mean that."

"Yes, I do."

"You don't."

"I do."

"You don't."

"Seymour, I don't love you. In fact, I don't think I even *like* you very much."

"Then I guess marriage is out of the question."

"Totally."

"Well, at least think it over."

Seymour handed me the empty Coke can and left the apartment.

When Sandy came home, an hour later, she found me staring at the empty can of soda. I felt as though I'd dreamed the whole conversation, or heard it on *Another World*.

I didn't see Seymour again for a long time. Sandy and I toured Europe that summer, visiting fourteen countries in eight weeks and hitting every church from Scotland to Yugoslavia.

In England, I hung around Windsor Castle for days on end hoping to get a glimpse of Prince Charles (still my number-one husband choice) but Sandy couldn't stand the dampness and finally convinced me to move on.

Naturally we faithfully called our parents once a week, on Sundays. The night I called home from Athens, Mom told me to find a television set because a man was going to moonwalk on network television. Sandy and I discovered a couple of televisions set up in the park so everyone could watch the historic event. Of course, we couldn't understand the language but the black-and-white still photograph of the moon being broadcast on the screen was easy enough to see. The picture never changed, so, after staring at it for a couple of hours, we got bored and went to get something to eat.

That particular summer was also the summer of Woodstock, which, of course, we also missed. Although both of those events took place a number of years ago, I'm still really peeved they happened the one summer I was out of the country and if I ever speak to anyone from NASA I'm going to give them a piece of my mind.

Senior year Jon moved off campus, to run a health food store in town. I promised Jon I'd remain faithful while he went on a month-long ashram retreat, but then Sandy introduced me to Marvin Rosenthal, who roomed with Bradley, Sandy's boyfriend, and two days later, I wrote a Dear John letter to dear Jon, enclosing his lavalier.

My parents assumed I had dumped Jon because of Marvin but the truth was I broke up with Jon because I couldn't possibly down another bowl of brown rice.

Marvin Rosenthal was a lot sexier than his name. He was a big bear of a guy, snuggly, like Hoss Cartwright from *Bonanza*, and although Marvin was real personable, he was not without one pressing flaw. Marvin was obsessed with ironing; wrinkles drove him into an absolute frenzy. We would go out for the evening, have a lovely time at the movies, dinner, whatever and then, about 1:00 in the morning, Marvin would stroll over to my closet and start rummaging through its contents.

He'd find a wrinkled dress and, like a man possessed, he'd get out Sandy's iron and go to work. Bradley, a psych major, said Marvin was enacting his desire to flatten women to the board, but I thought he was just being tidy. At first, I didn't mind Marvin's idiosyncrasy—in fact, my cotton shirts never looked better.

Marvin offered me his fraternity pin one night after we attended a Jefferson Airplane concert. I knew I was making a mistake, I didn't really love Marvin, but he was pre-med and getting pinned to him was the only way I could get my parents to speak to me again.

Mom had stopped answering my phone calls when she'd learned I'd rejected Seymour's marriage proposal. Even worse, Dad had stopped sending my monthly allowance checks and had all but threatened to cut off my tuition if I didn't "get serious with a pre-med and soon, Young Lady."

So, I accepted Marvin's pin and allowed his fraternity brothers to serenade me that night. I think they sounded real good, but after two hours of the Airplane, I couldn't hear very well.

Since Marvin had claimed my left breast with his pin, I figured he was entitled to it. So, with the advent of pinning I got into petting, under the blouse, over the bra. Eventually, the blouse came off and the bra quickly followed. I was saving below the waist for an engagement ring, but we never made it that far. I returned Marvin's pin one winter night after I caught him in my bathroom, ironing the shower curtain. Sure, it was wrinkled but as Marvin pressed, the plastic curtain melted all over the bathtub. I had no choice: Marvin's obsession with ironing was threatening to ruin every synthetic fabric in the house. Marvin eventually found happiness by marrying into the dry cleaning business, where his mania, if not quite controlled, at least became less obvious.

I didn't tell my parents about breaking up with Marvin, and when I went home for spring break, I borrowed Sandy's (rather Bradley's) pin so that they wouldn't get suspicious.

Sandy and Bradley were really in love and she started sleeping over at their apartment so often that I felt like I was living alone. I missed Sandy and, when she was home, all she talked about was her latest sexual exploits with Bulging Brad, as she called him. I was the only girl in our circle of friends who could still claim her virginity and, by then, it was nothing to brag about.

Confidentially, I had my first sexual experience senior year, although I never told anyone, not even Seymour, who thought I was a virgin on our wedding night.*

I can't go into a whole lot of detail, not because of Seymour, but because frankly, it all happened so quickly, I don't remember the event too well. The guy I was dating at the time was a future forest ranger from the agricultural department. I'll call him Smokey, mainly because I can't remember his real name.

Smokey was tall, I think, and he may have had a beard. Anyway, I *do* remember one night we were in his room studying pine cones and smoking unlabeled cigarettes. (Sorry, Dad.) We started necking on his bed, and pretty soon, our shirts were unbuttoned. (After Marvin, naked chests were no big deal.) Smokey was murmuring something about little acorns and big trees when, I guess, I sort of dozed off. The next thing I knew, Smokey was rolling over and lighting a cigarette.

"So, was it as good for you as it was for me?"

"Was what as good?" I asked, wondering why my skirt was wrapped around my neck.

He looked so hurt that I suspected something more important than a lecture about acorns had transpired during my brief catnap.

Smokey got out of bed and put a record on the stereo. Carol King sang a song about the earth moving under her feet and that's when I realized I had, in all

* He's in for a real shock when he reads about it here for the first time.

probability, lost my virginity. I searched the sheets but there were no blood stains or anything to indicate I was now a woman in the full sense of the word. Maybe I was imagining the whole thing. But then I noticed Smokey was scoring a notch on his wooden bedframe with a pocket knife and I realized I had finally joined the ranks of the sexual revolution.

Surprisingly, I didn't feel any different even though I was absolutely sure I was pregnant. For a moment I thought I could feel the baby kick but then I realized my reaction was probably a bit premature, which, I think, was also Smokey's problem, although I didn't know it at the time.

I was really mad at myself for falling asleep because, like Woodstock and the moonwalk, it seemed I was always out of the country when the good stuff went down.

Two days later, I discovered I wasn't pregnant when I got my friend, which is how we used to describe the advent of menstruation in college. Within a week, I got birth control pills, which I.took faithfully every day even though I didn't have another sexual experience for almost a year after that night. However, a pink wheel of pills was the required status symbol in the early 1970s and it was essential to either hide the pills someplace where your mother would find them or pack them in your purse in such a way that they would fall out every time you searched for your keys.

Right before graduation, I went to see *The Graduate* at a small theater near the college where the audience was packed with students. Halfway through the movie, before Dustin sleeps with Anne Bancroft, he's floating on a raft in his parents' pool and his father (who is now Dr. Craig on *St. Elsewhere*) asks him, "What was the point of four years of college, Ben?"

Dustin replies, "Beats me," and during the twenty-minute standing ovation that followed that line, it occurred to me this was a moment of truth for many kids in the audience, including myself—I cheered the loudest.

As I sat on the makeshift stage during graduation, I suddenly realized Dean Stanley had been right when he told us, as freshmen, that college didn't work miracles, academically or socially. Picking up on the same theme during his commencement address, Dean Stanley said, "Realize your potential. Recognize the things we've tried to teach you, even though the lessons might be painful."

The dean's speech made me conscious of the most important, and the most painful, lesson I had learned at college. The truth was I'd probably never even get to date the Prince of Wales, much less rule the British Empire by his side.

That whole summer, I tried not to think about Prince Charles by keeping busy attending engagement parties, bridal showers, and wedding ceremonies. I was Sandy's maid of honor when she married Bradley.

"Always a bridesmaid," Mom wailed as I dressed for Sandy's wedding in a pale pink gown. "When is it going to be your turn? And why hasn't Marvin come by all summer?"

"Mom, there's something I should tell you about Marvin."

"He's making you drive, again, tonight? What's wrong with that boy? Don't his parents ever give him the car?"

"It's not that, it's that Marvin and I split up."

"What?" Mom shrieked. "Why?"

"I just . . . because I didn't love him, Mom."

"But he was pre-med."

"So?"

"Oh, Bambi, Bambi, Bambi. First Seymour, now Marvin. What am I going to do with you? You're doing this just for spite, I know it."

"No, I'm not."

Mom looked up to the ceiling. "Why am I being punished like this?" she wailed.

I tried to explain about Marvin's ironing but Mom was too hysterical to listen to reason. She ran crying from my room.

How did I ever get into this family? I thought for the millionth time. But a little part of me couldn't help but wonder if maybe Mom was partly right. As I looked into my makeup mirror, I realized this was the fourth time in two months I was dressing up for somebody else's wedding. Even Cheryl Stanton, the radical, had gotten married during a sit-in at Columbia University.

After Sandy's wedding, things went from bad to worse with my mother. Aside from remaining unengaged, "a spinster with a college degree," according to Mom, I had gotten used to my independence at UC, which didn't sit well with my mom. She had a conniption fit every time I flicked my cigarette ashes on the kitchen floor, a habit I'd acquired in the school cafeteria.

One day, Mom raised hell when she searched my purse for some change (or so she claimed) and found, instead, the birth control pills and a few other suspicious items.

"The pills are Sandy's," I lied.

Mom seemed relieved by my lame explanation and, because sex was not a subject she cared to pursue, even under the best of circumstances, she turned her attention to the other items in my purse.

"And just what are you doing with this baggie of oregano?" she demanded.

Obviously, it was time for me to make some serious decisions about my living arrangements. My options, however, were limited. I didn't have enough money to move into my own apartment and I certainly didn't feel inclined to go out and get a job. (It was a crushing blow to my self-esteem to realize that with sixteen years of education, I hadn't acquired one saleable job skill.)

Of course, there was always graduate school.

It was my father who helped me to decide what to do with my life. One night we sat down to have a talk about my future and Daddy offered to buy me a Mustang on the condition that I forget about applying to graduate school and get married instead.

I spent the next few days debating what color Mustang to choose, finally settling on burnt orange with a brown leather interior. After that, my only problem was deciding who to recruit for the lucky spouse and, as I've already explained, I ultimately decided to marry Seymour for one perfectly logical reason. He was the only man who'd ever officially proposed to me. In defending this decision I have to add that I was understandably confused by all the watershed decisions life forces a woman to make at such a turning point. I spent weeks wondering:

How would I find one dress to satisfy all twelve of my bridesmaids?

Should the pigs-in-the-blanket be served before or after the potato latkes?

Should I invite cousin Estelle with or without an escort?

Did I love the bridegroom?

Really, I was much too busy counting my chickens before they hatched to give much attention to such details as compatibility, mutual respect and love. What mattered to me was that Seymour was six feet two inches tall and I could wear high heels with my wedding gown.

ANNULLED BUT EMPLOYED 10

I've already said everything I care to say about my marriage to Seymour.

I was very, very young at the time and under all kinds of pressure from my parents, peers and, I suppose, myself. See, I wanted to be like everyone else; you know, normal; like Robert Young, Jane Wyman, Princess, Bud and Kitten on *Father Knows Best*. I soon learned it was a mistake to think marriage would solve all my problems. But, then again, I divorced Seymour because I thought divorce would solve all my problems, which was sort of like trying to extinguish a fire by pouring gasoline on the flames.

Sure, marriage to Seymour was hard, but being single again wasn't exactly a reason to celebrate. Suddenly, I was confronted with a whole new mess of problems and I didn't have clue one about how to function as a divorcée.

The morning after I left Seymour and moved back into my parents' house, I awoke all alone in my little four-poster bed. For a moment, I forgot where I was; I rolled over looking for Seymour but, to my horror, kept on rolling. I landed on the carpet with a thud.

Still not fully cognizant of my surroundings (I have never been a morning person) I listened for the familiar sounds of my in-laws arguing.

(*"Get up, Sol!"*

"Five more minutes, Sadie, please!" ➤

*"What is this? Some kind of holiday? Get outa bed,
already, ya bum!")*

But my room was as quiet as a tomb.

I was alone, alone, all alone.

I sat up on the pale pink, deep pile carpeting and
noticed Elvis smiling down on me. I instantly remembered where I was . . . and why. A wave of loneliness
rolled over me, quickly followed by a wave of hunger.

I decided to tackle the most pressing problem immediately, grabbed my robe and headed for the
kitchen.

Over coffee and a glazed doughnut, I thought long
and hard about how I would handle the inevitably
traumatic events of the next few months. I needed to
organize my thoughts and devise a strategy for the
next crucial phase of my life.

I carefully weighed the principles and guidelines I
had been taught by my parents, my teachers, Rabbi
Zindl and the Beatles. After much soul searching, I
devised a two-pronged plan incorporating everything
I had learned, so far.

I wrote down the two things I most urgently needed
to do in the near future on a blank piece of paper. I
stared at the paper for a long time. By synthesizing
my complex deliberations into two simple rules, I devised a game plan that couldn't possibly fail:

1. I WOULD GET MORBIDLY DEPRESSED.
2. I WOULD EAT MYSELF SILLY.

The real beauty of this agenda was that I had cleverly utilized the two tactics that came most naturally
to me. "It's foolproof," I had to admit to myself.

Mom agreed.

"This plan has worked for me many, many times in
my life so I'm sure it'll work for you, too," she said,
encouragingly, as she stirred the pancake batter. "I'm
really happy to see you're using such sound judg-
ment." Mom promised to help as much as she could,
adding the ingredients for triple-layer chocolate

cake to her already crowded shopping list as we sat down to eat breakfast with my dad and *The Price is Right*.

Eating breakfast at home reminded me of my childhood days and how much my life had changed in the past year. I thought about my girlhood friend, Sasha Crest, and remembered all the times Sasha and I had shared our innermost secrets and desires. How I longed to confide in someone this morning! Then and there, I realized what I needed most, aside from a refill on the coffee, was a real best friend.

Impulsively, I got Sasha's telephone number from my old address book and dialed her house in Minneapolis. Sasha's mother answered the phone.

"Hello, Mrs. Crest," I said. "This is Bambi Goldbloom, Sasha's friend. Do you remember me?"

"Bambi!" she exclaimed, excitedly. "Of course I remember you, I was at your wedding a few months ago."

How could I've forgotten that Mr. and Mrs. Crest had come to my wedding, all the way from Minneapolis, in place of Sasha who had been unable to attend?* Where was my brain?

"So tell me dear, how are you?" Mrs. Crest was saying. "And how's that handsome doctor husband? What a catch, Bambi! A doctor, ach! I tell all my friends, that Bambi Goldbloom, she's one smart cookie . . . a chocolate chip cookie!" she added with a giggle.†

"Listen, Mrs. Crest," I said, "I called to talk to Sasha, is she home?"

"Sorry, dear, you just missed her. This is the time of day she goes downtown to toss her hat in the air."

"Excuse me?"

"You know, like that Mary girl from the TV. The one with the three names?"

---

* As a last-minute substitute for Sasha, Mrs. Crest had been a lovely bridesmaid.
† Oh, how I missed the famous Crest sense of humor!

"Mary Tyler Moore?"

"Right, the skinny one. Anyway Sasha thought it might bring her luck if she started tossing her hat in downtown Minneapolis. So, she finds a busy street corner, twirls around a couple of times, smiles a whole lot and tosses her beret in the air. I told her I thought it was crazy but, you know, if it helps her find a husband, I'm all for it."

"Ummm," I muttered thoughtfully, wondering if Sasha was really the person I wanted to consult for advice.

"I'll tell Sasha to call you when she gets home." Mrs. Crest promised. "And, by the way, dear, our wedding present is late in arriving because it was special ordered from the Avon distributor in Italy. I'm putting it in the mail tomorrow."

I hesitated for a moment before saying goodbye. I meant to tell Mrs. Crest not to mail the present but I got curious and wondered what she had bought me.*

I was more depressed than ever after talking to Mrs. Crest. Our conversation made me realize the tragic consequences of breaking up a marriage: I would have to return my wedding presents, even the ones I liked!

No, I thought in horror, this can't be true!

I quickly reviewed the list of wedding presents I had received, which Mom kept hidden in her kitchen drawer.† Scanning the list, I realized I could rather easily part with any of the nineteen ice buckets now stored in Mom's basement, but there was a lovely set of copper-plated pots Seymour would have to arm-wrestle away from me.

And what about all the cash Seymour and I had received from our closest relatives? I had already spent most of it at the cosmetic counters in Blooming-

---

* As a bridesmaid, she probably spent a bundle!
† The list helped Mom determine the proper amount of money to spend at reciprocal gift-giving occasions, like when Cousin David got married and Mom bought the bride and groom a pen and pencil set similar to the one David had given Seymour and me.

dale's. Frantically, I took a few deep breaths to regain my composure and consulted my parents.

Mom thought I should return all the unengraved and unmonogrammed presents but Daddy disagreed.

"She can return the gifts when the guests return my seventeen grand!" he emphatically declared.

I heaved a sigh of relief and poured myself another cup of coffee.

Sasha called back sometime later in the afternoon but the minute we started talking, I realized how far apart we'd grown. We had nothing in common anymore. Sasha wasn't the least bit interested in hearing about my problems; all she wanted to discuss was the latest episode of *The Mary Tyler Moore Show*.

"Don't you love the way Mary crushes Ted's hat when she hugs him?" she wanted to know.

Sasha had become obsessed with the popular television series, overidentifying with Mary Richards, the character played by Mary Tyler Moore, even going so far as to quit grad school in order to take a menial job at a local St. Paul television station.

"It's not Minneapolis," she apologized, "but it's as close as I could get. And, as Lou Grant said only last Saturday night, 'there are no menial jobs, Mary, only menial people.' I can't say it funny, like he did, but it was a riot because he was talking about that crazy Ted."

I later read in the *Daily Post Times* that Sasha's problem was

> *. . . not uncommon among longtime viewers of* The Mary Tyler Moore Show. *Other symptoms of* The Mary Syndrome *include: obsessive cheerfulness, compulsive neatness, pathological sweetness, persistent do-gooderness and the tendency to only feel comfortable with men named Murray, Ted or Mr. Grant.*
>
> *Today, on any given afternoon in Minne-*

*apolis, scores of young, single, cheerful girls
are tossing their hats into the air and smiling
like lunatics.*

Anyway, Sasha wouldn't stop talking about "that
obnoxious Sue Ann" long enough to hear about my
troubles with Seymour.

"I'm sorry I couldn't come to your wedding," Sasha
gushed, "but I had to antique my furniture and hang
an M on my wall."

I tried to go along with this craziness but when
Sasha started calling me Rhoda, I knew it was time to
hang up. (I didn't want to be the fat one!)

I've never forgotten Sasha's last words to me that
fateful afternoon: "Oh! Mr. Grant!"* she said with a
schoolgirl giggle.

As I hung up the phone I sighed and told myself
not to get depressed about Sasha, I had my *own* life to
depress me. In keeping with my plan of attack, I hurried into the kitchen to bake up a batch of brownies.

For the next few months, I stuck with my two-point
scheme and, I have to say, it worked like a charm. In
no time at all, I was twenty pounds overweight and
borderline suicidal. I had become a textbook example
of Jewish Bulemia, a common syndrome in which the
patient gorges herself on food and then decides, at the
last minute, not to vomit.

Seymour tried to phone me a couple of times but I
knew they were only duty calls because he always
called me from the office of his cousin Morris, the
lawyer.

"Morris wants to know how you're feeling," Seymour would sullenly begin every conversation.

Apparently, Morris was more concerned about my
feelings than my future ex-spouse. I thought Morris

---

* This was the last conversation I ever had with Sasha. Many years
later, I heard she became a total recluse when her favorite television show went into syndication and was shown three times a day.

was just protecting his client's interests until he called
one day and asked me out.

"Seymour told me about the *demands* you placed
on him while you two were living with Aunt Sadie
and Uncle Sol," Morris said, "and, listen, babe, I don't
think any of them were unnatural, immoral, *or* sex-
crazed."

I thanked Morris but politely declined his offer to
"grab a coupla cocktails" at the Tree Top Motor Inn
in Bayonne. The thought of going out with another
Weizentraobawitazeman was more than I could handle. Besides, at the moment, I was kind of down on
the entire male species.

Morris took it in his stride. "Listen, baby cakes, no
problayma!" he said. "After the settlement, we'll
talk."

As for Seymour, well, I heard from my (so-called)
friends he'd been seen around town with Tiffany Jerkowitz.

Of course, Seymour and I never discussed Tiffany,
which wasn't surprising; considering we'd rarely
talked when we were married, it was unlikely we'd
start sharing our secrets at this point in the ballgame.
We kept our phone conversations on neutral subjects
such as the weather and the upcoming Jewish holi-
days. By the third or fourth phone call, however, Seymour began musing about the division of our wedding
presents. It started when he casually asked to borrow
an ice bucket.

"Sure," I said, " you want Lucite, glass, brass, aluminum, copper or plastic?"

I didn't become alarmed until his next phone call,
when he started making noises about the copper pots.

I hung up the phone and called Aunt Selma's lawyer, Dick Shyster, "the best divorce man in the business," according to my aunt—and my uncle Melvin.

"Dick says you should be happy with the Lucite ice
bucket," I told Seymour the next time he called from
Morris' office. "You've gotten everything you're

gonna get out of me. I've given you the best eleven weeks of my life. The free ride is over, bub. I've got you dead to rights on cruel and unusual treatment, denial of conjugal rights and mentioning feces during my wedding ceremony. And, if you want to go to court, that's fine with us, but Dick says those pots are mine, come hell or high water."

"But you walked out of this marriage, not me," Seymour whined. "I thought we were happy. Why should I have to pay?"

Now, this was before divorce laws were concerned with equal rights. In those days, things were simple. It didn't matter who was right or wrong; who had the greater earning capacity (or the richer parents); who walked out on whom. Women were the weaker sex so we got everything. (Not a bad system if you ask me.)

Eventually, Seymour and I went to court and our afternoon in the judge's courtroom was not unlike Passover dinner at my in-laws' house.

Judge Levine arranged the folds of his black robe before asking Seymour a few questions. "Now Mr. Wisentra . . . uh, Mr. Whizentrap . . . can I call you Seymour?"

"Call him anything you want," quipped Sadie, "just don't call him late for dinner."

Seymour chuckled.

"Right," the Judge said. "Now, Seymour, I want to establish the nature of your relationship with Bambi . . ."

"Bride and groom," Seymour interjected.

"Yes, but . . ."

"Husband and wife."

"Yes, *I know* you two are married, Seymour. What I don't know is: Do you have any grounds for divorce?"

"Yes, sir. Mom and Dad just bought a couple of acres in central Florida."

Sadie clapped Seymour resoundingly on the top of his head. "Dummkopf!" she hissed. "Morris told you not to mention the real estate!"

"I'll try talking slower," the Judge said. "You see, Seymour, in settling your divorce petition, I need to assess the kind of marriage you have. For instance, do you beat Bambi up in the morning?"

"Yes, sir!" Seymour chuckled. "Every morning. My wife never gets out of bed before eleven."

"Eleven-thirty!" exclaimed Sadie. "And then she's in the bathroom for forty-five minutes!"

Seymour snickered.

Judge Levine rapped his gavel on his desk and demanded silence.

My lawyer glanced at me and smiled.

"Seymour, are you certain you want this divorce?" the judge asked.

"No, sir, I don't. It's my wife's idea, Your Honor. She says we don't communicate."

"Communicate! That word again!" Sadie scoffed. "Mister Judge, Your Honor, what's with the kinder these days? Did we know from communicate? We got married, had children and never once knew from communicate. We never thought divorce. Not my generation, am I right, Sol?" Sadie turned to Sol who was trying to hide behind a yellow legal pad.

"Sol, tell the judge I'm right," Sadie was gritting her teeth while smiling for the judge.

Sadie jabbed Sol in the ribs but he continued to doodle on his legal pad. She got really excited and smacked Sol's shoulder, hitting him so hard that Sol's false teeth flew out of his mouth and slid across the table, landing in front of Judge Levine.

Everybody in the room howled with laughter.

"Order in the court!" the judge screamed, slamming down his gavel and shattering Sol's bridge into a zillion pink plastic shards.

As my lawyer predicted, I was awarded all of the wedding presents, the cash from our joint checking account and the stocks and bonds in our savings. Seymour got to keep Simca's girdles.

Everyone in the family, my parents, grandparents,

Aunt Selma and all the cousins, agreed it was a fair and equitable settlement. "This is America," my mother's cousin Mamie declared, "what else did that nebbish Seymour expect?"

The only one who was really aggravated about the judge's decision was Simca. She sent me a nasty note, saying she was insulted, no infuriated. "I hope you always have to buy retail," she wrote.

"What a horrible curse to impose on my daughter's head!" my mother screeched, spitting twice on Simca's letter to ward off the evil spell.

After the divorce, I was a single (but slightly richer) woman again. Pretty soon it was time for me to think about either getting a job or finding someone else to marry me.

I was pretty much soured on marriage so I decided to get a job. The problem, of course, was trying to find someone to hire me. I was afraid to ask total strangers for work so I pursued a few job leads from my family and friends but my prospects were pretty dim and I was rapidly losing hope of ever obtaining gainful employment. And then one day I finally interviewed for a job with someone who seemed like the perfect employer. I was called back twice to talk to him and his staff. If ever I was going to get a job, it looked like this would be it!

I nervously waited for my prospective (I hoped!) employer to further consult with his business associates and (I prayed!) offer me a job. The day finally came when he had promised to call about the job and I hung around the house with Mom, nervously pacing up and down the living room and praying for him to call.

At last, about 4:30, the phone rang. Mom raced me for the phone and, being in better shape than me,* she picked up the receiver before I could get to it.

---

* Well, she hadn't just gone through one torturous annulment and two Sara Lee Cheesecakes!

"Hello, Bambi Goldbloom's residence." Mom smiled at me. We had a little joke going between us that she would answer the phone impersonating my secretary in order to "impress" my future boss. I couldn't believe she actually had the guts to do it!

"Oh, hello, Herman," Mother said stiffly, placing her hand over the receiver of the phone and silently mouthing the words, "It's your father."

"What was that, dear?" Mother said to my dad. Then her face lit up. "You got the job, Bambi!" She shouted, laughing and then crying at the same time.

I leaped into the air, thrilled to the very core. Daddy had offered me a job as receptionist in his office! I had passed the critical inspection of everyone else in the office, including Mildred, Daddy's secretary, and Bernie, the pattern cutter.

Oh, it was a happy day for me. I had a job! Someday, I would be eligible for my own checking account! A credit card! Unemployment!

Mom handed me the phone.

"Okay, princess, you're in," Daddy said. "It wasn't easy convincing these guys. I really had to sell Bernie on your *experience*." He coughed meaningfully.

(Daddy had lied to everyone in the office about my past experience, fabricating a detailed resume for me. I had played along with the deceit during my interviews with his staff but I think Bernie, the pattern cutter, was suspicious.

"So, *Miss Let's Cut Skorts*," Bernie said, "you were secretary to Howard Hughes?"

I nodded uncomfortably. I knew Daddy had chosen Hughes' name because no one would be able to verify my employment record with the famous recluse, but I felt guilty playing along with the lie.

"So, tell me, it's true?" Bernie demanded. "The meshuggener guy had six-inch fingernails and wouldn't touch the toilet without gloves?")

"Anyway," Daddy continued, "the scoop is you're now our official receptionist. But, you know, you'll get no favors just because you're related to the boss. You have to pull your weight just like everybody else!"

"Oh, Daddy, I'm so excited! But, like, I never even asked . . . how much does a receptionist make?"

"Umm, I'm starting you at, um . . ." My father lowered his voice almost to a whisper. "You're starting at forty-two thousand dollars a year," he mumbled into the receiver.

"How much is that a week?" I asked.

"$807.60," Mom said from the kitchen phone.

"Wow," I whistled, impressed. I had no idea receptionists got paid so well.

"Herman, how much vacation time does she have coming?" my mother wanted to know.

"None, Janice. First she works, then she gets vacation."

"What?" I screamed. "No vacation? What kind of slave-driver are you, Daddy?" I started to cry.

"Okay now, princess, now, come on, don't cry. We'll start you off with three weeks' vacation. How does that sound?"

"Four weeks sounds better," I said, sniffling into the back of my hand.

"Four weeks it is, then."

"OK, that's groovy, and Daddy, when do you want me to start?"

"How about tomorrow, kitten?"

"Tomorrow? Oh, Daddy, silly goose, tomorrow's Tuesday, you know Tuesdays I go for my manicure and pedicure." I chuckled at how forgetful my father could sometimes be.

"Then how about Wednesday?"

"No, Herman," Mom interrupted, "Wednesday we're shopping Loehmann's and then she's got a dermatologist appointment."

My father sighed heavily. "All right, let's discuss this when I get home tonight."

"Sure, Daddy, and thanks, you're the greatest! I promise, you won't be sorry. I'm going to be the best receptionist you ever had! Oh, you're just the best Daddy in the world!"

Daddy laughed quietly, he loved to be complimented. "Okay, baby, that sounds good. I got to go now, so here's kisses." Daddy made kissing noises into the phone and then we hung up.

It felt good to be taken seriously by my father. All I wanted from him was a square break, a chance to prove myself in the business world. And from all those baby kisses he sent me over the phone, it looked like he was finally going to start treating me like an adult. At last!

Then and there, I vowed to be dead serious about this job. I made up my mind that tomorrow, when I went for my manicure and pedicure, I'd select an earnest color like pale peach, maybe even clear varnish, to show Dad I meant business. No more Racy Ruby Rose, I was about to join the ranks of the working girls.

I could hardly wait to buy my first Calvin Klein three-piece suit.

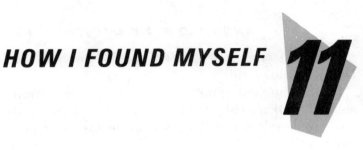

HOW I FOUND MYSELF

I used the bulk of my
   divorce settlement to buy a
proper business wardrobe for a working girl.

Using his connections, Daddy got me into the Calvin
Klein showroom so I could shop wholesale. The lady
who assisted me was ecstatic about my purchases.
"You've spent more than the Midwestern buyer for
the Petunia chain," she marveled.

I bought Calvin Klein, Anne Klein* and Bill Blass
until my closets fairly bulged. I was dressed for success with such a vengeance that I could've outfitted
all of Connecticut in navy blazers and paisley bow
ties.

I bought working shoes—low-heeled oxfords and
stadium pumps—but I couldn't resist purchasing several pairs of sling-back, rhinestone-studded black stiletto heels, which, of course, could only be worn with
something dressy like the fabulous magenta satin
strapless gown I discovered, on sale, in Lord and Tay-
lor's. The slinky gown bore such a striking resemblance to the Gilda dress of Barbie's that had caused
such a major turning point in my life that I simply had
to have it. I reasoned I might need such a dress for a
formal work-related dinner dance, and I wondered if
receptionists ever attended such affairs as I handed
Mom's charge card to the saleslady. Of course, I had

---

* I always wondered if Calvin and Anne were related.

no excuse for buying the cunning black negligee except to tell myself, what the heck, work wasn't everything.

Daddy grudgingly understood I had to delay starting work until my wardrobe was adequately stocked but he insisted we spend our evenings together so that he could teach me "the ropes." Although I was simply exhausted from shopping all day, I dutifully spent my evenings at home with my father. Daddy showed me his accounts payable receipts while I modeled my new clothes for him (excluding the black negligee, of course).

I began my job one bright October morning. Daddy and I drove into Manhattan together, and when we got to the office he told everyone how much he enjoyed having company in the car. I couldn't share Daddy's enthusiasm for joint commuting, since I had used the drive to catch up on some much-needed sleep. (I'd been up till 3:00 the previous night choosing an outfit to wear on my first day of work.)

I knew almost everyone at Patty Pants from the numerous Chanukah parties and bar mitzvahs we'd all attended so Daddy really didn't have to escort me around, but he seemed to get a kick out of introducing me to his staff and I obediently went along with him. There were so many compliments on my Calvin Klein lime-green suit, Anne Klein navy silk blouse, Louis Jourdan navy suede pumps, Judith Leiber navy bag with a whisper of green on the shoulder strap and Bill Blass tweed scarf in navy, lime and raspberry that, before long, it was lunchtime. To celebrate my first working day, Daddy took me to La Kosheriere, a glitzy garment-center dairy restaurant.

That afternoon, Daddy set me up at my desk in the waiting room. I was thrilled by the trappings of success. I had my very own stapler, Scotch tape dispenser and a box of paper clips. Daddy gave me one of his official Patty Pants coffee mugs. Then he assigned me the task of making coffee every morning which I flat-out refused. "Making coffee is not in my job description," I complained.

"What job description?" Daddy asked, but when I started to cry he backed down and said, "All right, princess, forget the coffee."

My duties were not overly complicated but the job required a certain amount of style and personality. I received everyone who visited or phoned the office (which is why I was called a receptionist) and Daddy depended on me to present Patty Pants in the best possible light. "Be people-oriented," Daddy instructed, which, in non-corporate terms, meant "Be nice and smile pretty." Therefore, I was charming and gracious to everyone, except when I was in a bad mood and couldn't be bothered.

The first week at work was really exciting. Daddy took me to wonderful lunches and everyone in the office treated me as if I was the Boss's daughter. By the second week, however, the staff's enthusiasm for my arrival had waned a bit and, by the third week, people were actually ignoring me. I felt twinges of discontent with my job, especially when Daddy escorted a group of hotshot buyers to lunch and didn't invite me along. (It really galled me to call La Kosheriere and make Daddy's luncheon reservation when I wasn't included in the party.)

The phone never stopped ringing, even when I was trying to concentrate on an interesting *Cosmo* article, and all day long I had to say, "Hello, Patty Pants. Can I help you?" I wouldn't have minded except that the calls were rarely, if ever, for me.

I had assumed that, in my new job, I would be meeting lots of handsome businessmen who wisecracked like Tony Franciosa and dressed like Gene Barry.* However, most of the guys I encountered

* I make reference here to the stars of a television series whose name I can't remember although I'm positive Susan Saint James played a secretary and the show took place in the offices of a magazine company or detective agency.

were messenger boys who looked more like out-
patients from Bellevue.

"I'm bored," I told my father one night when we
were stuck in traffic in the Lincoln Tunnel.

"Now, princess, you're the best-dressed girl at Patty
Pants," Daddy said, patting my shoulder.

"Big deal, aside from Mildred and Conceptia I'm
the *only* girl at Patty Pants."

"Don't you like your job, kitten?"

"It's okay, Daddy, but I need more interesting
things to do."

"How about if I let you open all the office mail for
me in the morning?"

Daddy's suggestion wasn't exactly what I had in
mind. I had been giving a great deal of thought to my
duties at the office and had decided, instead of being
the receptionist, I wanted to design Daddy's fall line.
However, knowing my father's mania for using only
experienced personnel, I hesitated to ask him for
the new position and decided to talk to my mother
first.

Mom thought I was showing great initiative and she
gladly presented the idea to my father. "Maybe it's
time to give the girl a promotion," Mom gently coaxed
Daddy.

"Janice, the girl's worked three weeks."

"But you said I've been doing a quote Excellent Job
unquote," I reminded him.

"An excellent job as a receptionist, which does not
qualify you to design the fall line."

"The girl has design experience," Mom argued.
"Bambi, show Daddy your portfolio."

"Portfolio?" My father looked bewildered.

"Yeah, Daddy, I've organized a retrospective of my
Katy Keene designs . . ."

My father's face reddened and he started to choke
on his coffee. "I t-t-told you NEVER to mention that
K-K-Katy name!" he exclaimed and stalked out of the
dining room without touching his chocolate pudding.

"Don't worry about him, dear," Mom advised, patting my hand. "Daddy'll come around."

It took a while but with both me and Mom hocking my father night and day, it was only a matter of time before Dad caved in. I was promoted to senior designer and everyone in the office congratulated me except for the two junior designers, who threw a fit when I moved into the only private office in the design area.

"So who needs those soreheads?" I asked my father but he just groaned and swallowed another shot of Maalox.

For my first line, I wanted to design something really special so I worked hard to come up with a new look. I shopped all the suburban stores, searching for ideas, or someone to copy, and then, when I was walking past Herman's Sporting Goods, I noticed these gigantic football shoulder pads in the window. I bought several pair of the pads and sewed them into our ladies' blouses. I was going for a look somewhere between the Dallas Cowboys and Mildred Pierce. Little did I know, at the time, I was inventing a whole new fashion phenomenon, which would later be dubbed "Stadium Chic" by *Women's Wear Daily*.

The line was a smash; massive shoulder pads became all the rage on Seventh Avenue. I got a big raise and Daddy's former junior designers finally stopped picketing the sidewalk in front of Patty Pants.

Reveling in my success, I stocked the water cooler with Cold Duck and took a well-deserved vacation to Club Med in Martinique, where I met Roger, the struggling director. Roger was my first serious affair following my divorce and he was everything Seymour wasn't: sexy, handsome and living in his own apartment.

There was an instant attraction between Roger and myself. We met at the check-in desk the day we both arrived at Club Med.

"How about a piña colada in my room?" said this tall guy with smoky gray eyes.

"Sounds great." (As I said, there was an instant attraction between us.)

We weren't in Roger's room for more than five minutes before he started running his fingers through my hair and whispering the naughtiest suggestions in my ear. This was unlike anything I'd experienced with Smokey or Seymour. I was astounded to discover it was not only possible, but quite exciting, to talk while having sex.

Afterward, exhausted, Roger and I lay in bed together and watched a tarantula climb the grass wall of his hut. All that week, Roger and I barely left the place. I don't recall even unpacking my bathing suit.

We started seeing each other back in the city and a whole new world of sexual possibilities opened up to me. Roger had great imagination and a vocabulary that was not to be believed. We were great in bed together although we rarely got as far as the bedroom. There was so much sexual energy between us that, most nights, we hardly got much farther than the foyer. Naturally, we spent most of our dates at his place, because I was certain Mom would not approve of our antics on her Persian foyer rug.

It was a happy, productive time in my life. I had finally found two things I was good at: designing clothes and sex. My happiness was complete, at least until everything fell apart.

While Roger kept me pretty busy at night,* during the day, I struggled to finish my spring line. I followed "Stadium Chic" with "Boxer Chic," which, unfortunately, was not quite as hot. The satin shorts sold well enough but those big gloves proved impractical for driving a car or putting on lipstick. Daddy lost a pretty penny, and his entire staff threatened to walk out, including Mildred, who was like a mother to my dad.

I know this will shock you (it shocked me), but the

* And sometimes in the morning.

fact is, I got fired from Patty Pants. "Either you go or I go bankrupt, *again*," was how Daddy put it.

I did not leave quietly or without adequate compensation; Daddy gave me two years' severance pay, but it was still quite a blow to my ego.

"It's bad enough to get fired," I explained to Roger, "but to get fired by your father is the ultimate humiliation."

"The ultimate what?" Roger asked, excitedly.

"The ultimate humiliation."

"Oh, babe, I love it when you talk dirty!" Roger threw me on the floor and I forgot about Patty Pants for the next forty-five minutes or so.

The next morning, however, I faced the question every middle-class, divorced, unemployed Jewish woman must eventually confront: Should I go to law school or not?

I had been out of college for some time and the thought of having to go back to class, to study, and to take tests made me want to puke, which I didn't think was a very encouraging sign. At Sandy's suggestion, I visited the NYU law library to, you know, check it out. I spent a whole afternoon in the stacks but I could not find one book by Jackie Susann or Rona Jaffe so I decided not to be a lawyer.

I tried hard to think of something constructive to do with my life but, frankly, I couldn't think of anything interesting that didn't require a charge card.

Once, Roger and I discussed marriage, but only in a very hypothetical, noncommittal way. Roger had also been divorced recently and he was a bit skeptical about going through the ritual again.

One morning while we were watching the *Today Show*, a paroled ax murderer said during an interview, "I have no intention of killing again. On the other hand, I cannot predict the future."

"That's exactly how I feel about marriage," Roger commented.

"Oh, really?" I asked but Roger refused to say anything more on the subject. He left the room to take a shower. (It was a habit of Roger's to leave the room whenever the conversation turned to marriage.)

One night, I casually mentioned to Roger that I thought it was time for us to live together, but unfortunately, my timing couldn't have been worse. The very next day, Roger decided to move to California to advance his stalled filmmaking career. We tearfully* said goodbye at the airport and, as I drove back to Hohokus, I decided never to date another unpredictable struggling artist, to get a job and to get my own apartment in Manhattan. Although I eventually found both employment and an apartment, I fudged a little on the first vow when I started dating Mack, the unpublished poet.

I met Mack at the makeshift bar in the Metropolitan Museum of Art, during a posh opening-night party. Mack was bartending.

As he poured Perrier, he kept staring at me, licking his lips in the most suggestive manner. Somehow, Mack got my name and number from one of my friends at the party (I'd come with Sandy and Bradley and a bunch of Bradley's shrink friends). He called me several times at home but I refused to go out with him.

"I don't date bartenders," I told Mack.

"I'm not a bartender. I'm a poet," he said.

"Published?"

"Not yet."

"Even worse," I said, recalling Roger.

One day, Mack mailed me a poem he'd written in my honor. It was entitled: *Bambi G., I Think of Thee.*†

OF ALL THE WOMEN IN THE WORLD
OF ALL THE OYSTERS, YOU'RE THE PEARL.
SO, TO A GOLDBLOOM BURNING BRIGHT
'TIS SHE I TURN TO IN THE NIGHT

---

* Roger had a tear in one eye, or so I thought; I was sobbing too hysterically to be absolutely positive.

† Copyright © by Mack Bernstein. Reprinted from *The Ode Not Taken* (unpublished).

AND LAY MY HEAD UPON HER BREAST,
BAMBI G., YOU ARE THE BEST!

I was quite flattered to be the inspiration for Mack's work, although the next time he called, I did suggest, "One minor change. One little word, if you don't mind."

"Which one?" Mack asked.

"Could you take out 'breast'? It's kind of, you know, personal."

After pouting for a few days, Mack changed the last two lines to: "And lay my head upon her ear/Bambi G., you are so dear!" and we started dating.

Around the same time, I got a job interview at DEF, the communications conglomerate, because my mother's friend Ceil played Mah-Jongg with the aunt of the chairman of the board.

I decided to make my best effort during the interview because I was hungry for a job that would offer a purpose to my life, especially since my unemployment benefits had all but run out.

After flirting for fifty minutes with the personnel director of DEF, Vinnie DeSalvo, I landed a job in broadcasting.

I worked for *Twisted Candid Camera*, an updated version of the old television show. In this new format, we went on location to surprise people by scaring them senseless. Our "surprises" included attempted rape; kidnaping a kid from a busy supermarket and keeping the 'victim' sequestered for four days; replacing a seeing-eye dog with the producer's schnauzer; sending singing telegrams to funerals; creating havoc in hospitals by switching X-rays, drugs and charts; rerouting welfare checks and well, you get the picture.

I was a production assistant, which sounded real glamourous until I discovered my main function was to supply the crew with tunafish sandwiches and Tab —not a whole lot more interesting than being a receptionist at Patty Pants, and the salary wasn't even close.

Mom couldn't understand why I wanted to work for "that imbecilic show. What's the point?" she asked.

"I'm trying to find myself."

"Find yourself what?"

I sighed. "Find myself something to do with my life."

"There's always mar—"

"Aside from marriage," I hastily added.

Mom slammed her iron on the ironing board, but didn't pursue the subject, for which I was thankful. We had a sort of unspoken pact that Mom would stop hocking me about getting married if I would stop threatening to commit matricide every time Mom slipped another issue of *Brides Magazine* into the bathroom.

Despite our pact, I knew, sooner or later, I would have to leave my parents' home. Aside from my problems with Mom, it was hard living in the same house with the man who had fired me. So, during my lunch hours from *Twisted*, I searched Manhattan for an affordable apartment.

I was thrilled when I signed a lease on a cute little Greenwich Village apartment—a five-story walk-up situated on a historic block, right between two neighborhood shops, the House of Leather and Ears Pierced: Your Choice With or Without Pain.

It was such a sweet little one bedroom apartment and a real steal for the price. Of course, I had to invest a chunk of my severance settlement in decorating because, like any new place, the apartment needed some minor work to make it homey. A fresh coat of paint, wall-to-wall carpeting, nine or ten new glass panes for broken windows, a couple of electrical outlets, a stove, a refrigerator, a radiator, a working toilet, a couple of closets and like nothing, the place was ready for occupancy.

My landlord was so ecstatic about my home improvements that he quadrupled my rent, on the spot, which was only fair because, as he explained, the apartment was worth more money now that it was fully renovated.

The apartment changed my self-image. Like all of my friends, I was officially rent-poor and could boast that 95 percent of my salary went toward paying the rent. "I'm a real New Yorker now," I thought as I spent the other 5 percent of my income on necessities: taxi fares, fresh flowers and *New York Magazine*.

My first neighborhood friend was Guido, the exterminator, who visited my apartment three or four times a day. Guido claimed the mice in my kitchen had been trained in Lebanon for their exceptional commando tactics, but I was more upset with the roaches, since they were just about the same size and weight as the new Volkswagen Rabbit.

Yet, in spite of the unwanted roommates behind my new General Electric refrigerator, I loved living in the city. From my window overlooking Sixth Avenue, I could witness the sights and sounds of Manhattan. One day it might be a three-car collision; another day a violent domestic quarrel, or a man with a powerful microphone preaching the end of the world right in front of my building. One summer, a foursome of black kids sang "Stayin' Alive," at fifteen-minute intervals, every single night, even in the pouring rain.

"Ah, New York City," I would think as I sat in my Azuma rocking chair and experienced this panoply of sights and sounds, "there's no other place in the world quite like it!"

Yes, the Village was exciting, and a little intimidating, since all the men were better dressed than me; except for the guys who only wore studded black leather pants, jackets, armbands, and hats, with their hairy naked chests, a look that didn't appeal to me at all, even though Mack liked it a lot.

Most of my dates with Mack were spent in my new apartment. I wallpapered or varnished while he talked about his epic poem-in-progress. I had to constantly boost Mack's flagging ego by insisting his poetry was incisive and he didn't have to be published to be a great writer.

"Oh, yeah?" Mack would scowl, "if that's true, name me one other great author who isn't published," which put a real dent in my argument and, after a while, I got pretty bored discussing his problems. Our relationship improved slightly when Mack picked up a few extra bartending gigs and we started going out double-dutch, which was a lot better than when I had to pay for everything myself.

One night Roger called from LA and he sounded sad and lonely; obviously he wasn't all that enamored with Hollywood.

"Tip the world over and everything loose falls into LA," Roger sighed. "Listen, I was just soaking in the Jacuzzi, wondering when you'd be moving out here."

"When you ask me, I suppose," I answered, disguising my utter shock.

"I was thinking you could get your own apartment and, with your TV experience, a good job."

"Are you asking me to move to LA?"

"Oops, there's someone at the door. I'll call you soon," he promised.

I never heard from him again. But Roger's call made me realize something was missing from my relationship with Mack, namely, great sex, which was why I broke up with him and started dating lots of other men.

I had been relatively monogamous up to that point in my life but I quickly made up for lost opportunities. I gave up searching for the perfect man, which was a good thing, considering the guys I dated during the next few years. Having abandoned all hope of meeting Mr. Right, I learned to settle for Mr. Mediocre.

One night, a fireman arrived at my apartment to check out a carbon monoxide complaint and we dated for a couple of weeks.

"Your eyes are like green pools," crooned Fireman Fred.

"My eyes are brown," I pointed out.

"Sure, but they remind me of green pools."

Fred's poor brain was partially incinerated but at least he had a full-time job and very nicely developed shoulder muscles. Eventually, we broke up because Fred couldn't tolerate my smoking, especially in bed.

Then Sandy fixed me up with Donald, an associate shrink of Bradley's, who I kind of liked until the night we had dinner in his apartment. The only piece of furniture Donald owned was a snake-like couch, twenty-five feet of a velvet-covered tube that coiled around like a long strand of spaghetti. The couch was dreadfully uncomfortable and, even though this was the era of beanbag furniture, I kept wondering about the subconscious message behind that gigantic phallic symbol.

I also dated an assistant rabbi I met at a blackjack table in Puerto Rico. His name was Aaron and the poor guy suffered from severe manic depression. "People are always coming to me with the most horrendous problems," Aaron groaned. "Death, adultery, divorce, illness . . . You can't imagine what a downer it is."

One afternoon, winded from a strenuous bike ride in Central Park, zigzagging taxicabs and horse-drawn carriages, I parked myself on a bench to catch my breath. A guy in skintight black shorts rode past, braked his racing bike and sat down on the bench to admire my thighs.

His name was Jack and he was a lawyer specializing in corporate ambulance chasing. This meant he hung out at faltering companies, patiently waiting for them to go bankrupt, so he could make his living settling insolvency cases—Jack was fabulously rich.

Jack's professional ethics made my skin crawl, especially after he closed down a local lending library on a trumped-up tax evasion charge. Still, we dated for many months. I guess Leroy, his chauffeur, was the key to our longevity as a couple. It was Jack who introduced me to the convenience of getting around town in a limo so the relationship was not a total wash.

I loved riding through Manhattan in the black-windowed stretch Caddy with Leroy at the wheel in his smart little driver's cap. Now when I see a limo drive by, I don't have to wonder what the passengers inside are thinking; I know for certain I am being snubbed.

After Jack, I got fixed up with Robby, who had been ditched by so many women that I could almost see the tread marks on his forehead. A friend from work, Gloria, had been dating Robby until she dumped him in favor of marriage to a previous boyfriend. In the true spirit of sisterhood, Gloria gave Robby my telephone number.

Over coffee at the local deli, Robby only wanted to talk about the horrendous blind dates he'd had in the past and, let me tell you, his experiences were heartbreaking; a girl once abandoned him on the Staten Island ferry by jumping overboard and swimming to shore.

"Now tell me about your worst blind date," Ronny said, but, of course, I was too kind to point out the gentleman in question was sitting across the table from me.

I met Kenny in my dentist's office. Kenny said he worked freelance for the government. His job was to "float trial balloons."

"I come up with WHAT-IF scenarios," he said, "like WHAT IF the Arabs decided to buy up all the television stations in America?"

"And you get *paid* for that?" I laughed.

"Yeah? Well, you won't think it's so funny when you're stuck watching *My Favorite Moslem* five times a day," he retorted.

Kenny had a queer midtown office stocked with strange volumes of statistical and analytical data and a telex machine that clattered away at all hours of the day and night. We were often in his office at night because Kenny refused to take me to his apartment.

We had been dating for about a month when Kenny started asking me strange questions. "Why did you travel to San Francisco three years ago and only stay for the weekend? Who was the prisoner you visited at Riker's Island in 1974? Why was your American Express bill $1,376 last month?"

What scared me was that all his information was correct, even the Riker's Island part (I'd once visited my landlord there to pay my rent).

Kenny said he had "run a check" on me, claiming he was tapped into all the important computer lines of the government.

I told Kenny I didn't like the idea he had invaded my privacy.

"What privacy?" Kenny laughed. "Every time you sign your name to a credit card or make a plane reservation, it goes into some computer. You think I'm the only guy in the world with access to that information?"

"No, but you're the only guy I ever *dated* with access to that kind of information."

I told Kenny I didn't want to see him anymore, which, of course, made me much more attractive to him. He started calling constantly and sending me little notes on Charlie Brown* cards. I began to feel as if I was being followed. So I resorted to the one sure-fire method for getting rid of a guy: I told Kenny I was pregnant. I never heard from him again.

I spent a couple of evenings in singles bars on the Upper East Side but they were so awful that I can't even think of anything funny to say about them.

And then there were the married men. Sooner or later, every unattached woman in Manhattan is tempted, at least once, by a married man. The truth is, in New York City, falling in love with a married guy is as inevitable as co-op conversions.

Dating married men had several advantages: a) there were so many of them, and b) they tended to take me to really nice restaurants or, at the very least, to hotels with great room service. I also discovered I really enjoyed having sex in the daylight, particularly during lunch hour.

* Why doesn't someone put Snoopy to sleep already?

But eventually, I got pretty bored by the endless succession of men, married or single, who trooped through my apartment. I suspected there had to be more to life than dressing for a date, straightening my living room, hiding my Tampax box and mixing Bloody Marys for men I hardly knew.

I would've loved to throw myself into work but, unfortunately, I was suddenly unemployed. Our show had become a smash hit when it was moved to a new time slot, opposite *Masterpiece Theater* and the News. Everyone was in high spirits until the day our cameraman was fatally shot by an irate grocery-store owner during one of our "staged" robberies. I quit that afternoon.

On line at the unemployment office I met several people whose lives had been changed by est and Silva Mind Control, so I experimented with both disciplines. I became quickly disillusioned, however, when I learned the leader of est was a former encyclopedia salesman and that most of the Silva Mind Control fanatics used the procedure to will themselves parking spaces on the streets of Manhattan.

It was a confusing time in my life: no job, no boyfriend. I was right back where I had been when Roger had split for the Coast, and I was none too happy about it. My life was taking on a distinctly roller-coaster-like quality. I felt older, but no wiser, and I despaired. Then, just when I thought things couldn't get worse, they did.

Daddy called to tell me Grandpa Max had suddenly passed away, on the dance floor at Roseland.

"In the middle of a fox trot," Daddy reported, his voice cracking with emotion. "The funeral's tomorrow. Nana Yetta wants to sit shiva in your apartment so Grandpa's garment-center friends don't have to schlep out to Jersey."

It was a request I could hardly refuse. So, following the funeral, the whole congregation of mourners taxied down to Greenwich Village.

It was sort of pitiful to watch all those old people

climb five flights of stairs to my apartment, although we set up chairs and refreshments on each landing to make the trip a little easier.

There was barely enough elbow room in my packed apartment to shmear a bagel but everyone was too busy talking and stuffing themselves with kasha knishes and gefilte fish to notice. It was a sad, and very fattening, event because Nana Yetta catered the shiva from Zabar's Deli.

I chatted with relatives I had not seen since my wedding. And, because these were all family or close friends, no one was shy about asking really tactless questions.

"So, when're you going to get married again?" my mother's cousin Mamie asked.

It was the tenth time in twenty minutes I'd been asked the same question. "Oh, I don't know. I'm really into my career."

"With your degree in electrical engineering, it's understandable."

"No, that's Estelle, Uncle Maurie's daughter," I said. "Estelle is the electrical engineer in the family."

"Of course, and you're an . . ."

"Actually, I'm on unemployment at the moment."

"Oh? And how much do you take home a week?"

"Not much."

"Then how can you afford to live in Manhattan? Is your father footing the bills or do your alimony payments cover your expenses?"

"Excuse me, I have to see about making coffee."

Halfway to the kitchen Uncle Shelley grabbed my arm. "Bambi!" he exclaimed, "I hear Herman fired you from Patty Pants! Wait! Don't tell me why. Let me guess, you were stealing from petty cash? No . . . no . . . you were taking two-hour lunches?" Shelley was doubled up with laughter.

I was rescued by my aunt Selma. "Never mind Shelley, he's got a brain like a sieve," she said, sending her husband to buy some more paper napkins.

"So, Bambi dear. You dating someone special yet? It's been quite a while since the divorce."

"I want to dance at your wedding again, tsatske-leh," Nana Hannah said.

Nana Yetta burst into tears. "Me, too, darling, but without my Maxie, who'll dance with me?"

This went on for six more days. Occasionally, the family forgot about my spinsterhood while discussing Grandpa Max and his colorful life. As I roamed from room to room, emptying ash trays and throwing away paper cups, I picked up snatches of conversations about my grandfather.

"He was the only immigrant on Ellis Island who spoke English," boasted my father, "with a Boston accent no less!"

"It took him months to learn to pronounce *shiksa* correctly," noted Nana Hannah.

"Imagine? The man was bar mitzvahed at twenty-four," marveled the Rabbi.

"When he first moved to the Lower East Side, he didn't know a dradle from a menorah," laughed Aunt Selma.

"He thought chicken soup was only made by Campbells," Mom explained.

"Ach! But he loved ready-to-wear!" sighed Bernie, the pants cutter.

"No one loved ready-to-wear more than Max Gold-bloom," declared Shmuel Rubin, grandpa's zipper salesman.

Listening to these anecdotes, I realized it had taken real guts for my grandfather to defy his family in order to "do his own thing," as they said in the seventies. I wondered if I would ever have a thing to call my own.

I thought about what I really loved to do and it struck me that, aside from sex and Calvin Klein, books were what I loved best. Ever since the days of *True Confessions* and *Gone With The Wind*, I'd been a voracious reader. I was an English major. Many times I had toyed with the idea of getting into publishing but two obstacles had always stopped me: insecurity and inexperience. But, I asked myself, what experience had Grandpa Max had when he fled Beacon Hill?

I was, after all, a Haveford Huntington Goldbloom and it was time for me to prove it by showing a little initiative.

The day after Grandpa's shiva, I called my only contact in the media, Vinnie DeSalvo, the personnel director at DEF. (The corporation owned Haphazard House, a well-known publishing company.) Vinnie wouldn't return my phone calls so I was forced to use a more drastic tactic.

Cutting up a magazine, I picked apart letters and pasted together a ransom note that read: "Hire Bambi or you'll regret it!"

A week later, Vinnie got me an interview with Wanda Rondalee, the Editor-in-Chief at Haphazard. I felt great going into the meeting, but as I interviewed with Miss Rondalee, my confidence waned.

"Can you type?" asked Wanda Rondalee.

"No," I replied.

"Take dictation?"

"No."

"Shorthand?"

"No, but I could learn, I guess."

"Listen, this is not much of a job." She tossed my application onto her desk. "Editorial assistant. It's mostly a secretarial position and you're a bit older than most of our assistants."

"Oh," I said.

"I have to be up front and tell you the pay is lousy." If she was trying to talk me out of wanting the job, she was succeeding.

"One thing, though, you certainly have the right clothes for this place. That's a fabulous suit," Miss Rondalee added admiringly.

"Thanks," I said, feeling a little better.

"It's Calvin?"

"Yeah."

"I just adore his clothes but they're so expensive."

"Mmm," I murmured, "My father's in the business so I buy wholesale. Listen, I can get you up to Calvin's showroom, if you'd like."

"Wholesale?" Her brown eyes widened in amazement. "Calvin Klein, wholesale?"

"Forty percent off."

"Bambi, the job is yours. Say the word."

"Why thanks, but I don't know. It doesn't sound at all what I had in mind."

"Perhaps I painted too gloomy a picture, this is really a wonderful place to work."

"Can I think about it, Miss Rondalee?"

"Wanda, please. Sure, think about it, give me a call." Wanda helped me on with my coat and walked me to the door. "You'll have fun here, really," she said as I entered the elevator. "Maybe I could do a little better on the salary," she added as the doors closed.

I watched the numbers on the panel light up. I guess I had a misguided notion of what it meant to be an editor. I'd thought editors spent their days reading wonderful manuscripts, discovering geniuses, eating fancy lunches, making brilliant editorial suggestions that instantly unblocked writers and having fabulous affairs with the best minds in the country. Typing, shorthand and dictation had definitely not been part of the big picture.

I needed to do some serious considering before committing myself to Kathryn Gibbs, so I hailed a cab and directed the driver to the only oasis in Manhattan and my favorite spot for contemplation: Susan Bennis/ Warren Edwards, the most fabulous shoe store in the world.

Alighting on Park Avenue, I pushed open the enormous gilded doors to the shop and, sighing with relief, propelled myself into the lush, heavily carpeted interior.

Astonishingly, the saleslady who greeted me was none other than Tiffany Jerkowitz.

"Why, Bambi Goldbloom, what in heaven's name are *you* doing here?" Tiffany had lost twenty pounds since college. She wore a Norma Kamali black and white checked dress. Her hair was Sassoon cut and hennaed a deep rich auburn.

"I came to buy a pair of shoes, naturally." I said, sucking in my stomach.

"You know, of course, our shoes are terribly expensive." Tiffany laughed gaily, shaking her head, which accentuated the Dorothy Hamill movement of her hair.

"You work here, Tiffany? Selling shoes?"

"Actually, I'm manager of the store. Can I have Phillippe show you anything in particular?" She snapped her fingers and a short man dressed in tuxedo pants and an oversized sport jacket appeared. "These are quite lovely," Tiffany pointed her foot at me. She was wearing the most exquisite pair of red lizard heels I'd ever seen. "On sale this week. Only $575."

"I think I'll browse awhile."

"Of course."

I refused to let Tiffany think I couldn't afford a pair of shoes so I selected a pair of the lizard heels Tiffany had suggested, since they were the cheapest shoes in the store.

"So, what've you been doing since your divorce?" Tiffany asked after Phillippe disappeared with my charge card.

I tried not to grind my teeth. "At the moment, I'm considering a job in publishing. I just met with the editor-in-chief of Haphazard House and she's dying for me to take the job but I don't know." I sighed. "I just can't make up my mind."

"Haphazard? I'm impressed. What's the job?"

"Editorial," I said, deleting the "assistant" part of the title.

Phillippe appeared from the back room. "I'm sorry, Miss Goldbloom, but there's a problem with your credit card," he said. "It seems you're over your credit line." He clucked his tongue. "Naughty, naughty."

"Publishing's glamorous but I guess it doesn't pay too well," Tiffany snickered.

"It's not that," I said, stalling until I could fabricate a plausible lie. "Yesterday I went shopping—Bonwits—and I guess I went overboard in the, um, fur department. I couldn't resist the raccoon jacket."

She suspiciously eyed my camel cloth Calvin coat. "I'll take your personal check."

"Sure, Tiffany. Thanks." What did she care I only had $87.54 in the bank? I hastily wrote out a check and handed it to her.

Tiffany scrutinized my check. "Can I see some identification?"

She pawed through every piece of plastic in my wallet; she called my savings bank, my tax accountant, my stockbroker and my mother before she was satisfied. "I'll approve your check on one condition," she purred, "you have to say Pepsi-Cola."

I turned and headed toward the door.

"Only kidding!" Tiffany shouted and chased after me with my new shoes.

I left the shoe store and, at the first available phone booth, called Haphazard House.

"I'll take the job, Wanda." I said.

"Great. You're sure?"

"I'm sure. When can I start?"

Standing in that phone booth on Park and Fifty-sixth, I vowed to myself that I would succeed at Haphazard House. I'd be the best damned typist in publishing. I'd learn shorthand. I'd take dictation. I'd even make coffee, if that's what it took. Nothing was going to stop me. The next time I shopped Tiffany's store, I'd buy two, maybe three, pairs of shoes.

I had found myself at last and now I realized the motivating factor that had been missing from my life: revenge.

CAREER GIRL

I quickly discovered it was dog eat dog at Haphazard House.

After filling out my W2 form, I was immediately sent to Daniel Boreman's office. Boreman was the publisher at HH and, according to Vinnie, he had a ferocious temper. "Don't cross him and don't keep him waiting," Vinnie advised.

I ran up the stairs to Boreman's office and, while I waited for my appointment with him, I struck up a conversation with Jeanette, one of Boreman's six secretaries.

"So, you work for Wanda?" Jeanette asked.

"Yes."

"I suppose you've already heard all about Wanda and Vinnie."

"Vinnie DeSalvo? From Personnel?"

"The same. Watch out for that guy, he's a real hot ticket. Ask Wanda." Jeanette laughed. "I don't mean that literally, of course. Now that Wanda's married, she doesn't even want to *hear* the name Vinnie De-Salvo. Vinnie dropped her like a hot potato at the last Christmas party. Vinnie's married, you know, but his wife plays deaf, dumb and blind, if you know what I mean.

"Anyhoo," she continued before I could respond, "Vinnie is like really weird, has this thing for the Xerox machine."

"Xerox machine?"

Jeanette leaned across her desk and whispered. "You know, he likes to photocopy himself, especially the more prominent parts of his anatomy, which, as I understand it, are *very* prominent. Of course, I don't know this firsthand, but I have a friend in Payroll, Cyrisse. Know her?"

"No."

"She's a doll. Really, you'd love her. She lives near me, in Queens, so sometimes we ride the train home together. Well, one day Cyrisse is minding her own beeswax and has some stuff she needs to copy, so she walks into the Xerox room, the big one on the nineteenth floor, and—" Jeanette giggled "—the machine is going full blast and Cyrisse catches Wanda and Vin—"

"Send in Miss Goldbloom," barked a voice over Jeanette's speaker phone.

The voice startled Jeanette, she sort of bounced on her chair, then she pointed to the door of Boreman's office. "Hurreee," she hissed, "he hates to be kept waiting."

"Oh, yeah, right." I hastened toward the door.

"Fabulous shoes, Bambi," Jeanette called after me.

The other five secretaries stopped typing and glanced at my feet. I thought I heard the blonde one say, "Susan Bennis/Warren Edwards. On sale last week."

Opening Boreman's door, I walked into a huge corner office, all windows, marble and chrome. Boreman signaled me to take a seat while he talked on the phone, I should point out, for the next forty-five minutes.

So, I had plenty of time to make a few personal observations. Boreman was a very big man who wore his shirt impeccably tapered to hug his beefy torso. His initials were embroidered on his cuffs, breast pocket and collar tabs. Similarly, everything on Boreman's desk, including his marble pen holder, crystal ash tray, silver telephone and cigarette lighter in the shape of a small handgun was monogrammed DB. The sole wall in the office that wasn't sheeted in glass was lined with shelves of carved duck decoys. Occasionally, Boreman aimed his lighter/gun at one of the ducks and clicked it. The phrase "sitting duck" kept running through my mind.

Boreman gazed at me intensely as he barked into the phone. He was cutting some kind of deal; I could tell because he spoke in the same tone of voice my father used when he hondled with the Puerto Ricans in his factory. But, unlike my father, who hunched over the phone and stared intently at a scratch pad of paper while he talked, Boreman read his mail, took his pulse, did a crossword puzzle, chain-smoked and straightened his picture frames while parading back and forth behind his desk with the telephone receiver glued to one ear.

Finally, Boreman hung up the phone and leaned back in his enormous black leather chair. "I have just one piece of advice for you, Miss Goldbloom." He paused dramatically. "F.U."

I didn't quite know how to respond. "Excuse me?" I said.

"F.U.," he repeated, with a grin. His teeth were capped to perfection.

"Right," I replied, for lack of anything more specific to say.

"F.U." Boreman laughed. "Follow Up!" He went on to explain how no one ever finished a project without a clear-cut follow-up plan.

"Yes, well, thank you for that piece of advice, sir. I'll try to remember it."

"Try?"

"I *will* remember it, sir," I promised.

"Good. And if you're smart, you'll get to know Sybil Weinberg, the marketing director. Pronto. The trouble with most you editorial people is none of you knows diddalee-squat about sales."

"Yes, sir. I'll go introduce myself to Miss Weinberg

right now." (I couldn't believe I was being such a goody two-shoes, "a real brown nose," as Bruce Berger would've said.)

Boreman got up from his chair, leaned against the side of his desk and crossed his arms over his chest. "You know, Bambi, Wanda's a great editor. She works well with authors, the artsy types. You can learn something from her.

"But Wanda don't know beans about discounts, remainders or advancing books into the chains. And she conveniently forgets she works for Sybil.

"Sybil sells the product so she gets to be boss. *Sybil*. She can show you how books sell in the real world.

"If you learn something around here, Bambi, you might succeed. If not, you're out. That's the deal."

"Thank you." I didn't know why I thanked him except I felt kind of challenged by the prospect of proving myself to Boreman. I liked the way he talked to me, as an adult (for what seemed like the first time in my life).

"That's the spirit, Bambi."

I hurried out of Boreman's office to find the marketing department.

Several people were lined up outside Sybil's office, all of them holding legal pads or computer printouts. I took my place and waited in line. The guy behind me introduced himself as an advertising director named Gary. I told him my name and mentioned it was my first day of work.

"Oh, good," he said, "then you haven't yet heard this morning's most vicious rumor about Sybil and Vinnie DeSalvo in Personnel."

"Sybil? You mean Wanda, don't you?"

"Wanda and Vinnie? Since when?"

"Well, I . . ."

"Never mind. I'll call Lisa, she knows everything."

Gary rushed off and, a few minutes later, I walked into Sybil's office, which was about half the size of Boreman's.

Sybil was quite tall and wore her salt-and-pepper hair very short, in a style we used to call a "pixie cut." She had a look of fierce determination about her, especially as she kicked a hardcover, green-jacketed book across the floor. Sybil cursed at the book and then asked who the hell I was.

I introduced myself. As I spoke, Sybil chewed a red pen, which must've been cracked or something because red ink dotted the corner of her mouth. Then I noticed her white blouse was splotched with ink blobs, and, when I politely pointed this out to her, she growled that all her clothes were similarly stained to add a more "industrious" look to her appearance. Sybil offered me her red Pentel and, when I refused to ruin my favorite suede skirt, she accused me of not "having the right attitude for Haphazard House."

I felt I was not getting off to a good start.

I asked Sybil if there were any particular kinds of books she liked to publish. "We publish books to be read by women under hair dryers, period," Sybil said, "and the quicker Editorial finds that out, the better off they'll be."

"That's interesting. Perhaps we could discuss it further at lunch sometime."

"I don't lunch."

"Never?"

"Never, I'm in therapy five times a week; I use lunch hours for my sessions."

"Oh, well, thanks for talking to me. I appreciate your time."

"Goldbloom, just remember one thing . . ."

"I know," I said with a friendly smile, "F.U."

Sybil sucked in her breath; her face reddened. "What did you say to me?" She pointed her Pentel at me, stabbing it in my direction.

"F.U.? I, ah, thought you were telling me to F.U." I could feel myself start to sweat. "Like *Follow Up*? It's like a joke."

"That's your idea of a joke?" She tossed her pen on the desk. "Goldbloom, stay away from humor books."

"Right." I wanted to leave Sybil's office in the worst way.

"What I was going to say was just remember one thing: Green jackets don't sell!" She gave another kick to the green-covered book, *Money is Everything*, on the floor.

"Thank you," I said as I ducked out of Sybil's office.

Wanda was annoyed when I told her I had been to meet Sybil. "Who said you could meet Sybil?" she demanded.

"Boreman. He told me to."

"Oh. What did you think? Of her, I mean."

"Well, I don't know," I said, not knowing which position to take after the events of that morning.

Wanda snickered. "Phony baloney. Gushing insincerity. She acts so sweet and then stabs you in the back. Don't trust that baby talk of hers."

"No, she was really kind of mean to me."

"Oh?" Wanda frowned. "That means she likes you," she said. "Just remember one thing."

I kept silent.

"You work for me, not Sybil."

Later I found out more about the great rivalry that existed between Wanda and Sybil. Part of it was caused by the nature of their jobs. At almost every publishing house, there's a struggle for power between Sales and Editorial but, at Haphazard, this conflict was compounded by personal considerations.

After her affair with Vinnie ended, Wanda had married a stockbroker and was now "rich as the dickens," which she took every opportunity to remind everyone, especially Sybil, who had never married. Sybil desperately wanted a husband like Wanda's. Actually, Sybil wanted a husband like Jack Lord on *Hawaii Five-O* but, realistically, she would *settle* for a husband like Wanda's. As for Wanda, she wanted Sybil's job.

The two women had attempted to reconcile their differences when Boreman called them into his office one morning and said, "You two stay in this room and work out your problems or you're both out on the street." After two days, they emerged from the Executive Suite, glassy-eyed and thinner, but apparently resolved to end their rivalry, at least until Sybil refused to approve Wanda's American Express bill and Wanda scribbled "Sybil loves Vinnie" all over the walls of the Xerox room and they stopped talking again. It was clear to me that Wanda and Sybil had something more than Vinnie in common. Obviously, as kids, both of them had served some time at sleep-away camp.

While it was true I worked for Wanda, I wanted to remain on good terms with Sybil, who approved all raises and promotions and had a very close relationship with Boreman. In the months that followed, I worked real hard for Wanda while secretly playing up to Sybil every opportunity I got. Let me tell you, it wasn't easy.

I soon discovered that typing, dictation and shorthand weren't exactly required, since none of the other editorial assistants could perform any of these tasks. However, I was so determined to outshine the other assistants, I took night courses and learned to be the fastest typist on editorial row.

I also answered phones, opened mail, returned manuscripts and kept Wanda's appointments running smoothly. I performed all the tasks required of an editorial assistant and constantly asked for more. I also became adept at writing copy, so Wanda let me write all the mountains of boring stuff she was supposed to write. When Wanda wasn't in the office, I visited Sybil and asked her if I could do any writing for the Sales Department.

Among other things, Sybil controlled the mail order division of HH and she asked me to write blurbs (short descriptions) of the books they were selling through the mail. I became quite proficient at describing thousand-page books in one sentence.

In exchange, Sybil taught me the business side of publishing. She showed me how to read a computer

printout, estimate overhead expenses and decipher
book-buying trends through mail order sales. Wanda
couldn't prevent me from associating with Sybil, but
did become quite short-tempered when she suspected I was going to Sybil for advice.

I attended as many meetings as I could, especially
Wanda's weekly editorial meeting where she constantly reminded the editors that "the cardinal law of
publishing can be summed up in one word: spin-off."

"That's two words, or one hyphenated word," I remarked.

"And that kind of thinking will land you a job as a
proofreader," snapped Wanda.

Editors at HH had to draw up contracts, so I took a
few contract law classes at NYU. I was particularly
interested in the "sex clause" of HH's contract.

Sybil claimed that well-written sex scenes were
crucial to book sales and HH had a hard and fast rule
about including sexual descriptions in the books we
published. A special clause in our standard contract
insured the inclusion of plenty of good sex scenes:

CLAUSE 103: UNLESS A SEXUAL ACT IS EITHER
DESCRIBED, INTIMATED, SUGGESTED OR IMPLIED
APPROXIMATELY EVERY TWELFTH OR THIR-
TEENTH PARAGRAPH THROUGHOUT THE MANU-
SCRIPT, THE PUBLISHER IS UNDER NO LEGAL
OBLIGATION TO PRINT, PUBLISH, PROMOTE THE
WORK OR PAY ANY ADDITIONAL MONIES TO THE
AUTHOR FOR THIS PARTICULAR WORK OR ANY
OTHER WORK THE AUTHOR MAY WRITE (OR HAS
ALREADY WRITTEN) DURING THE COURSE OF THE
AUTHOR'S LIFETIME AND THE SUBSEQUENT
LIFETIMES OF ANY FUTURE HEIRS, ASSIGNEES,
RELATIVES, LOVERS, CASUAL ACQUAINTANCES OR
HOUSEHOLD PETS OF THE AUTHOR.

Clause 103 caused some problems for our more serious writers, but even the author of *The Life and
Times of Mohandas K. Gandhi* managed to include a
chapter entitled "Mr. G Tells All."

I wrote more jacket copy for Wanda, and blurbs for Sybil and took courses at the New School in book design, editorial evaluation and power lunching. One time, Wanda let me write an introduction for one of our books, *The Complete Book of Fingerpainting,** because the author had been thrown in jail on a drug rap.

Yet despite all my hard work, after almost two years, I was still an editorial assistant and I realized that, in order to advance, I would have to bring in a book of my own. But from where? I didn't know any agents and the only author I knew was in the slammer. I turned to the slush pile.

When unpublished writers mailed their unsolicited manuscripts to Haphazard House, one of the assistants (usually me) would log in the name of the author, the title of the work, and the date the submission was received and then stash the manuscript in a closet, which was opened again only to throw in more manuscripts. My coworkers claimed there was never anything of value in the slush pile but I disagreed.

"Somewhere in that mass of manuscripts, there has got to be a gem waiting to be discovered," I told the staff. "I am going to find that diamond in the rough and make its author famous. I am striking a blow for all the unknown writers who work in total obscurity." The assistant editors snickered and, I think, started some kind of lottery in which the winner predicted the date I would get fired.

I let them scoff as I opened the door to the slush pile closet. However, after speed reading 374 manuscripts, I began to realize they didn't call it slush for nothing. I was about to give up the project and then decided to read one more. I selected the fattest manila envelope in the closet and lugged it home with me.

The manuscript I happened to choose was a self-help primer written by a therapist named Moe Nagel-

---

* It was heaven to see my name in print: "Introduction by Bambi Goldbloom."

man. Dr. Nagelman's therapy was based on his theory of hugging—he claimed people could solve all their problems if they would only learn to hug themselves.

"Hug yourself, and soon someone else will want to hug you, too!" wrote Moe Nagelman, who, of course, lived on the West Coast.

I fought hard to convince Wanda and Sybil to publish *Hug Yourself.*

"Not another California Charlatan," Sybil moaned when I presented the project at our weekly editorial meeting. "Besides, it's impossible to hug yourself."

"Not if you have long arms," commented Wanda, who seemed interested in the project only after Sybil had objected to it.

"True," I said, happy for any show of support. "And just look at Dr. Nagelman's client list." I passed copies of the client list around the conference table.

Wanda was obviously impressed with the names of the Hollywood starlets who endorsed the Nagelman therapy, especially since the group included two of Charlie's Angels.

Marianna, the publicity director, glanced at Moe's biography and author's photo and announced she thought the project "had legs." * She held Moe's photo to the flourescent light. "He's not bad looking," Marianna declared, "and he's already made several appearances on *Good Morning San Luis Obispo.*"

"Let me see that photo," Sybil snapped. "Okay, so he's cute. Is he married?"

"No," I said, "he's divorced and spends most of his time in Hawaii."

"Hawaii?" Sybil smiled for the first time that morning.

"Tell Sybil Moe knows Jack Lord," Wanda whispered and, for a moment, I thought she was serious.

"Why don't we get a copy of the San Luis Obispo tape?" suggested Marianna's assistant.

* In publishing terms, this meant the book would walk out of the stores; although in his author's photo, Moe's legs weren't bad either.

"Good idea," Marianna agreed. "Let's see if he's got any sex appeal on video."

"Right, and if he looks as good as his photo, we'll publish his stupid book," Sybil announced, stuffing Moe's photo in her purse.

Moe turned out to be super interview material—he was smart, funny, sexy and, most important, totally huggable. Sybil flew out to Maui to take a private meeting with him and eventually convinced Moe to sign a contract without reading it.

Hug Yourself was published six months later, after Moe fulfilled his obligation to Clause 103 and added lots of sexy stuff to his manuscript. The book was then vetted by our crack team of lawyers, who insisted Moe's sex scenes were libelous and ordered them deleted from the manuscript. Moe was really peeved when Haphazard charged him for the legal opinion, which ate up most of his advance, but at least it taught Moe to always read a contract before signing it.

The printing press sent me a dozen advance copies of *Hug Yourself* and I was really dismayed when none of the books were stolen off my desk. You see, in publishing, the likelihood of having a bestseller is directly proportionate to the number of copies ripped off in the office. (The quicker the books "disappear," the surer you can be you've got a bestseller.) Piles of Moe's book remained untouched on my visitor's chair. In the bookstores, the book moved very slowly. The *Village Voice* reviewed the book in two words, "It stinks," which I did not think was a considered evaluation.

Wanda tried to cheer me up. "It could happen to any editor," she said at the next marketing meeting.

"Sure, it happens to Wanda all the time," commented Sybil.

Then, unexpectedly, *The Daily Times Post* bought first serial rights and ran excerpts from the book for a whole week. Moe was a little irked the paper chose the more sensational aspects of his work, running the piece under the two-inch headline, "I Hugged Marilyn Monroe!" but, because of the newspaper series, Marianna was able to wrangle a booking on *Donahue* for Moe and one of his Hollywood clients.

On network television, Moe taught Phil Donahue how to execute the perfect hug. "Marlo will love this!" quipped Phil and the audience sighed with envy.

"I lost twenty-three pounds hugging myself and Moe Nagelman's therapy improved my sex life 100 percent!" declared one of Charlie's Angels, and *Hug Yourself* sold 18,746 copies that day in Chicago.

Every one of my copies of the book was stolen from my cubicle. Within two weeks, the book soared to Number One on the bestseller lists.

In house, all the credit for discovering Nagelman was divided between Wanda, who published the book, Marianna, who booked *Donahue,* and Sybil, who tricked Moe into signing the contract.

"I made Moe's book," Marianna bragged.

"And Sybil made Moe," Wanda remarked.

I was upset because no one gave me credit for discovering Moe Nagelman in the slush pile. But then Wanda called me into her office, thanked me for finding *Hug* and said Sybil had approved my promotion to editor. I asked her if I could attend the next ABA convention but Wanda said no; only she, Wanda, was attending the ABA from Editorial. "I worked here seven years before I was sent to ABA," Wanda added. "Come talk to me in four years."

Two days later, Sybil asked me to write blurbs for the 647 new titles she'd just purchased from another publisher for the mail order operation. "It's for a special Dostoevsky's Birthday Sale. I need the copy by the end of the week."

I hesitated because I had Moe's new manuscript on my desk and it needed a ton of editing.

Sybil said she would send me to the ABA if I wrote the copy for her.

Wanda blew a fuse when she learned I was going to the ABA but, since Sybil had approved the airline tickets, there wasn't anything Wanda could do except order me to carry four heavy cartons of our latest books on the plane to California.

The American Booksellers Association convention was held in a different city each year. That May, the ABA was taking place at Disneyland, in Anaheim. I was thrilled to be able to hobnob with the movers and shakers of publishing and see Mickey Mouse at the same time.

The theme of the convention was "Overcome Illiteracy—Toward a Reading Society," and the slogan was plastered everywhere. Supporting the cause were speeches and book signings by such important writers as a very famous actress who wrote a book about her previous lives,* a distinguished psychiatrist who described grief survival in his book *When Bad Things Happen to Good Pets*, a world-reknowned photographer whose picture essay was entitled *Pectorals and Posteriors*, and a 450 pound gorilla who had learned sign language and written his first novel.

I felt so proud to be among such a distinguished gathering but the highlight was when I finally got to wear my magenta satin gown to a cocktail party in Frontier Land.

There, I met an editor from Porpoise Publications, Ariel Abrams, who remembered my name from the introduction I'd written for *Fingerpainting*.

"I love your work," she said. "Call me if you ever decide to write your own book."

During the day, I worked the Haphazard House booth and spoke with bookstore owners, buyers, salesmen, agents, and other people who visited our area. At one point, Daniel Boreman made an appearance at our booth, walking around and greeting everybody like a visiting dignitary.

* A book I'm planning to read in my next life.

I hadn't seen much of Boreman since my first day in his office and I was anxious for his opinion about the work I'd been doing for the past three years. So I was pretty excited when he approached me. I smiled. He smiled. "Daniel Boreman," he said, extending his hand to me. "Who're you?"

"Bambi. Bambi Goldbloom."

"Nice to meet you, Bambi. You work at HH?"

Apparently I had not made as big an impression on Boreman as I thought!

Moe Nagelman attended the ABA and manned a "Come Hug Moe!" booth which was enormously popular. As with all profitable books, we followed the success of *Hug Yourself* with a calendar, "The Nagelman Hug-a-Day Desk Diary," which was moderately successful and allowed Sybil another trip to the Islands.

Because Moe's book made so much money, we adhered to our spin-off philosophy and milked the project for all it was worth. The next season we published two Nagelman books: *Hug Your Wife* and *Hug Your Hubby*. In subsequent years, Moe adapted his theory for the parental guidance market (*Hug Your Kids!*), the self-help market (*I'm Huggable, You're Huggable*), the How To market (*How to Hug*), the El-Hi market (*Hug Your Guidance Counselor*), the college market (*Hug Your Prof*) and the gay market (*Hug Your Roommate*).

Moe even started writing a monthly column for *Cosmo* called "Hug Your Breasts!" Ultimately Moe became the darling of late-night television and a real voice of the decade, partying with politicians and rock stars. His close friend, the mayor, got in on Moe's act by adapting "Hug New York!" as the city slogan. Bumper stickers with the slogan in a heart were distributed during the mayor's run for re-election and, when he won the race, "Hug Cleveland!" and "Hug Houston!" started appearing on out-of-town limosines.

Naturally, Moe's work was imitated by several

smaller publishers, and Haphazard brought suit against the publishers of such rip-off books as *Embrace Yourself* and *Cuddle Your Spouse*, but the judge ruled Moe didn't own the copyright on the act of hugging.

"An oversight in our legal department," declared Daniel Boreman before firing all of Haphazard's staff lawyers.

After a while, the success of Moe's books brought me to the attention of Daniel Boreman and made me the envy of the editorial staff. At one marketing meeting, Boreman singled me out as his star editor, which was sort of like "teacher's pet" except that the toys were better. After that, I got asked to Boreman's invitation-only publishing parties, private screenings and celebrity dinners where I met such famous people as Prairie Haze, the Channel 16 weatherman. A few times, I got driven around town in Boreman's limo and, once, even hopped in his private jet* to a sales conference. Some people wrongly accused me of sleeping with Boreman, which wasn't at all surprising since stories of Boreman's sexual adventures with his female employees ran rampant at HH. (I later learned that each of the duck decoys in Boreman's office had the name of a woman, usually a previous employee, carved on its underbelly.)

As a full-fledged editor, I worked even longer hours than I had as an editorial assistant. Sybil's theory was that editors had four opportunities a day to entertain prospective authors—breakfast, lunch, drinks and dinner. "Four opportunities a day, five days a week—equals twenty meals a week to conduct business for Haphazard," Sybil explained. "I expect all editors to use their American Express cards at least seventeen times a week." I was grateful for the chance to eat breakfast at home three times a week but, as I said, I had little time for myself. My social life revolved almost entirely around entertaining agents and writers and gossiping with co-workers.

* Fully stocked with champagne and fresh shrimp!

I tried meeting men outside of the business. I attended a convention for plastic surgeons, ostensively to find an author for a book Sybil wanted to publish called *After 40, It's Suture, Suture, Suture!*

By the hotel pool, I met a doctor named Chuck who was fascinated by the stretch marks on my tummy and said, "With proper surgery, you can get rid of those ugly marks."

"Right," I said. "But it might be easier to get rid of you."

For a short time, I dated a guy named Joel who lived in my building. I fell in love the first time I laid eyes on Joel. He was removing sheets from the washing machine in the basement. (I'm a pushover for men who do their own laundry.)

Joel was a truly generous guy, giving out compliments as freely as Tic Tacs. He particularly liked the maroon Calvin Klein dress I wore the first night we went out to the movies. I thought he was making a pass as he fondled the dress fabric all through *Grease*. Of course, I realized I was mistaken when, over coffee, he asked to borrow the outfit.

One fall, I took a film course at the New School, hoping to meet a new man. I carefully dressed for the night class, which was a waste of time and panty hose because only women attended Course 317: The Ali McGraw Film Retrospective. Obviously, I wasn't the only lonely girl in the auditorium where the level of sniffling during a screening of *Love Story* was not to be believed.

I confided my failure to Sybil who suggested I join her dance class to get back in shape but, at first, I hesitated.

"I look awful in a leotard and I can't lift my leg all that high."

"Oh, don't worry, nobody cares how well you dance. It's not like people are judging you or anything."

"No? That's funny. I must be the only one; I'm real critical of everyone in dance class."

"Me, too," admitted Sybil. "Especially the really klutzy girls."

In spite of my insecurity, I decided to take the class with Sybil. Naturally, I bought a stunning new wardrobe of high-gloss leotards but the more classes I took, the more I began to realize the really good dancers wore torn leotards and frayed sweatshirts.

It struck me that I might have stumbled on a new fashion trend, so I wore my dance outfit to Daddy's office one evening to show him the complete look: seven pairs of leg warmers, two sweat bandannas, pink tights with two runs in them, a black leotard with ripped sleeves and holes in the back, several strategically placed safety pins and a multicolored elastic belt. A frayed sweatshirt was piled over this outfit with one long-sleeved tee-shirt tied at the waist, fashioning a kind of flap over my rear end.

"A pile of rags," laughed Mildred.

I tried to convince Dad Patty Pants should cash in on the trend by shredding his line of ladies' blouses. Dad gently hinted I had lost touch with my fashion savvy and Bernie acted as if I were totally meshugge.

"You hear this? The girl wants we should rip the garments before shipping them! Mistah Goldbloom, I beg you, remember the skorts!"

"And the boxing gloves!" Mildred cattily added.

Anyway, Daddy never made a dime off the Irene Cara/Jennifer Beals look that swept Seventh Avenue a few seasons later and I tried hard not to tell my father, "I told you so!" because Mom said it every fifteen minutes or so.

Wanda did not like the fact that Sybil and I went to dance class together but, since it was an exercise class, I only lasted six weeks before dropping out.

I traveled a lot on my job—visiting authors in various cities around the country and attending foreign book conventions—and developed many long-distance romances.

"A guy in every airport," joked Sybil, who understood my situation, being in the same place herself. By then, I had formulated the philosophy that the best way to keep a relationship exciting was not to see the other person very often. A passionate, yet meaningful, four-day weekend, once or twice a season, was just the thing to keep the fires flaming.

Meanwhile, Wanda got pregnant and, during her maternity leave, she was fired from Haphazard House. It was a lousy thing, really, but Sybil had warned her not to leave the office for more than two weeks at a stretch since Boreman had a very short attention span, especially for pregnant women. Or so Sybil told me the morning she announced I was the new editor-in-chief.

Naturally, I was thrilled by the promotion which meant I would move up to Karl Lagerfeld suits, Bottega Venetta briefcases and $120 Suga haircuts. I did, however, suffer some twinges of guilt over my ex-boss who had, after all, given me my first break in publishing.

I called Wanda to tell her I felt bad about taking her job. She cried on the phone, which she claimed was only due to postpartum blues but it made me feel so guilty that I offered to refuse the promotion. She said, "Oh, you can't do that, not really," and, I admit, I was pretty relieved. I promised I would keep in touch even though we both knew that my reputation at HH would be seriously hampered if I was ever seen in Wanda's company.

"It's best not to hang out with ex-employees," Sybil once advised me. "The aura of failure is contagious."

So although I didn't see Wanda, I thought of her often as I assumed the duties of editor-in-chief and tried to avoid making the same mistakes she had. I treated Sybil with respect and honesty except when I lied through my teeth to compliment her at least once every day. I hoped my friendship with Sybil would make my job easier than it had been for Wanda and it did; until I wrote my own book.

Books about American business were selling strong at the time and, after my varied experiences at Patty Pants, *Twisted Candid Camera* and HH, I had a theory on the subject which I neatly summarized in the title of my book: *In Search of Mediocrity*. In the introduction, I wrote, "H.L. Mencken once said: Nobody ever went broke underestimating the taste of the American public. This was a pretty amazing observation considering Mencken, who died in 1956, probably never shopped K-Mart, watched *Family Feud* or ate a Big Mac."

In *Mediocrity*, I applied the principles of American capitalism to my own personal life. I compared (and contrasted) my early education (the teaching/tap dancing routines of Mr. Wall) to the business techniques of Lee Iacocca and Colonel Sanders. I synthesized the workings of American factory workers with the morals of the Five Town girls from Camp Kenico. I melded the theories of the United Steel Workers to the "blue-balls" theories of Rocky Rissotto. I analyzed the failure of my marriage in light of the Edsel's economic catastrophe. I noted how blue-collar workers invariably failed to dress for success.* In short, I personalized the strengths and weaknesses of American business by symbolically portraying one woman's journey through the complexities of life in suburban New Jersey. It was a radical treatise, to put it mildly.

The analogy evaded many of the editors and agents who read the proposal. "What do poodle skirts have to do with the AFL-CIO?" whined one agent.

At first, I had trouble placing the book with a publisher.

The manuscript went through a series of rejections or, I should say, a series of editors who really wanted to publish it but either couldn't get support from their editorial boards or had lost my phone number.

---

* Footnoting that only Ralph Lauren could work in denim with any class.

Some editors asked pertinent questions like, "Why don't you write a book about Swedish architecture?" or "Why don't you write a Gail Parent novel?"

Even my own family was not all that encouraging about my first attempts at being a writer. In fact, their reaction to the first draft of *Mediocrity* was less than enthusiastic.

"If this is great literature, I'll eat my yarmulke," cracked Uncle Shelley.

"She can hardly write a postcard—go know from a book," Nana Hannah commented.

However, when Ariel Abrams from Porpoise Publications was interested in my book and I became one of her authors, with a contract and advance in hand, my family was much more receptive. Mom threw a contract-signing dinner and my cousin David asked to borrow a grand.

"Here's to the most successful member of our family," David said, raising his glass to toast me.

It was a proud moment for me, as we raised our champagne glasses; at least until my mother's cousin Mamie piped in with, "Ach! But who's the happiest?"

"Oh, well, the happiest?" In unison, my relatives lowered their glasses to contemplate Mamie's question.

I took a sizeable chunk of my *Mediocrity* advance to the shoe store where I'd last seen Tiffany. Once there, I talked to Phillippe, the new manager. Tiffany had either quit or been fired, Phillippe couldn't remember which. "I think she was getting married," Phillippe said, "although maybe she was starting her own business." I was disappointed that Phillippe didn't have the memory for details that made gossip such a sport at HH.

As a writer, it felt strange to be on the other side of the desk. I was dismayed but not surprised when, after signing my book, Ariel refused to answer my phone calls. I didn't take it personally because it was standard procedure at Haphazard to ignore an author once we had signed his or her book.

"The only good author is a dead author," Sybil would often remark, which is why she preferred to publish posthumous works. Sybil said her general philosophy of life was simple: "Everything's going to go wrong so expect the worst." Which is why, I guess, she was most comfortable with dead authors, who at least weren't calling her every minute of the day complaining their books weren't in the stores.

Sybil also refused to publish any book written by someone on the staff of Haphazard, which was the real reason she turned down my book, not because of the "stick-figure characters," as she told Marianna.

It was a decision Sybil came to regret.

In Search of Mediocrity was, as they say in the trade, "an instant bestseller!"

"At last, a business book with boobs!" wrote Ellen Curly Beige in her monthly magazine column.

A reviewer in *Ms. Magazine* christened my book, "The businesswoman's *Portnoy's Complaint*—without the calf's liver, of course!"

"You were always my favorite grandchild, tsatskeleh!" declared Nana Hannah.

Mom was disappointed, however, when I placed the finished book in her hand. "It's so thin," she commented.

"Thin?" I barely ever heard that word pass through my mother's lips.

"I thought you'd write a longer book—more pages, like Janet.* Herman, don't you think Bambi should've used more words to write her book?"

"Janice, if the girl needed more words, she would've used more words," said Dad, who'd been in a foul mood ever since *Woman's Wear* devoted an entire issue to "Tattered Chic."

Anyway, although the reactions at home to *Mediocrity* were mixed, the sales of my book were brisk and

---

* Janet Dailey was my mother's favorite author.

I achieved a certain amount of fame and fortune, at least in places like Detroit and Sacramento where I was a big hit on local television.

I spent a lot of time preparing for the day Barbara Walters would call and ask me to be a guest on one of her specials.*

Being famous has its rewards but I discovered the pitfalls as well. Following my television appearance on the Detroit version of the *Today* show, I was besieged by people in the airport.

"You're Bambi Goldbloom!" squealed a middle-aged woman who was toting seven shopping bags. "I seen you on TV this morning. You wrote a book or something? Yeah, my sister Belle read it, and she said it stinks! Ha-ha! No offense, but that's really what she said!"

"Yo! Bambi," called out a young man with a gigantic tape recorder balanced on his left shoulder. "Hey, pretty mama! Gimme a dollar or I'll smack you upside yo' head!"

I returned from Detroit to discover my apartment had been burglarized. The burglars had ripped off everything of value including my three lamps, a toaster oven and my lizard shoes from Susan Bennis/ Warren Edwards. They had left my apartment in total disarray—clothes, books and records were scattered everywhere. "They could've at least folded the sweaters that were too ratty to steal!" I fumed to the police officer who arrived on the scene.

None of my possessions were recovered and, a month later, I moved into a glitzy skyscraper on the Upper East Side, which was a very different environment from the funky West Village. On the Upper East Side, the women wore mink coats to walk their poodles and the shopping was extremely limited. There were no food stores, delis or dry cleaners in sight although, anytime I wanted, I could rush out and purchase an expensive oil or watercolor painting from

* I'm still waiting, Barbara!

any one of a hundred art galleries on Madison Avenue.

Sybil was not sympathetic to my taking off time for my author's tour or to move. She accused me of not working hard enough for HH and piled me with work, which was okay because, by then, I had my own editorial assistant, who was doing the bulk of my work for me anyway.

Despite my new job and fabulous new apartment, I, of course, was still looking for a nice guy—someone like Alan Alda or Wanda's husband—but the chances of meeting such a man seemed more and more remote, since I was having a difficult time finding a date for my cousin Estelle's wedding, much less a lifetime mate.

Then, Prince Charles decided to marry a plump schoolmarm, just so he could have a virgin on the throne. I wondered how Queen Elizabeth would react to a royal divorce. (She must have been nervous, I reasoned, because I was, conspicuously, not invited to the wedding.)

I was haunted by the massive press coverage of Lady Di. Every time I turned around in the supermarket there she was—grinning at me from beneath one of her whimsical garden hats. "And I look so good in hats," I would enviously groan to myself.

I thought I had buried my obsession with Prince Charles when I graduated college but I couldn't help feeling it should've been *me* in that black, off-the-shoulder ball gown that scandalized all of London!

I had waited half my adult life for Charles to pick up the phone and call.

Sure, I joked about the marriage of Prince Charles, but those photographs of Princess Di in her two-block-long wedding gown threw me into a deep depression.

I was desperate enough to consider looking up old boyfriends when, one day, I almost tripped over my old Camp Kenico heart throb, Igor Stein, who, I soon

learned, lived in the neighborhood. We went for coffee and I was delighted to discover Igor still had his
great sense of humor, showing me his old match burn
trick twice and fooling me into fifty-two pick-up right
there in the Bon Jour Croissant!* shop. Igor, now a
urologist at Beth Israel, expressed interest in escort-
ing me to Estelle's wedding but I turned down the
offer when he mentioned his wife had just given birth
to their fourth child.

After I left Igor, I returned to my office more depressed than ever. I tried to hide my mental state during our afternoon marketing meeting but it was hard
to escape Sybil's eagle eye.

"Who's sobbing hysterically under the conference
table?" she asked. "Bambi? 'Zat you down there?"

Sybil let me leave work early and, when I got home,
I found a registered letter waiting with the doorman.

The New York City authorities had traced me to my
new address in the East 70s. "Dear Miss Goldbloom,"
the letter read, "It is now our duty to inform you that
as a thirty-year-old, single, Jewish girl living alone in
Manhattan—incredibly successful and unbelievably
depressed—you are required by city ordinance to
enter psychotherapy within thirty days of receipt of
this notification."

I showed the letter to Sybil who verified its authen-
ticity. "Yup," she said. "I got the same notice myself
—that's why I started seeing Dr. Yesandno."

I had to swallow two glasses of Soave Bolla before
I could summon the courage to call a shrink, but once
I'd made an appointment for an introductory session,
I felt kind of elated.

"Therapy might be fun," I thought to myself, imagining a few pleasant afternoons, chatting and giggling
over my ex-husband's hubba-hubba school of love-
making.

Little did I know that giggles were the last thing to
expect from psychoanalysis.

* Translation: "Hello, Toast!"

THE COLOR MAUVE

13

*M*y therapist's name was
Sheila Bergman-Horowitz
and she had been recommended by
Sybil's shrink, which proved to
be a boon to my relationship with my boss.
Sybil and I spent many hours analyzing our analysts.
Together, we also commiserated over all the Claude
Montana leather coats we could've purchased with
the money we were throwing into therapy.

Sheila Bergman-Horowitz's*office was located at a
busy cross street on the Upper West Side; the block
was affectionately dubbed "Therapist Row" by the
hundreds of New Yorkers who made daily pilgrim-
ages to see their psychoanalysts on that street. In recognition of the historic block, The NYC Transit
Authority thoughtfully provided free boxes of Kleenex at the local subway exit, which was great if you
didn't mind blowing your nose in a tissue spray-
painted "Garcia 116."

The first time I saw Sheila B-H, she was holding
several cumbersome packages and struggling to unlock her office door. I quickly diagnosed her problem;
she was trying to unlock her door with a set of brightly

---

* I figured the hyphenated name was her solution to keeping a
measure of independence when she'd married; I wondered what
her husband was like.

colored, plastic baby keys. I pointed to the teething keys in her hand; she laughed, threw the toy into her purse and unlocked the door with a metal key, the kind adults use. I wondered which one of us needed help as I followed her into the office.

Sheila wore a pale green Chanel suit accented with tons of rope jewelry. She was better dressed than I was, I bitterly noted.

I guess Sheila was middle-aged, although I can't describe her too well. For most of my sessions, I lay on her couch and she sat behind me so I never got a really good look at her. After my forty-five minutes expired, I avoided looking her directly in the face, embarrassed by all the intimate details of my life I had revealed. I did, however, spend lots of time observing the art on Sheila's walls.

The office was decorated with African tribal masks and other (expensive) primitive art objects. An antique quilt hung near the door. Behind Sheila's desk was a modern art painting, which resembled, to my artistic eye, a gigantic Hebrew National frankfurter slathered with green mustard.

During my first session, Sheila said, "So, why're you here, Miss Goldbloom?" which, I suspected, was some kind of psychoanalytic screening test. I thought carefully about my answer and replied, "I'm not sure."

"Hmm," Sheila murmured.

I didn't know how to begin the session so I avoided getting down to business. I talked about the weather, the subways, the latest episode of *60 Minutes*. I complimented Sheila on her African masks and her patchwork quilt but I carefully refrained from even mentioning the incredibly phallic painting behind her desk.

I kept waiting for Sheila to say, "What's a normal person like you doing here? You don't need therapy. Go, buy yourself a new pair of boots."

Instead, Sheila suggested we begin with three sessions a week.

We discussed Sheila's fees and possible payment schedules. Sheila was sympathetic to the financial burden I was undertaking and offered to cosign a low-interest loan for me.

During my second session, I confessed my social life was no bed of roses. I talked about men and what I expected from my relationships. Sheila listened attentively, muttering, "I see," several times. Then, when I ran out of complaints, she offered me her advice.

"Forget Prince Charles," she said. "He's married, his old lady's pregnant and he lives with his mother. Guys like that *never* leave their wives."

Sheila's argument was persuasive but I resisted, still fantasizing about the ball gowns, the country house in Wales, command performances at Albert Hall and, especially, that diamond tiara.

We spent hours analyzing my obsession with Prince Charles until we traced the development of my neurosis to a favorite early game show of mine, *Queen for a Day!* Sheila said my problem was that I had taken the show too literally as a child and, thus, was reenacting my lifelong desire to wear a crown and win a Maytag washer-dryer of my own.

"Forget Charles," Sheila repeated. "I'm interested in what's right for you. Now, tell me what you really want."

"Ankle-length pearls the size of Ping-Pong balls," I said, naming the first thing that came into my mind.

"Seriously," Sheila insisted. "Go home and make a list."

All night I worked on my list, which I presented to Sheila the next morning.

"Let's see what we have here," Sheila said and proceeded to read the list out loud. "I want: 1) Victoria Principal's body; 2) Sandra Day O'Connor's career; 3) Margaret Mead's brains; 4) Suzanne Somers' hair and 5) Baryshnikov's children." Sheila cleared her throat but didn't comment.*

---

* Sheila's silences were deafening.

"Well, it sounds better when you read it to yourself," I offered.

Sheila didn't respond so I took my copy of the list and looked it over once more. "I guess I shouldn't complain since I've got Victoria's brains, O'Connor's hair, Mead's body and Somers' career," I half-heartedly joked.

Sheila mentioned something about self-confidence and, for no apparent reason, I started to cry. In fact, I cried a lot in therapy. Usually, I sobbed pretty steadily for the first part of my session and then spent the remainder of my time talking about why I was crying. Pretty soon, Sheila got to know me real well and she took over the talking part, freeing me to spend the entire session choking on my tears.

At first, I never quite made it to my appointments on time, which Sheila called "resisting treatment." However, if I was on time, Sheila said I was compulsive; if I was early, she said I was obsessive. I felt I couldn't win, which, I think, is called the Hopelessness Phase and, after it ended, I settled into a routine of arriving fifteen minutes early for each session because I was most comfortable with obsessive behavior.*

After a time, I decided I liked therapy, because I'd always been fond of talking about myself. (I tend to agree with most of my own opinions.) I also enjoyed hearing Sheila's viewpoint, especially the real catty stuff she said about Tiffany Jerkowitz.

Therapy allowed me to relive my childhood, at least as much of it as I could remember. Sheila encouraged me to think, feel and act like a child, which was hard because she nixed playing Barbie dolls; even though, for reasons of security, I occasionally brought Barbie along to my sessions.

After a while, Sheila helped me realize I had endowed Barbie with powers she didn't really possess and, all these years, I had used the doll as a substitute

---

* Especially involving expensive shoes or any foodstuff baked with fresh blueberries or apricot jam.

older sister/mother. "That was fine when you were a child," Sheila said, "but don't you think, now, it's Barbie's turn to cry?" It was quite a revelation, as you can well imagine; and when I informed Barbie, in no uncertain terms, she was only a plastic doll, well, she didn't take the news like a sport. Barbie flung herself into my new toaster oven, accidentally melting her favorite pair of plastic stiletto heels.

Naturally, I talked a lot about my parents, especially my mother. I discovered, deep down, I was furious with my parents for having typecast me as "doctor's wife" since I was six months old. I was so enraged, in fact, that for a while, I considered suing my parents for therapy fees and damages. I even consulted a lawyer, who charged me two hundred dollars and said that, although I had grounds for such a suit, it was unlikely a judge would uphold a settlement, especially since most judges were parents themselves.

Neither Mom nor Dad approved of psychiatry. Dad thought it was "best not to air your dirty laundry in some stranger's office."

"Give me ninety bucks an hour," Mom said, "and I'll listen to anything you want to say."

I got around the issue by not mentioning my analysis to my parents. Mom got suspicious when she noticed Barbie's semi-melted stilettoes in my toaster oven but I jabbered away about drying rain-soaked shoes, which put Mom off her guard and off my back. If nothing else, therapy taught me how to duck my mother's questions more effectively.

Therapy also taught me to be more productive since I had to take on a ton of free-lance work to pay for my sessions.

One day I made an astute observation that, I think, impressed Sheila. "All my life I've been surrounded by people whose names begin with the letter S— Sasha, Sandy, Aunt Selma, Miss Singer, Seymour, Sybil and now Sheila. Do you think that means anything?"

"What do you think?" *

"I don't know, that's why I'm asking you."

"I think, subconsciously, you are seeking your mother in all of your friends and relationships."

"But Mom's name is Janice," I protested.

No response.

"With the letter J," I added for clarity.

No response.

"It makes no sense."

"How do you feel about that?" †

Of course, I worried about becoming too dependent on Sheila as I didn't want to spend the next ten years in therapy. I thought I had everything under control until the night I paid my monthly bills and Sheila's fee was the exact same amount as my paycheck. I checked my calendar and discovered I'd seen Sheila sixteen times that month or, you could say, every other day.

I began to realize I hardly ever made a decision anymore without first consulting my shrink. I checked with Sheila before negotiating any new author's contract, approving an advertising budget or editing a manuscript.‡ I called Sheila's office hourly when a big meeting was being planned at Haphazard House. (Sybil suggested I install a Watts line in Sheila's office so that I could do business during my sessions.)

I was conferring with Sheila about whether to buy Lavoris mouthwash or Scope when, bingo! I realized I was into the dependency stage of my therapy.

At about the time I made this revelation, Sheila announced she was going away for the month of August. I couldn't believe she would leave New York when I was in such a crucial stage of my treatment. And, no matter how much I begged and pleaded, she wouldn't

---

* Sheila's favorite expression; next to "How do you feel about that?"

† I told you.

‡ Sheila grasped the ins and outs of the publishing business in almost no time. (She also began dropping hints about a book she was planning to write.)

tell me where she was going for the summer or who she was going with. Listen, I wasn't being neurotic or anything, I was merely curious, at least until Sheila's silence convinced me she was going away with a patient she liked better than me or, possibly, with her mother.

The day Sheila left for vacation, just for spite, I called her answering machine at my regularly scheduled time and talked on her tape for forty-five minutes.

After that, I was feeling kind of low so I left my office and walked across town to Horn & Hardart for an early lunch. There, I picked up my favorite comfort food, chicken pot pie, and settled myself at a table near the window.

I was eating quietly, minding my own business, when someone placed a tray across the table. The food on the tray made me gag: rare, rare steak oozing blood, a mountain of greasy fries, mucousy okra, a huge glass of milk and a slice of white cake with white frosting.

The man behind the tray peered intently at me. "Bambi? Is that you?" he asked.

I was certain I'd never crossed paths with this pot-bellied man whose brown hair was cut in a ridiculously dated porcupine crew cut. He wore the most awful polyester, plaid, three-piece suit with a wide striped tie. Although I couldn't see his feet, I was certain he wore white socks and Florsheim-type shoes. He looked as if he was an FBI agent, or a bank teller, so I became instantly paranoid that he knew my name.

"My name happens to be Bambi, but you must be confusing me with another Bambi."

"Bambi Goldbloom?" He leaned over to kiss me but backed off after I screamed.

"You don't know who I am?" He looked hurt.

"No."

"It's me Jon . . . Jonathan . . . Jonathan Siegel . . . Jonathan Livingston Siegel."

"No! Jon?" I laughed, embarrassed. "I guess I didn't recognize you without the pony tail, the beard, the sheet."

Jon grinned as he plopped down in his chair and began carving his steak. He stuffed an enormous wedge of meat into his mouth and chewed vigorously. Brown gravy trickled down his chin.

"I see you're no longer a vegetarian," I commented.

"Gave that up years ago. After you dumped me for that Marvin guy. Joined the army, the real world." He gulped his milk. "Stayed ten years. Now, I'm into sneakers. I own the Qantas franchise for the tri-state region."

"Qantas?"

"Australian sneakers. Great sole support. Forty-seven outlets in Manhattan alone." He quickly polished off the white cake in three bites. "Been married, oh, fourteen years, got six kids. Here, I'll show you pictures."

Jon pulled out his wallet and unfolded his plastic photo holder. The color photos displayed a huge brood of kids; kids at the beach, in the driveway, dressed in Little League uniforms and graduation caps. His wife was plump and red-haired and looked, well, content. Tired, but content.

Something about those photos triggered a deep response in me and, when Sheila eventually returned from vacation, I spent seven weeks discussing my chance meeting with Jon. I wondered if I would ever be a happy face surrounded by a couple of kids in someone's wallet.

"You know, when I dated Jon," I told Sheila, "I often fantasized about the kids Jon and I would have. We'd live on a commune, raise our own food, educate the children ourselves." I sighed. "If it wasn't for all that brown rice, I might be the mother of Jonathan's kids."

"How does that make you feel?" Sheila asked.

"Like a biological time clock ready to explode," I finally admitted.

I started dreaming about garage sales and Tupperware parties. Sheila analyzed my Tupperware dreams back to the happy times of my childhood in Mrs. Crest's apartment with Sasha. I discovered I had channeled all maternal feelings into my job, giving "birth" to books instead of babies. Underneath my silk blouse and wool cashmere jackets, there was a housewife just screaming to come out.

I decided to get married, have a baby and throw a Tupperware party, which, I know, was not the most original idea but it seemed, at the time, the logical solution to my problem. Once again, I set out to snag myself a husband.

I quickly eliminated, as candidates, the men in my office, as I had already dated most of them.

The only guy who was proposing at the time was Guido, my ex-exterminator from Greenwich Village. I discovered, after I moved to the Upper East Side, Guido was madly in love with me and, for years, he had been undercharging me for insect bomb and monthly maintenance. A dozen times, I had turned down Guido's marriage proposal and a dozen times he said, "Hey, I deal with New York City cockroaches, I'm persistent."

Sheila thought I was being a bit hasty in turning down Guido's proposal.

"Perhaps your expectations need to be lowered," she said.

"How low can they go?" I wailed. "I only want two things: a guy who can hold down a steady job and isn't carrying any infectious diseases."

"And Guido?"

"And a guy that doesn't smell like insecticide."

"That's three things," Sheila observed.

I turned to the singles ads in *New York Magazine*.

After a few weeks, an ad caught my eye: "Nice guy, nice job, wants to meet nice girl for (guess what?) nice time. Photo would be nice. Have a nice day. Write Box 67."

Was this the nice guy of my dreams?

I responded immediately: "Nice ad (I wrote). I'm a nice gal hoping to meet a nice guy. I don't have a recent photo but I look exactly like: a) Jane Fonda b) Dolly Parton c) my mother. (Guess which?) A phone call would be nice. Signed, B. Crest."

Just to be on the safe side I used a phony name. I mean, who knew? I could be sending my phone number to the Son of Sam.

Mr. Nice Guy called me a week later. He said his name was John Beresford Tipton* and he was a used carpeting salesman.

"Used carpeting?" I inquired politely.

"Right, mainly wool blends and deep pile."

I asked John what kind of response he had gotten from his ad and he told me he'd received 250 letters, so far.

I was astonished. "Did the letters have anything in common?"

"Yeah, every woman who answered the ad claims to have a great sense of humor," he said. "So, who do you look like, Jane or Dolly?"

"More like my mom, I guess."

"I had a feeling that was going to be your answer." Did he sound disappointed or was I imagining things? "By the way, what does the B stand for?"

I still didn't want to reveal my identity so I tried to fabricate a clever reply but nothing came to me. "It's just a B," I finally blurted out.

"Oh, like B.F. Goodrich without the F—or the Goodrich."

"Yeah, like that." I was not exactly honored at being compared with radial tires.

John asked a ton of semi-personal questions about my personality and, naturally, I mentioned my great sense of humor, but he sounded skeptical.

"Look, how about we meet for a drink tomorrow?" he said.

"Where?"

* The name sounded familiar but I just couldn't place it.

"Under the clock at the Biltmore Hotel, Forty-third between Park and Lex."

"They tore that building down."

"Oh, how about Bloomingdale's? You know where it is, right?"

I laughed.

"Men's cashmere sweaters, around seven?"

"How will I know you?" I asked.

"I'll be wearing jeans and a gray sweatshirt. My hair is brown."

"Okay," I said, thinking he sounded kind of cute.

The next night, I was in Bloomie's by 6:45, hoping to get a first glance at this guy (and perhaps make a quick getaway.) I couldn't decide if I was just nervous or I was actually having a cardiac infarction.

I was standing next to Designer Belts when I recognized, over in Silk Ties, a man wearing jeans and a sweatshirt. He was walking toward me. He looked familiar although his Al Pacino/Serpico beard and hair confused me for a minute. Then I realized he was Bruce Berger!

At first, Bruce stood near the 100 percent Lambs Wool Sweaters as if he were waiting for someone. I was trying to decide whether or not to approach him when he walked over and asked if my name was B!

Was this my life, I wondered, or the plot of a Charles Dickens novel?

Six weeks later, Bruce and I were married at his parent's house in Bayonne. We made a pact never to tell anyone about the ads in *New York Magazine*.*

My second wedding was a lot different from my first. Because both of us had been previously married, we had a small ceremony in Bruce's parents' living room and a major barbeque in their backyard. My father did the honors at the grill even though he was no

---

* Bruce didn't talk to me for two days after he read this chapter. I told him to shoot me for being honest but, fortunately, he didn't follow my advice.

great shakes as a chef. It took Dad about an hour and forty minutes to light the coals; he used the whole can of lighter fluid and the entire Travel section of the Sunday *New York Times* and, I tell you, the franks were charred beyond recognition and tasted a lot like kerosene. But Dad worked so hard that no one had the heart to complain. Aunt Selma made a dynamite potato salad and Mom supplied her fabulous triple-layer chocolate cake.

After the wedding, Bruce and I began our hunt for an apartment. We soon discovered that finding a large, affordable apartment in Manhattan was next to impossible so we decided to move back to the suburbs. We borrowed money from our folks and bought a cute split-level in Hohokus, not far from my parents' house. I spent weeks decorating the house which proved to be an almost religious experience. I can't tell you how many times I reverently wondered: If God could create the color mauve, why couldn't He create matching carpeting?

For a while, I commuted to work every morning but I found it was difficult, if not impossible, to be taken seriously by New Yorkers. "HOHOKUS!" people would scream with laughter. "What is that, some kind of stuttering disease?"*

I soon grew tired of the Jersey jokes and the endless hours of commuting and, after talking to Bruce, decided to quit the city altogether.

Sybil was furious when I announced I was leaving Haphazard House. "How could you do this to me? After I promoted you? You can't leave!"

"I can. I am."

"You're going to live off a *man*," she sneered, as if it were a crime or something.

"Yeah," I grinned. "I rather like the idea."

* They say there's no place like home but I've traveled the world and it seems to me there are plenty of places like home. The truth, however, is that there's no place like New Jersey. Only in America would they name the site of so much toxic waste The Garden State!

"You'll be sorry," she warned. "No one walks out on Sybil Weinberg."

There were about fifteen guys I knew personally who had walked, no, ran, out on Sybil but I was too polite to contradict her, especially in mid-tantrum.

After two hours, Sybil gave up trying to dissuade me from quitting my job. She was almost as upset as Sheila was when I quit therapy; only Sheila's reaction was more concrete.

"You can't quit now," Sheila screeched. "I'm in the midst of renovating my kitchen!"

"Sorry."

"Sorry? What good is *sorry?* Who's going to pay for the double-door fridge? The marble counter tops? Bambi," she cried, "I was counting on you!"

"Sheila, I'm out of here."

In truth, I found Bruce just in time, and I don't mean because my apartment was going co-op that summer; Bruce saved me from any more marketing meetings, blind dates or therapy fees.

After I severed my ties with the city, a whole new world opened up to me. With no job and no therapy, I was able to devote almost all my time to raising houseplants and looking after my new husband.

Most of the time, I liked being married to Bruce. He was sexy, he encouraged me to be myself and he didn't mind doing the dishes. We enjoyed a lot of the same things, like reading for instance, although our taste in books couldn't be more different. While my favorite books were *Scruples, Clan of the Cave Bear* and *Garp,* Bruce enjoyed reading L. Ron Hubbard, a writer for whom my respect was (and is) well under control. (Bruce thought that dumb book, *Diuretics,* was like a Bible or something.)

My life with Bruce was blissful but not without problems, and their names were Darla and Dirk, his children from his first marriage. I discovered, quite early in motherhood, that the longest and most painful deliveries occur when you give birth to stepchildren. Bruce's kids didn't exactly welcome me into the family with open arms. Darla nicknamed me "The Bitch on Wheels" and claimed I had wrecked her parents' marriage.

"But Darla, dear," I patiently explained, "your parents were divorced two years before I even met your daddy."

She glared at me from beneath her purple streaked hair and a silver lightning bolt painted above one of her eyelids. "Because of you, Mom and Dad will never remarry."

"Honey, your mother doesn't want to remarry your dad."

"What makes you such an expert?"

"She told me I'd married her leftover garbage."

Even though it was a verbatim quotation, Darla didn't believe me and, for the next eighteen months, she refused to speak to me, which put a real strain on our relationship.

Fortunately, Darla and Dirk lived with their mother during the week, which gave Bruce and me lots of time alone to fight about his kids. While Bruce argued for more understanding and perhaps a family ski trip to Vermont, I was in favor of weekend boarding schools.

During the really trying times, I remembered my mother's sage advice and found myself constantly repeating Mom's words to my new step-kids.

"Laugh and the world laughs with you," I would tell them. "Sulk and you go to your room."

I also had to contend with Bruce's twin sister, Ethel, who hadn't changed much from our childhood days. Ethel still had the infuriating habit of copying everything I did. I bought red shoes, she bought red shoes. I joined a swim club, she joined a swim club. I married a used carpeting salesman, she married a used carpeting salesman; namely, Bruce's store manager, Mr. Lockjaw, as we nicknamed him for his winning facial expression and flair for telling one joke over and over, "Tissue? I don't even know you."

Ethel was married in her parents' house and had

the matzo balls to ask my father to be her chef for the barbeque.*

I once complained when Ethel bought an identical blue velvet gown and then wore it to the same family affair. She didn't understand why it bothered me so much.

"I don't like to make decisions," Ethel remarked. "So I borrow yours."

"I'm *really* flattered," I said, my voice dripping with sarcasm, as yet another wedding guest, walking by, asked if Ethel and I were twins.

"No, I'm much younger," my sister-in-law purred.

"Two months!" I exclaimed, grabbing the luckless wedding guest by the lapels of her mink stole. "She's only *two months* younger."

"Two months and six days," Ethel sang out as she waltzed off with my husband. (I often thought Ethel had a thing for Bruce but, of course, incest was not a proper topic of discussion in Jewish households.)

I tried not to make a big hassle over my problems with Ethel as I didn't want to come between Bruce and his family. I handled the situation very cleverly, I thought, by ignoring Ethel and her husband during the few family gatherings where I was forced to sit within speaking distance of them.

Bruce and I wanted children, so we worked real hard getting pregnant. My gynecologist suggested I keep an ovulation calendar and take my temperature every fifteen minutes but Bruce insisted on using the old-fashioned method of marathon sex so we made love almost continually. Bruce developed back problems and I had trouble walking; but otherwise, we both felt great and we obviously did something right. I got pregnant. Of course, Ethel got pregnant two weeks later.

My step-kids did not take the news of my pregnancy with as much joy as I had anticipated. Dirk, who was kind of shy around me, seemed perplexed. "Gosh,

* Dad felt he wouldn't be able to look the mishpuka in the face if he declined the honor.

Dad, I thought you guys were, you know, too old to, you know, um, do it."

"Ugh! Gross!" exclaimed Darla. "Like I'm totally grossed out. I'm going upstairs to barf my brains out."

Bruce joked about the kid's reaction but I was not amused since, at the time, barfing was no laughing matter to me.

Okay, I hate to admit this, but I was not one of those brave, everything natural, pregnant women. I liked the part about eating for two but I didn't really enjoy being thirty pounds overweight or what pregnancy did to my appearance. For six months, my navel looked like a light switch, brown freckled patches covered my face, my breasts sagged over my stomach and my thighs rubbed together even when I wasn't walking.

Once, when I was in the tub, Darla burst into the bathroom, took one look at me naked and shrieked, "Your body is totally gross. I'm never having a baby!"

"What a loss for mankind," I muttered as Darla flounced out again.

Since I'm on a confessional roll here, I'll also admit I wasn't very good about the pain. I started screaming for painkillers after the third contraction and didn't stop until my daughter was eating solid food.

In all fairness, I'd say giving birth is a real life experience but, then, so are many really disgusting bodily functions. I love my baby a lot but, if I had my druthers, my husband would experience hard labor and I'd stand next to him with the whistle.

Ethel's baby, a boy, was born a day after my daughter and the whole family was sobered by the thought of a baby Mr. Lockjaw.

Bruce and I named our daughter Sara. After a lifetime of receiving copies of *Bambi* for every birthday, I chose to give my little girl a less unusual name. Actually, my first choice had been Krystle but Bruce was afraid people would think we'd named her after Krystle Carrington, which was really silly. We didn't even watch *Dynasty!*

Naturally, I had my share of newborn adventures—
the first time my baby slept through the night* and
the time she almost swallowed my pearl earring.

Sara admirably performed all the jobs required of a
newborn: she stared at light bulbs, screamed through
the wee small hours of the night, polished off her
strained apricots and drooled like a real trooper. For
recreation, she enjoyed playing "Go Boom" and a
rudimentary version of "Clap Hands." She did however, seem bored to tears by "Where's Mama?" and
"Where's Papa?" even when we diversified the game
with "Where's Nana Janice?" or "Where's your
nose?"

I thought she was a real happy baby because she
smiled all the time but the pediatrician said, "Those
ain't smiles, Bambi, that's gas."

Sara had a perfect heart shaped mouth, two big dimples, a lock of curly hair on top of her head, the cutest
little tushie and, well, you know how adorable babies
can be especially in those teeny, tiny little outfits like
Sara's pink, tie-dyed, spandex dress with the rhinestones or her red cotton playsuit strapped together
with a baby whale on the left shoulder. I loved buying
little-girl clothes. My daughter was even more fun to
dress up than my dolls had been, even though Sara
did tend to spit up a lot more than Barbie.

Once the baby was born, even Darla got excited
about playing with her. She took Bruce's Master
Charge card into the city one day and, at a posh Manhattan children's store, City Kidettes, Darla bought
Sara a black leather skirt with a matching leather vest
lined with fake leopard fur. "Now Sara will look just
like the dudes on Christopher Street," she said, refer-
ring to my old stomping grounds in Greenwich Village. It wasn't exactly the kind of outfit I would've
selected for Sara, but it was the nicest thing Darla had
done since I'd married her Dad, so I didn't complain.

Darla had also picked up a cute little football jersey
for Buddy, Ethel's new baby. I told Darla it was

* I woke her up at dawn just to make sure she was still breathing.

sweet, not feeling particularly generous after I had spent weeks knitting a baby bunting for Ethel's newborn while my sister-in-law bought Sara a three-dollar undershirt painted with her name, which washed out the minute the shirt got wet.

Actually, I have no complaints about a lack of clothing for my little girl. Mom filled several of Sara's drawers with Izod undershirts and unbelievably expensive Japanese designer pajamas. Because Sara was my parents' first, and possibly sole, grandchild, my mother was always available for babysitting. In fact, Mom often came over to babysit when Bruce and I stayed home for the evening.

What scared me, though, was finding myself sounding so much like my mother when I talked to my little girl. One day I overheard Darla doing a vicious imitation of me over the phone. *"Oy vey!"* Darla mimicked. *"I gained so much weight when I was pregnant. You shouldn't know from the pain!"*

I almost dropped my pot roast. Did I really make the same complaints as my mother? In the same voice? I sat down at the table and tried to remember the list I'd made as a youngster of all the things I was never, ever, ever going to do to my kid when I became a mother. But, somewhere along the road to motherhood, I had forgotten many of those complaints.

I did gasp, however, when I remembered the day we brought Sara home from the hospital and Bruce said to her, "Did you like all those nice doctors at the hospital? Maybe someday you'll marry one of them," and I told Sara to listen to her daddy.

I couldn't get these thoughts out of my head as I left the house to take my Rabbit to the Midas transmission shop in Bayonne (for the third time in six months).

As I strapped Sara into her infant car seat, I had to stifle the urge to tell her to "Sit Up Straight!" Next, I'll be telling her to take her elbows off the table and get her hair out of her eyes, I thought to myself and almost cried.

I was in the waiting office of the shop, worrying

some more about Jewish genetics, when I recognized my ex-husband, Seymour, driving up to the garage— in a Jaguar, no less. Naturally, I was wearing my rattiest jeans and no makeup, so I raced into the ladies room and did wonders with a little lip gloss and some of my daughter's plastic barrettes. (Sara didn't mind when I pulled the barrettes from her hair. I only wished I could fit into the stunning mauve suede snowsuit she was wearing.)

I confronted Seymour in the waiting room.

He looked pretty good, except that his hair was thinner and his belly rounder. He still carried the same pen and pencil set in his shirt pocket. It was the first time we had seen each other since our divorce. Seymour and I shared a Diet Coke, ogled Sara and caught up on each other's lives. As he talked, I got to wondering why I'd ever divorced such a nice man, but then he mentioned his parents and I remembered all too well.

Seymour's father, Sol, was gone.

"Oh, I'm so sorry," I said. "When did he pass away?"

"What pass away? I said he was gone. He ran off with his bookkeeper. They're living together, *in sin*, in a condo near Pompano Beach. Mom lives with us."

After our divorce, Seymour had married Tiffany Jerkowitz and finished his degree at vet school, where he specialized in doggie dentistry. Later, he opened his own clinic, the Yuppie Puppy, on the Upper East Side, which was now enormously successful. His specialty was Akita Periodontics and Seymour was perfectly content to work on doggie gums all day and then dine poolside with Tiffany at their lovely Scarsdale colonial.

"I guess I should thank you for leaving me," Seymour said with a wry laugh. "If we hadn't split, I might never have married Tiffany. You know, she's the best darned wife a man could have!"

I excused myself to throw up in the ladies room and, when I returned, Seymour was revving the motor of his black Jag. He waved goodbye as he drove the sleek car out of the garage.

Since I was now a mature woman with a husband, a family, a bestselling book and several months of analysis under my belt, I no longer felt bitter or vengeful. I told myself I was happy to see my ex-husband doing so well but, even so, I was sorry Seymour left before I had gotten the chance to scratch his leather upholstery with my car key.

When I got home from the Midas shop, I opened the mailbox and, to my surprise, discovered a letter from Q (now Mrs. Q), my childhood ex-best friend. Well, actually, the letter was from Q's secretary.

"The purpose of this letter is to inform you that, as former Class President, Mrs. Q is planning the program for the twentieth-anniversary reunion of your high school class. The committee asked us to inquire if you would be interested in delivering the keynote address.

"They say you've put Hohokus on the map with your book, *In Search of Mediocrity*," wrote Q's secretary, "which we're told was adopted for all social studies and home ec classes at Ho High. Of course, neither Mrs. Q nor myself has ever heard of your book but there seems to be some enthusiasm here for your writing career.

"Please write us if you want to speak at the reunion.

"P.S. I am writing on behalf of Mrs. Q because she still has not forgiven you for what she calls 'the school bus incident.' Please address all future correspondence to my attention."

I was, of course, flattered by the request but not at all certain I wanted to attend the reunion. The thought that it had been *twenty years* since high school was more than I could bear and, after seeing Seymour that afternoon, I was not exactly anxious to take another stroll down memory lane.

Bruce, however, was excited about the prospect of meeting our old high school chums.

"What's wrong?" he asked. "You have a wonderful life. You've got nothing to be ashamed of."

"I'm not ashamed of my life now," I tried to explain. "I'm ashamed of my life back then."

Bruce didn't understand so I pulled out our high school yearbook and turned to my graduation picture. "Look at that," I said. "Do you think I want to confront people who knew me when I looked like this?"

"I knew you when you looked like this," Bruce pointed out.

"Just look at the photo."

"Okay," Bruce admitted, "so your makeup was a little extreme."

"Three pairs of false eyelashes and enough black eyeliner to make up the Statue of Liberty is not a little extreme, it's embarrassing."

"So what? You were a Bopper's moll. Think of it as an expression of your individuality. You're the only girl in this book who posed for her graduation picture in a motorcycle jacket."

"Let's see," Darla exclaimed, pulling the yearbook from Bruce's hand. "Pretty cool, you look like a real punker compared to these geeks in the stretch hairbands." Reflecting on Darla's sense of style, which included lots of rusty safety pins and scabs, I realized the photo was even worse than I feared.

Although Bruce laughed off my high school affectations, the picture in that yearbook made me cringe. I looked preposterous and the worst part was that, at the time I'd thought I was coolness personified. No, I didn't want to be reminded of those times or spend an evening with people who did.

I tried every plausible excuse but Bruce was really adamant so, eventually, I said, "Okay, I'll go but only if I get a new fur coat out of the deal," which was how I got my lovely silver-tipped raccoon and, coincidentally, the inspiration for this book.

SERIOUS PLEASURES

My twentieth-anniversary high school reunion was everything I thought it would be: boring and embarrassing.

Boring to listen to all my old girlfriends talk about diapers, housekeepers and stretch marks; and embarrassing when people asked, "So, what's new?" which is not an easy question to answer when you haven't seen someone in over nineteen years.

The reunion was held in the Cresskill Bowling Lanes in Garfield, New Jersey. The Lanes were elaborately decorated to resemble the theme of our senior prom, "A Night of Knights." The decorating committee resurrected the papier mâché drawbridge and the fiery, crepe-paper-breathing, flying dragon, who by now was practically bald of his tissue-paper carnations, which had all but rotted away after all those years in someone's basement. The dragon oozed his stuffing all over Lanes 7 and 8.

I barely paid attention to the decorations as I was nervously searching the room for Tiffany and Seymour. I dreaded seeing them together.

There were, of course, a few surprises, like when Ethel made her grand entrance in a brand-new raccoon coat and when Sandy arrived without Bradley, which I didn't understand until she explained Bradley had divorced her two years before and was now paying her a meager $86.50 a week to cover expenses for herself and her three kids. Sandy had barely left her house for the past six months. We promised to get together after the reunion, although I told Sandy I wasn't interested in cruising the singles bars in Fort Lee with her.

Anyway, Sandy had a lot in common with Ronnie, Kar, Bev, Cyn, Bobbi and Nita. All of them were divorcées, working mothers and real estate agents.

Ronnie, in fact, had even been divorced twice and was working on her third. She looked a lot better than in her high school days, with her contact lenses and now stylish frizzed hair. "I didn't blossom until I hit thirty, so now I'm making up for lost time," Ronnie told us.

Lesley still had traces of her former cheerleader prettiness but she now was puffy, wrinkled and pregnant with her ninth child.

"You had to go and marry an Italian," Ronnie remarked.

The biggest shock was quiet, unassuming Kimberly Katz, who had escaped Hohokus by hitchhiking to Vegas. After an implantation and plastic surgery, Kimberly stripped for a living, "a stripper on the strip," as she said, while putting herself through school to become a blackjack dealer. During a particularly exciting game, she met Vito Marchioni, who proposed after Kimberly dealt him four blackjacks in a row. Kimberly was now a happy housewife living in a suite at Caesar's Palace.

Kimberly and Vito sat next to us during dinner and our husbands became fast friends after Vito mentioned a chain of motels he was constructing on the strip.

"Vito, have you given any thought to used carpeting?" Bruce asked.

"No, we usually go with the new stuff. Brucie, our motels are pretty classy joints—water beds, flocked wallpaper, X-rated cable TV, slot machines in every room."

"Vito, used carpeting is where it's at. And talk about cheap!"

"OK, talk," Vito said.

Also at our table were Lesley and her husband, Kar, Bev, Nita, Ronnie, Bobbi and Sandy. Among us we had nineteen children, which became the main topic of conversation as we ate dinner. No one ate very much however, because the reunion was catered by the staff of the high school cafeteria. The Shepherd's Pie was cold, the cartons of milk were warm, and the waitresses wore hairnets and orthopedic shoes.

After dinner, the evening's ceremonies were chaired by Mrs. Wall, the former Miss Singer, who'd advanced through the Hohokus school system to her current position as principal of Ho High. Mrs. Wall stood at the podium and read from our yearbook the names of the kids we'd elected Who's Who twenty years ago, insisting that each of those poor people come up to the stage and say a few words.

It was not a pretty sight.

Most Popular hadn't brought a date to the reunion. "Always an usher, never a groom," he quipped.

Class Sophisticate wore a miniskirt, fringed vest, white go-go boots, love beads and several silver rings made from the tips of spoons.

Cutest Couple held hands on stage, kissed passionately and disappeared for several hours. (They were married but not to each other.)

Most School Spirit kept muttering, "This reunion sucks."

Class Clown, an insurance salesman, gave a long-winded speech comparing whole life to term insurance.

Neither Most Likely to Succeed nor Most Happy-Go-Lucky were in attendance. Most Likely to Succeed was serving ten to fifteen at Allentown and Most Happy-Go-Lucky had been committed to Bellevue.

Class Chatterbox hadn't changed much, she talked

non-stop for twenty minutes until Class Politician ruthlessly shoved her off the stage.

Best Dressed looked stunning, as always, if I do say so myself.

Mrs. Wall announced it was time for my keynote address and everyone applauded except Q who took that particular moment to drill new holes in her bowling ball.

I had barely gotten into my speech when I was interrupted by a messenger who carried a huge horseshoe bouquet of green carnations. He placed them on the stage and handed me a telegram.

"Read it!" shouted someone from the floor so I opened the envelope.

"Good luck to our old classmates," I read. "We're sorry we can't be with you tonight. Stop. We're vacationing in the Mediterranean on a yacht that costs fifteen hundred dollars a day. Stop. Love to Ho High! Stop. Doctor Seymour Weisnetroubwitz and his wife, the former Tiffany Jerkowitz."

"Who's Seymour what's-his-heimer?" shouted Class Sophisticate.

"Who gives a crap?" demanded Most School Spirit.

Everyone started talking and making jokes about the telegram. "Fifteen hundred a day is chicken feed," declared Q, who was wearing a floor-length sable coat that probably cost more than my split-level. "Dunstan and I have our own yacht, don't we Dunny?" Q's husband nodded proudly.

"Properly insured?" asked Class Clown.

The crowd was too excited to pay attention to my speech, so I wound it up in five minutes and chucked the remaining twenty-seven pages into the trash.

"Whad'ya expect from these Bozos?" asked Pride of the Faculty as I walked off the stage.

As I started back to my table, Mr. Wall approached me and kissed my cheek. I couldn't believe how ancient he was and, try as I might, I couldn't find one trace of gorgeous Cubby in this decrepit old man who wore a wide-lapeled blue suit covered with chalk dust.

"So, Bambi, what're you writing now?"

"Oh, I'm working on a few ideas."

"You know, I always thought someone should write a book about the educational system in Hohokus."

"That's an interesting idea."

"You think so? It's yours. By the way, Bambi, I was just thinking of a conversation we had, years and years ago, about younger women. Do you recall it?" He squeezed my arm. "You know, you're still cute as the dickens."

"Oh, there's my husband," I said. "Excuse me, Mr. Wall."

"If you need a ride home," he said, but I pretended not to hear as I turned and raced over to Bruce. "Let's go," I whispered to him.

Bruce was still in animated conversation with Vito and it took quite a while to break up their negotiations and then say goodbye to everyone.

On the drive home, Bruce talked excitedly about the deal he had struck with Vito to carpet the Vegas motels. He was so certain that the deal was going to come through that, the next day, we went out and bought a Volvo station wagon, trading in the Rabbit.

The day the Volvo arrived, however, Vito was indicted on some kind of loan-sharking charge and his deal with Bruce fell through, which was a real blow to our financial picture. We were desperate to make some cash to cover the car payments and Bruce politely suggested I start writing again, at least until his business picked up a little.

I hadn't written since Sara was born. When I was pregnant, I thought motherhood would provide the perfect environment for a writer. Sara would sleep most of the day and I'd write while listening to her happy baby gurgles in the background. Well, any woman who's a mother knows how quickly Sara shot that fantasy to hell.

The only writing I had done was a journal I had been keeping since my days in therapy, which was more an encyclopedia of kvetching than anything else. For days, I searched my brain for a book idea but I was long out of touch with the marketplace and didn't have a clue what to write.

I called Ariel and asked her to take me to lunch, where I told her I needed a project other than keeping a journal, which was productive but not profitable.

"Make it profitable," Ariel advised. "Turn it into an autobiography. If you don't want to stick to reality, make it a novel."

"I don't think I could do that Ariel. I've never written anything without lots of facts and quotations to fill space. I was thinking more of a business book, maybe a how-to-succeed type of thing."

"Business books aren't selling anymore."

"What is?"

"Cat books, sex guides for women who pick up the wrong men, bios of Winnie Mandela, AIDS."

"I hate cats. South Africa I know from nothing. Forget AIDS, I don't even want to think about it and I'm too much of a prude to write about sex."

"You hate cats?" Ariel asked, arching an eyebrow.

I remembered a long-ago lunch at which an assistant editor said Ariel lived with eleven cats. "Well, maybe it's a good idea to rewrite the journal as an autobiography. Tell the world what it's like to grow up in New Jersey."

"It's about time somebody did," Ariel said, pointing her breadstick at me. "I grew up in South Orange, you know."

"No, I didn't know. I thought you said you grew up in Beverly Hills."

"Well, we moved to Beverly Hills when I was a kid."

"How old?"

"I forget, seventeen, eighteen."

"That must've been some culture shock."

"For sure. I was teased unmercifully for my Jersey

accent, my Rah Rah clothes. It was hell. Well, you can imagine."

"Oh, Ariel, who'd be interested in my autobiography?" I asked. "It's not like I married Elvis Presley or slept with Rod Stewart. I'm just your average, ordinary woman."

Ariel wasn't listening. "I see a Jackie-Collins-type jacket, bright colors, expensive piece of jewelry. Hardcover. Medium price range. What d'ya think of this as a title: *My Life, My Loves, My Tsuris.* Women all over Bergen County will identify with that!" Ariel exclaimed, becoming more and more excited. "Westchester, too! Bambi, your story is all of our life stories —my secretary, my sister-in-law, my dressmaker." Ariel placed her hand on my shoulder. "Bambi Goldbloom, *c'est moi!*" she declared.

The next day, I sat down to expand my journal into an autobiography, which caused quite a stir among my relatives.

"You're not going to include *all* of us in the book, are you?" asked my mother's cousin Mamie.

"What are you going to say about Uncle Melvin?" Aunt Selma demanded to know.

"Be sure to include lots of sex," my "Uncle" Shelley advised, "and if you need any expert advice, my fees are reasonable."*

Seymour's lawyer and cousin, Morris, wrote a threatening letter cautioning me not to expose any confidentialities from my first marriage. Morris also called a few days later and asked if we could meet for drinks to discuss the issue but when I suggested we make it a date with spouses, Morris was suddenly engaged for the evening.

My mother was more upset than anyone else about the prospect of my autobiography. "Bambi is writing this book just to get back at me," she swore to Aunt Selma.

A few times, Mom snuck into my office while baby-

---

* Please note: "Uncle" Shelley got the quotation marks put back in his name after that particular remark.

sitting for Sara and stole pages from my typewriter, especially the scenes from my childhood.

Bruce, who was all excited about the big advance, tended to go blue in the face if I so much as inferred anything about our sex life.

I also had several arguments with Ariel, especially over bio copy for the press release and book jacket. I wanted something elegant like in those fancy Knoff books. Short, simple, sophisticated, like:

> BAMBI GOLDBLOOM IS THE AUTHOR OF *IN SEARCH OF MEDIOCRITY*. SHE LIVES WITH HER HUSBAND AND DAUGHTER IN NEW JERSEY.

Instead, Ariel wrote the following:

> THEY CALL HER BAMBI GOLDBLOOM. THEY HAVE TO. IT'S HER NAME. THIS BOOK IS THE STORY OF HER LIFE. SHE IS A BESTSELLING AUTHOR; A WIFE, DIVORCÉE, SECOND WIFE, MOTHER AND STEPMOTHER; A HOMEMAKER, A CAREER GIRL AND ALWAYS AND FOREVER, AN IN-CONSIDERATE DAUGHTER WHO NEVER BOTHERS CALLING TO FIND OUT IF HER POOR MOTHER HAS FROZEN TO DEATH DURING THE LAST SNOW-STORM. AFTER DIVORCING HER FIRST HUSBAND ("A REAL NOGOODNIK," AS DESCRIBED BY HER AUNT SELMA) SHE MARRIED HER NURSERY SCHOOL SWEETHEART, A USED-CARPETING SALES-MAN. THE COUPLE LIVE, WITH SEVERAL CHIL-DREN FROM PREVIOUS MARRIAGES, NEXT TO A TOXIC WASTE DUMP IN CENTRAL NEW JERSEY. "LIVING NEXT TO TOXIC WASTE IS NO LAUGH-ING MATTER," CLAIMS MS. GOLDBLOOM, "BUT SOMEHOW WE MANAGE."
>
> THIS IS THE AUTHOR'S SECOND BOOK, AND HER PUBLISHER BELIEVES THIS LAUGH-RIOT, UN-PUT-DOWN-ABLE, NO-HOLDS-BARRED AUTOBI-OGRAPHY IS, BY FAR, HER MOST ACCOMPLISHED

WORK. THE CRITICS SEEM TO AGREE. "SHE AIN'T NO ANNA KARENINA," COMMENTED *THE NEW YORK DAILY POST TIMES,* "BUT NEITHER IS JOAN COLLINS."

I sort of resented Ariel's making my life sound like a Gilda Radner—Jane Curtin skit from *Saturday Night Live,* but she'd gotten all the facts right, which is what you get for writing an autobiography. And despite Ariel and my family, I learned a lot in the process of putting my life story on paper (well, actually, on computer disc.)

As I career toward forty, I realize some of my options are gone forever. I suppose I'll never dance in toe shoes on stage, look great in a bikini or write decisions for the Supreme Court and I'm learning to live with it. I've come to understand my life has been ruled by the three F words: fashion, food and you know the third one.*

I've always been torn about spending time and energy on clothes, even though I truly enjoyed my short career in the garment center. Part of me thinks it's totally superficial to care about how I look but I also know I have the best times when I'm dressed really well, which I don't think is a complete coincidence.

Today's fashions, though, are confusing to me. I'm utterly perplexed by the punk look. I know the look has a special message to convey but, frankly, all it says to me is: Don't touch without surgical gloves. But then I remember how Class Sophisticate looked in her sixties outfit and I realize I have some nerve to criticize.

Yet it really bothers me when I see a young man wearing the same earrings as I am, especially when they look better on him.

On a more serious note, I believe that an earring on a male lobe is more than a fashion statement. Earrings have added a profound new meaning to the mating

* I've already explained about being a prude.

rituals of the eighties generation. This phenomenon is clearly exemplified in the decade's seminal movie, *Purple Rain*, where: Boy meets girl. Boy gives girl his earring. Boy gets girl.

A feminist variation of this rite of passage can be viewed in another classic film, *The Breakfast Club*. Here, in an extraordinary reversal: Girl meets boy. Girl gives boy her *diamond* earring. (Need I add?) Girl gets boy.

If only things had been this simple in my day, we wouldn't have sweated over where to position our circle pins!

As for food, well, I was twenty-three years old before I realized I was no longer on demand feeding and I've regretted it ever since.

If you ask me, there are four states of consciousness in this life: pigging out, thinking about pigging out, dieting and thinking about dieting. At any given point in your life, you are locked into one of these states (or bordering on another). In the final analysis, I think everything revolves around food. Oh, I know love makes the world go round and money changes everything but, honestly, you have to eat every day of your life.

As for the last F word, I have to say this is one area that has always been a mystery to me. I can't give a whole lot of advice about sex because, it seems to me, I'm no expert. I've held my own a couple of times in my life but I don't think that qualifies me as an expert.

I think it's true that, like Mick Jagger said, you can't always get what you want; you get what you need. As a corollary proposition, I also believe many women think they can't get what they want when, in truth, what they need is to want what they can't get. Frankly, it's not my happiest thought.

But, whenever I get really depressed, I think about Sasha, tossing her hat in Minneapolis, trying to re-create the life of a made-up character on television. Or I go to the local A&P and watch the really, really fat women pushing around their shopping carts. I find it very reassuring to note there are women who are even more overweight than me. "Things could always be worse," I guiltily remind myself. "I'm not as crazy as Sasha or as fat as that lady in baked goods." *

At any rate, I've just about come to the end of my story except to say that last night I microwaved Lean Cuisine for dinner. (We each had six or seven portions and it almost felt like a real meal.) Then we watched Sue Ellen Ewing and Jamie Ewing Barnes get blown to bits in *Dallas*. Later, I perused the latest women's magazines, learning all about Growing Up Kennedy; Bette Midler's sassy lifestyle; and where to give a toddler's birthday party in Manhattan for just under twelve hundred dollars.

During my nightly 7:15 phone call with Mom I learned Aunt Selma and "Uncle" Shelley are having fun redecorating their new place in the Catskills. (They took up permanent residence at the Nevele, where Shelley enjoys chasing the middle-aged ladies around the indoor pool.) My mother's cousin Mamie is still searching for Mr. Right, who's probably well into his seventies by now. Mom and Dad are considering moving to Florida and, as always, I'm encouraging them.

Ethel and her husband dropped by earlier this evening in an effort to bring the family together; she just can't accept the fact that no one likes her husband. "Why can't we all kiss and make up?" she whined.

"Tissue? I don't even know you!" Darla replied and I laughed.

Darla and I settled many of our differences after I introduced her to Zeke, Sandy Rasabinsky's oldest son. According to Darla, Zeke is really "fresh," which is the highest of Darla's accolades.

I still see Wanda and Sybil—separately of course, since Wanda never forgave Sybil for the firing and all.

* It's sort of a mean-spirited way to think but sometimes it really works.

Wanda is on her third pregnancy and Sybil's on her second therapist.

As for the future, my plans remain uncertain. Bruce and I are considering having another child if we don't get divorced or kill one another before the miracle of conception. In my heart of hearts, I'm still hoping I'll wake up one day and Bruce will have changed a little bit. In his new state, he'll be more like Kevin Kline.*

And that, dear reader, brings me to the end of my book. After tomorrow, I can start living the sequel.

The Punchline

Writing this book, my memoirs, was an act of serious pleasure.

Ariel edited the manuscript, and in red pencil, she filled the margins with: "Why have you included this scene?" or "What's the point of this chapter?"

I said, "The point is: This is what really happened, more or less."

I wanted to write about who I was so I had to include almost everything that's happened to me. As I kept telling Ariel, I'm not just the person you see today, an almost-forty-year-old woman, a wife, a mother, a writer. I'm also a mad divorcée, a blushing bride, a college girl, Sweet Sixteen with a hickey on my neck, the Wicked Witch in a black hula skirt wig, a mouther, a young sleuth, a spelling bee champ, the conductor of "The Itsy Bitsy Spider," a baby chewing on a spare rib. I am all of the layers of my life, even the real embarrassing stuff I've tried so hard to forget (or "repress," as Sheila would say).

As a child of the sixties, a careerist of the seventies and a parent of the eighties, I can't help but ask the one question that most perplexes my generation: "Oh,

* See *The Big Chill* for further reference.

God," I want to cry, "how did I ever get to be so old that now *I'm the grownup?*"

And God, in all his or her infinite wisdom, looks down upon me and replies, "Young Lady, Don't Use That Tone of Voice With Me!"

That, epis, is a punchline.

About the Author

When Linda Sunshine's first humor book, *Plain Jane Works Out*, became an international bestseller, her mother said, "But, darling, I never knew you had a sense of humor!"

Although Sunshine grew up in Fair Lawn, New Jersey, she vehemently denies any resemblance between her life and the life of Bambi Goldbloom, much to the amusement of her psychotherapist.

Currently, the author lives in New York where she is trying to decide whether to write a second novel or get a real job.